SEE YOU
ON THE
ICE

SEE YOU
ON THE
ICE

Trevor Horsley

Typeset in 11.5/15pt Adobe Garamond by Falcon Oast Graphic Art Ltd
Printed and bound in Great Britain by ImprintDigital

Quirinus

Chapter 1

The banging on the door increased.

'Fuck off!'

'Let me in! What you doing in there? I NEED TO GO TO THE TOILET!'

Bang! Bang! Bang!

'In a minute!' Picking up the dryer and curling the hair round the brush, he had almost finished, now just for the hair spray. Spraying a cloud across the back, top, sides and front of his hair, the vapour settled and turned solid, like concrete. A slight flick, *umm,* he thought, *not enough, another blast across the back should do it.*

Bang! Bang! Bang! . . . 'Come on!' . . .

Looking in the mirror for the last time, satisfied that the curls were just about perfect and the hair wouldn't move, he opened the door and pushed past his sister. 'Shift!' he said, making his way into his bedroom.

Slamming the bathroom door and shouting 'ABOUT TIME!' she proceeded to adjust the headphones, taking a seat on the toilet, and pressed play on the cassette player.

Tony looked again in the mirror, *looks good,* he smiled, *now? Brut, and then what to wear?*

Opening the wardrobe door, he surveyed the ten or twelve shirts and five different jackets with an assortment of trousers.

Dark trousers tonight, he thought, talking to himself. Sliding into a nice dark brown pair of Burtons with a 12 inch flare, *that should do it. Shirt? Could go for the yellow, nice collar and then I could wear the square brown tie.*

Wonder what Pete's wearing tonight. Blue I expect, he normally does. Think I'll go for the brown shirt, yellow tie and brown velvet.

Pulling the shirt off the hanger, his eyes caught sight of the sleeve. 'Shit! It's got a crease in the sleeve' he said out loud, 'what's wrong with her?'. *The amount of ironing she does you'd think she could iron my shirts better. I can't fucking wear this! Just wrong! Right, in the laundry bin with it. Now what?* he pondered.

How about the yellow flowers with the green velvet? Yes, that could look good, flared collar, not worn it for a while.

Ok, he thought. Making sure there were no crinkles, creases or marks on the shirt, he pulled it on. He adjusted the cuffs, folded the collar down and looked in the mirror. 'You're fucking kidding me!' he shouted at the mirror. The reflection showed that where he had pulled down the collar it had flicked the tip of a shaving mark and left a tiny speck of blood on the collar crease.

Looking closely, touching it with his fingernail. *'Bollocks, made it worse. Fuck! FUCK! Can't wear that now!'* Tearing the shirt off, lobbing it in the bin next to the brown shirt, he cast his eyes back to the rail. *'Going to be the plain yellow then!'* he fumed.

'*Collars ok though, could wear the green Paige tie or the brown or the red, but then what jacket? Umm . . . How about the cream pattern shirt, brown trousers, and green velvet? Not worn the green one yet, 75 quid at Burtons, not bad, week's wages, but it's the price you pay to look good. Anyway, might see Claire tonight at the Top Rank. Got a dance with her last week, bit of a grope, almost got a snog. Never know, might get one this week.* The thoughts drifted through his mind, contemplating the night ahead.

Right, just the shoes, brown, small plat tonight, one and a half inch rounded toe, nicely polished. He pulled the boots on, zipped them up and carefully made sure that the flares covered the whole shoe. *Nice* . . . looking in his mirror.

Keys, wallet, fags. Oh yes, and don't forget the Sobranie Black Russian ciggies. Bit expensive, but well worth it. Nice opener when chatting to someone like Claire. Plus, two lighters. One was for the Sobranies, a nice gold Dunhill, and the other a Zippo he'd picked up at the base last year. Dropping them into his jacket pocket. *Sorted.* Looking for the final time in the mirror. *Need another quick spray*, he thought.

Bursting into the bathroom, he grabbed the hairspray for one last squirt of liquid concrete.

'GET OUT! WHAT YOU DOING? I'M ON THE TOILET!' screamed his sister.

'No one's looking at you so shut the fuck up!'

'Right I'm done, see you later,' he said as he chucked the can into the sink and bounded down the stairs. 'Want me to bring you back a drink?' he shouted.

'BABYCHAM!' came the reply.

Getting into his car, sliding it into reverse, he pulled out and made his way onto the main road, over the bridge, through the country lane, across the top of the moor. Pushing it around a few bends, he slipped it into top gear on the straight. *Such a nice feeling to have a decent powerful car at your fingertips*, he thought. Round and down the hill, he drove alongside the river and entered the village of Woodcote. Nice little village on the outskirts of Reading, not overpopulated, one pub dating back about 300 years, small inside with a low roof, as was the norm with all country pubs. It seemed to Tony that the people back then were obviously a lot shorter than the people of today. Him and Pete didn't drink in the local pub. They'd been in there once, one Friday, early evening, but it was mainly for the country types who liked real ale, which was not something he and Pete did. Other than that, the village housed a couple of shops and that was about it. Pulling up outside a small bungalow, a short blast on the horn as he slowed. Pete was just coming out of the door.

Knew he'd wear blue, Tony thought.

They'd known each other for a couple of years. Pete ran the snooker hall in Reading, and when one night he was there playing, Pete had had a bit of trouble with a couple of blokes who had started to fight each other. Tony helped Pete throw them out. Sitting at the bar afterwards they spent most of the night drinking, and since then they had become firm friends and virtually inseparable. When Pete was working, which was most nights and every other weekend, Tony would come down and play snooker all night and into the early hours. *After all this time, playing, I still can't get more than a 15 break,* thought Tony. Snooker was not the game for him no matter how hard he tried.

One of the good things about playing at the hall so regularly was that, after hours, Pete used to let in most of the bar workers, waiters/waitresses and managers of all the other pubs and clubs in the area, and they played for free. The two of them never had any trouble in any club or pub they went into nor any problem getting in.

'Alright mate,' as Pete got into the passenger seat. 'Yeah good. Fag?'. 'Cheers.'

Pulling away with a quick glance at the watch: 5:45pm Friday night.

'Let's go to No. 25 first for a couple, then onto The Railway,' Tony said looking at Pete. 'Ok,' Pete replied. 'Why The Railway though, bit of a dump and full of paddys.'

'Said I'd see if Dave is in there. Might catch the football next Saturday. You want to come?'

'Not really. Reading are shit. Who they playing, Watford?'
'Yes, I think so.'

Pulling out of Woodcote, Tony pressed his foot down and the car easily slid up to 70mph. 'In the mood?' asked Pete. 'Yeah, why not?' replied Tony.

Gripping his cigarette in his mouth, Pete pulled on the seatbelt and clipped it into place, as Tony powered towards the first corner.

The MKII 3L Ford Capri was a handsome beast of a car. Tony had bought it about a year ago and he loved the power the car could give. Feeling the smooth walnut stick in his hand, Tony dropped a cog and shot into the first of the 13 bends of death. The tyres, new, held the road, and Tony whipped from one bend to the next, shifting the gears quickly to gain the maximum traction the car could give without losing the back end.

He'd crashed his Vauxhall a few years earlier on the A4 between Thatcham and Theale. An absolute dream of a road to drive, speed in excess in places was well over 100mph: his record from Theale to Thatcham was 11 minutes. His old man had done it quicker, but he was in a cop car at the time so that didn't really count. On this one occasion he was burning through Woolhampton and on the exit of this small village was a sweeping left-hand bend heading towards Reading, 100mph his way 90mph the other. As he exited the bend on the cusp of the white line he overtook the car he had spotted before he'd hit the bend; this unfortunately put him in the middle of the road Ordinarily that wouldn't have been a problem as the road was easily wide enough for three cars and any approaching vehicle would be cleared with room to spare. On this occasion, however, he saw a milk lorry in the middle of the road about to turn across in front of him to a dairy farm. Not able to swerve to the nearside of the lorry as cars were behind it, unable to break hard and pull into his own nearside as he would have hit the car he was overtaking, his only other options were a head on crash with the lorry, which really as far as Tony was concerned was not much of an option as he thought it would be instant death. Instead, his decision was to drop a gear and accelerate as hard as he could. He swung past the car he was overtaking and went straight over the curb, crashed through the hedge and into a field.

In a matter of seconds, the Vauxhall, heavy as the car was, made it through the fence, between two telephone poles and came to rest about 60 feet into the field. Fortunately, there was no ditch to fall into so the car, although smashed from the fence assault and with a damaged chassis, came to rest on all four wheels, much to the relief of Tony.

Swinging out of six, through into seven, Tony felt the car wiggle a touch as the rear tyre tried to gain grip on the white line. Accelerating hard to compensate for the loss, the car responded and pushed itself out of seven and into eight. The adrenalin pumped through Tony's veins as he whistled from one tight bend to the next. Over each small hump and through each blind bend, ten through to thirteen were done in a matter of what seemed like lightning seconds. Coming out of the last bend, Tony slowed the car to a more normal speed. Pete exhaled the smoke in his lungs and said, 'Fucked it up again on seven.'

'Yeah, I know, not sure why.' replied Tony.

'Could be the camber as you approach, puts the car off slightly, I think. Have to have a word with the council,' laughed Pete.

Coming into Reading at the top they made their way into Caversham and pulled up in a small carpark. Walking across the road they went down a few steps to the basement of No. 25. Tony knocked on the door. The small window in the door opened and a face peered through.

Tony thought it was a bit theatrical and 1920s American

speakeasies with the window in the door. Everyone knew what the place was and was not. As if it was ever going to get raided. But Colin liked it.

'Hi Winston, let us in mate,' said Tony.

The door opened and Tony shook hands with Winston. Winston bear hugged Pete and the two of them went into the bar area.

No. 25 overlooked the Thames, and in the summer, you could get a drink at the bar and go onto the terrace, sit in the sunshine, and just relax watching the water and the occasional boat drift by.

The place was owed by Colin Johnson. He'd owed a couple of places abroad, and when he settled back in the UK he wanted to create a place similar to what he was used to. High end, nice furnishings, a distinguished clientele, those who could afford the expensive wines and spirits. Tony liked the smooth and stylish environment, all the things that No, 25 was.

He too played snooker, as did Winston. Although Winston was more brawn than brain. On this Friday night, the small jazz band were setting up, and as Tony shook hands with Colin and exchanged the weekly pleasantries, Pete and Tony picked up a couple of bottles of beer and sat in one of the many comfortable chairs.

Lighting up a cigarette he looked around, quiet now but wouldn't be long before it picked up. Colin did a bit of food on a Friday night, only for a couple of hours or so. Lobster, prawns and the like. Not to Tony's taste, but it always smelt good. It attracted some of the local company bosses who would like to come in and eat and throw the cash around. Just as Colin liked it. Tony wanted to tee up Winston so that he knew they may well go to Valbonnes later. Winston would be on the door from 12. He would then know to expect them.

Finishing the second bottle, Pete put it down on the table, 'Ready?'

'Yeah, let's go,' said Tony.

It was not the sort of place him and Pete would spend all night in, especially at the prices Colin charged. Whilst they both made a few quid more than many it still didn't stretch to the cost of drinking there all night, but it was always a good place to start a Friday night, and every now and again they would visit late if the club they were in wasn't lively enough.

Most clubs and pubs in Reading these days were getting a decent name, and it was drawing in several thousand on a Friday night, which wasn't a problem as they were both local and regulars and avoided any trouble.

Waving to Colin, Tony and Pete shook hands with Winston and left. Picking up the car, they drove the short distance through to St Marys Butts. Pulling into the car park, the pair of them walked into The Railway.

'Fag,' offered Pete. 'Ta, I'll get the drinks,' said Tony. 'What you want?'

'Bass,' said his mate.

Passing the drink to Pete, Tony glanced around the room. About thirty or so in, couple of suits, mainly workers though, construction guys from the new M4. *Get busier later,* he thought.

The Railway was a standard town centre pub, two smoke-filled bars, lots of tables, small jukebox, pool table out the back and a variety of fruit machines and electronic table games. They were always busy playing Packman or Asteroids. Tonight though, was Friday and they were not there to play games. It was a drinking night.

Moving through the crowd at the bar and finding an ashtray on one of the many tables, he crushed his fag end out, took a couple of swigs, and his eyes settled on a group of four workers on the table near the toilet. Tony put a few coins into the fruit machine and idly pressed the buttons, watching the men out of the corner of his eye. It appeared to Tony, and if anyone else looked at them, that they were just four blokes having a drink after work, no deep conversations, just idly chatting. Not winning at the machine and taking another swig of his lager, he looked around the rest of the room to see if anyone was looking at him or them. Didn't really expect anyone to be, so with that he put his pint down on the table and walked over to Pete.

'Hey mate, left my fags in the car. Back in a sec. Look after my pint,' pointing at his pint on the table.

'Ok.'

Tony made his way outside, walked around the corner and spotted a phone box. A quick look over his shoulder to make sure Pete had stayed inside and he entered the box. Lifting the receiver, he dialled a London number and pulled a couple of 50p's out of his pocket. Too much he knew, but he couldn't take the risk of not connecting properly. On hearing a voice, he pressed the coin into the slot and waited for it to register.

'Hi, it's Tony,' he said. 'I'm in The Railway, Reading. Two new blokes are with the O'Dowd brothers.'

'Thanks,' came the reply, and the phone went dead.

Leaving the phone box, Tony slid his hand into his side pocket and pulled out a packet of Bensons. Lighting a new one, he made his way back into the pub and offered Pete a fag. 'Want another one' as he downed his drink, 'or do you want to wander round to The Bell?'

'No birds in here, let's go. Can't see Dave either.'

'I'll catch up with him later. Come on then,' said Tony.

Chapter 2

Stepping out of Lechfield House, he crossed over Curzon Street and made his way down Derby Street. A short, powerfully built man, walking with a purpose, it was a short walk to Green Park, which he cut across to get onto The Mall. Through St James's Park, he entered Horse Guards Parade and into Whitehall. Glancing at his watch, noting the 26 minutes it had taken him, he entered one of the many unremarkable offices aligning the street. He handed his badge to the doorman. On signing the register he was informed that someone would be down for him shortly.

The foyer was sparse but hanging on the wall over a small leather chair and occasional table was an oil painting. Recognising the figure, he stepped forward for a closer look. Major General Sir Henry Havelock astride an imposing stallion. The backdrop was an Indian village with the village leaders deep in thought. *Had problems back then with insurgents and terrorists did you not?* he thought.

'Good morning Sir', his thoughts broken, turning, he met the gaze of Hilary Smallbrook. 'I'll take you up,' she said. He'd met her once before on his appointment as section head four months ago. Polite, efficient and discreet was his impression. The lift to the third floor took moments, and as they walked along the corridor and into the outer office, he smiled to himself. *Carpet, ornate doors, brass fittings, stained glass and nice mahogany desks. Bit different from my small office: lino floor, tin desk and padlocked filing cabinet Mind you*, he thought, *I do have a window so not all bad.*

'He will see you now,' Ms. Smallbrook said and guided him into the minister's office. 'Geoffrey, good to see you again.' The minister, hand outstretched, came around the desk and shook Lieutenant General Geoffrey Palmer-Siddely's hand. 'Take a seat.'

'Thank you for your time, Sir. It's good to see you again,' responded Geoffrey.

'I've read your briefing report,' as they both sat. 'Interesting concept: however, I have to warn you that I'm not overly convinced it's a good idea, but, one of the reasons for getting you on board was for a young blood to breathe some new ideas across our dusty desks.'

Young blood, thought Geoffrey. Never thought of himself like that before. Forty-eight made him one of the youngest lieutenant generals the Army had. Having graduated Sandhurst twenty-five years ago, he had had a varied, hard but enjoyable time over the years, but as for young blood, well!

'I got you over to talk me through it. Your report was fine, but I need the bigger picture if I'm going to take it upstairs. So over to you.'

Geoffrey was prepared as always and had gone through this meeting in his mind several times over the weekend, looking for as many objections, questions and counters he could think of.

'As you know, the IRA are stepping up their activities across Northern Ireland and to quite some extent here. Whilst we have people on the ground over there and of course some valuable expertise here, I am concerned that we are missing a trick.' 'Let me explain,' he continued.

'Focussing just on mainland Britain for a moment, there are many men out there who could be a valuable source of information to us. They know people, they have base jobs and average lives. What I mean by that is, your electricians, plumbers, painters, builders, council workers and more, working, going to the football each week, down the pub on payday, holidaying in Blackpool, Bournemouth, year in year out etc. Just average run of the mill men making a living and living normal everyday lives.'

'Some of these have one thing in common: they have friends or know of people who have suffered at the hands of the IRA. It could be one of the football team, a school mate, the bloke who was in the snooker team, they joined up and either were injured or worse still, killed when doing a tour. Or even someone who was hurt in a recent bombing. And as you are only too aware, Sir, early this year there were four car bombs in London; thankfully, two were disarmed, one of which was just down the road.'

Nodding, the minster gestured for Geoffrey to continue.

'Now, intelligence is paramount if we are going to succeed in stopping further attacks. The information we currently gather from our men on the ground here and, of course, the intelligence briefing we get from the office in Belfast is good, can and will serve us well; however, the more information we have the better informed we are, which will enable us to act quicker and more decisively against what is in essence our enemy.'

'Ok, I understand that but we don't have the money nor will it play well to start recruiting members of the public into the service. You know there is a well-defined chain of how we get people on board, and I can tell you now that changing that will not happen for a long time,' said the minister. 'And this is the part that I'm struggling with, Geoffrey,' the Minister continued, 'engaging people who are, as you describe, at best, average, is not where we are, it's not the sort of thing we do, and to be honest, having a gang of chaps hurtling around the country playing spy games is really, really, not going to be a starter for ten. I'm sorry, but whilst on the surface your briefing paper was intriguing I see nothing that I can hold onto.'

'Sir, I'm not suggesting that for one moment. What I'm saying is that there is a wealth of information out there that we can use. We would take a few people, maybe twenty or thirty, who have been recommended to us. The type of person would be resourceful, have a high level of integrity, intelligent, blend in well in any group, probably knows a lot of people, acts well under pressure, not be afraid of change and, of course, will have known or know someone who has been treated badly at the hands of the IRA. All that would be required of them,' continued Geoffrey, 'is to look and listen and then pass on information.'

'Geoffrey, that's a tall order and finding men like that would take time, effort, money and resources, which we can ill afford. And, as I said, we can't afford it, we do not have the budget for any more staff.'

'That's where the difference lies, we would play on their loyalty and sense of helping. We would not need to pay anything to these people, they would be on the fringe of the department, if at all, know exactly what they are doing, they wouldn't get involved in anything apart from passing on information, and if we get the right sort of people that sort of information is given free of charge.'

'Well, thank you for coming by, Geoffrey,' said the minister, cutting Geoffrey off, rising from his seat. 'It is an idea, and in some ways a good idea, but I can't see anyone upstairs going for it at this moment. I'll keep your notes and if things change then maybe we can look at it again.'

Shaking his hand and thanking him for his time, Geoffrey made his way down and out onto Whitehall. Sighing, he made his way up towards Nelson's Column and The Admiralty pub on the corner. Sitting in the corner with a pint of London Pride he thought back over his meeting. He knew that it was a stretch for the minister to get on board, but the idea was sound. *Maybe it's a bit too early for any change*, he thought.

Back in the office he opened his safe, securing the briefing notes on the operation inside, then settled down to read through the wires placed on his desk, which had accumulated over the last three hours he had been out of the office. The Met were the main group who looked after terrorist incidents and intelligence in the UK currently, but more and more information was being shared between the two organisations as both groups had different ways of collecting it. He had a meeting later at Scotland Yard to go through this month's key points, so he had to make sure that what was given to them was sufficient. *They can have some info*, he thought, but there were some things that were left out. *I expect they do the same to us,* Geoffrey thought.

A few months later, Geoffrey was sat at his desk going through the myriad of reports that constantly updated him on a range of activities of the section he controlled and the updates from his extensive team, both on the mainland and in Northern Ireland. The pressure of identifying, keeping track and monitoring potential suspects was enormous. Every day lead to a different, urgent situation which could lead to a possible terrorist attack. That morning, on the 10th September 1973, just before he made his way out for lunch, the phone rang on his desk. Answering, he listened intently for a few minutes.

'Casualties?' he asked.

'Keep me updated,' with a deep sigh Geoffrey replaced the receiver. A bomb had exploded in the booking hall of Kings Cross at 12.24 p.m., causing extensive damage and injuring six people, some seriously. Witnesses had said that is was thrown in the hall by a young man, who then ran off.

Minutes later, the phone rang again; thinking it was an update, Geoffrey picked up the phone.

Letting out an involuntary gasp, Geoffrey shook his head: another bomb had exploded close to a snack bar in Euston

Station injuring eight people. The Metropolitan Police had received a three-minute warning and were unable to evacuate the station completely; fortunately, British Transport Police evacuated much of the area just before the explosion.

With a knock on the door, Geoffrey raised his head and he called out,

'Enter! Hello Mary,' he said, 'what can I do for you?'

'The Home Secretary called; he would like to see you.'

'Ok,' said Geoffrey. 'When?'

'Now.'

Chapter 3

Declan Cassidy climbed into his van and made his way out of Tallanstown, onto the main road and headed south towards Rosslare. By-passing Dublin, the journey would take all day, but as his ferry was at 7am tomorrow morning, he was in no rush. With little traffic around and very few Garda on the road he knew that the van would not warrant a second look. Having loaded up with a pallet of paper yesterday, the load was legit and all his paperwork in order so it was highly unlikely that he would attract any attention at either Rosslare or Fishguard when he got there.

Mid 40s, well-built, he had been in the Army for just over 20 years. It had got him out of the small village he lived in and he'd had a good grounding in how to use firearms and make/defuse explosives. His father Seamus was a member of the Irish Republican Army during the 1950s and he had indoctrinated the young Declan on the persecution the Irish had experienced at the hands of the British. It was always a plan for the young Declan to follow in his father's footsteps so he made sure to remember and learn everything he could whilst he was in the Army. The following years provided him with a wealth of experience, most of which he had now started to put to good use. As one of only four proven skilled bomb makers in the IRA he knew that at some point the British would know his whereabouts, but for now, keeping out of sight most of the time was working to his advantage.

On arriving in Rosselair, he made his way into the vast car parking area and settled down to sleep. The ferry was at 7am; what with the anticipated adrenalin and being an early riser, he knew he'd be awake a few hours before he needed to be. Customs was simple, they looked in the van and saw a pallet of paper. Paperwork in order, he drove onto the ferry with dozens of other vans and lorries, most making their way to England but some going further, down to Dover and then onto Europe.

The journey from Fishguard to Reading was uneventful. Stopping off a couple of times for fuel and something to eat, he pulled into the estate at around 10pm. As they didn't know what time he was arriving, he settled down once more for a few hours' sleep. He'd arranged that they would be at the yard at 7 o'clock.

Donny O'Dowd drove his Cortina across town to the small industrial estate, past the ten or so run down warehouses and around the back of Oxford Road to the high chain-linked fence that surrounded about half an acre of yard that he owned. Opening the heavy padlock and pushing the gates open, he drove through the scrap yard to his Portacabin, which was hidden from the road. Stepping out, he walked over to the two main buildings, both of which were about 10,000sq ft. of garage space; both used for the dismantling of cars. Some legal, some not so much. His business was selling on the scrap to several recycling plants who turned the metal into a block. In turn, they sold the metal on to the car manufacturers who made the blocks into cars, which then eventually ended up in his yard. Not quite that simple but easy enough to explain to those who came to buy a wing mirror, battery, car door etc. when theirs had been damaged, which was always much cheaper for the punter than going back to the manufacturer for spare parts.

He'd set the yard up back in the late '60s when he and his brother Patrick had come across to England as budding speedway riders. The site they bought was very close to the Reading speedway track and had made an ideal base to repair and test their bikes. The land had been going cheap as it had flooded a few years earlier and the local council had decided that building on it was too risky. Soon as they had moved in, they had created an earth barrier around the back end of the site next to the river in the hope that that would stop any further flooding. Hadn't been tested yet, fortunately.

They had a gift for repairing and maintaining bikes, and the garage had been busy in the early years. They made money out of bike repairs and, with the Reading team racing at the Tilehurst Stadium around the corner, business had been good. In 1973, the stadium closed and was relocated a few miles away. For a while, people still came, but they had started scrapping cars by then and had been getting closer to some friends back home so were less inclined to welcome visitors to the site. The site now had some 200 scrap cars piled high across it, which made trying to see into the yard extremely difficult, which of course, was what the O'Dowd brothers wanted.

Sean Keating was born and raised in Ballinskelligs by his grandparents. His father had died in World War II, his mother had left around that time and went to live somewhere in Dublin so it fell to his grandparents to look after the boy of ten. His grandfather had lived in poverty for most of his early life, and the district they lived in was one of a few in Ireland that fell under a poor law union. Having married Edith at eighteen, Sean's father was born in 1905, one of eight children; life had been tough for the whole family. His Grandfather Niall had joined up at the outbreak of World War I, fought on the Somme and was one of the lucky ones to get home in 1919.

Niall hated the British and blamed them for the poverty he and his parents had endured, for the punishment and harassment the Irish suffered at their hands, little or no work and even less money. His escape into the Army for him was a way to use the British by taking their money and sending his meagre wage back home to Edith. On his return, he had fought in the War of Independence; he was responsible, so rumour had it, for burning down the local coast guard station. Rumours again suggested he'd helped with the smuggling of food and spirits into the area. The influence he had over Sean was immense and forged a strong Irish mantra into the boy for many years, so it was with no surprise that Sean ended up in the IRA.

Sean used brute force to gain whatever he needed and was constantly in fights at school then later late-night brawls in the local pub. Although having a high level of intelligence, it was easier for him to resolve situations with his hands rather than by talking. He joined the local boxing club and fast became a very good amateur boxer. Temper though stopped him from moving up into the professional arena. To make money he sold illegal booze to the locals. He broke into many warehouses containing beer and cigarettes, which he quickly moved on to both local hotels, pubs and many of the people he had grown up with. Venturing into the Belfast area in 1968, where pickings were more lucrative, he quickly made a name for himself linked to violence and contraband delivery. It wasn't long before he came to the attention of the Provisional IRA.

Sean had caught the ferry from Dublin over to Liverpool. With just hand luggage, he went through customs simply enough and made his way to the train station. Catching a train from Liverpool, he changed at Coventry and waited for the next train to Reading. It would get him in at 4pm. As arranged, he rang the number on his arrival and waited outside the station to be collected. Patrick O'Dowd arrived within a few minutes, collected Sean and took him to the guest house he had booked for him. He told Sean that he would pick him up at 7:30am the next morning and take him to the yard.

After booking in and putting his bag in the bedroom, he went downstairs to the small dining room and had an evening meal. He then settled down in his room for the night.

On seeing the gates being opened by Donny, Declan fired

up the van and drove into the yard. Following Donny down the track, he pulled up outside the main warehouse. Getting out, he shook hands with Donny.

'No problems with getting here?' asked Donny.

'No, easy enough. Where's Sean?'

'Patrick is picking him up. He got in yesterday and is at the bed and breakfast. Be here in a bit,' said Donny, still with a strong Irish accent as neither of the brothers had lost their twang even after having spent many years now in England.

Declan's father Seamus had gone to school with Donny's uncle who had been as opinionated as Seamus was when it came to the British, so it was a natural extension that when anyone needed anything in the South of England, the O'Dowd brothers would be there to help. This, however, did flag a light to the security services, but because the brothers were so low key and every time either the police or MI5 had looked at them, nothing raised their suspicions thereby giving the brothers a reasonable amount of anonymity.

'There's a kettle and some coffee in the cabin if you want a drink; there's also a bit of a washroom if you need to have a wash,' said Donny.

'Thanks, I will,' replied Declan.

Donny turned and walked back up the track and padlocked the gate. Returning to the Portacabin, he made himself a coffee.

'When Sean gets here I'll walk you around the place and show you what we have. If there is anything you need I can get it within a day or so depending on what it is,' he said to Declan.

'Ok good, the sooner we get started the better,' said Declan, sipping his coffee.

They both pulled up a chair and sat at the desk waiting for Sean and Patrick to arrive.

Just after 7:30am, Patrick arrived at the gates, unlocked them, drove the van down the track and pulled up next to Donny's car. Showing Sean into the cabin, they exchanged handshakes and Declan introduced everyone. Sean had worked with Declan before, albeit briefly. Declan outlined his role and how all four of them fitted together in this ASU.

Patrick walked back up to the gate, locked up and then with Donny proceeded to show the other two around and what they had already brought in. Gathering around a work bench in one of the garages after the tour, during the following hours, the four of them planned out the logistics of the attack, the equipment still needed, the routes, the target date and the exact location.

Chapter 4

Tony knew the way to the yard because he had followed Patrick there a couple of weeks ago after he had seen him in the pub on a Saturday lunchtime. He had already decided on his way in so drove along Oxford Road to Mill Street. Leaving the car in the side street, he got out, locked the door and made his way through the industrial estate to the end where the yard was.

Making sure no one was around, he walked along the fence around the back towards where the earth had been dug up as a barricade. The chain link fence was easy enough to climb so he clambered over and jumped to the ground. Trying to be as quiet as he could, he made his way towards the two main warehouses. He knew both of them were being used as garages as Pete had been in there a month or two ago looking for a wing mirror for his Celica.

He could see the lights on in the warehouse next to the Portacabin. There were piles of cars all over the yard and it seemed simple enough to climb up between two columns, one of which rested against the side of the first building with easy access to the fire escape, which came off the mezzanine floor. Crawling across the top of a rusty old Escort, he managed to grasp hold of the rail onto the fire escape landing and carefully, trying not to make too much noise, jumped onto it. Trying the door, it was of course locked, but it was next to one of the windows, which had rusted over the years and fortunately for Tony had a broken pane of glass. Sliding his hand through the window, he unlatched it from the frame and pulled it open. With both hands, he managed to haul himself inside onto the mezzanine floor.

The floor was dimly lit so each step took an age, having carefully placed each foot down before putting his full weight on it. He could hear the talk on the ground floor below him, and after a few minutes he was able to look over the edge of the mezzanine floor and saw two of them next to a van. Carefully leaning over, he looked across the warehouse floor to see if he could see or even hear the others, when moments later, both Sean and Declan came out of a side office and made their way towards the other two.

Ducking back down, unsure if they could see him, he peered between the railings that ran along the edge of the mezzanine floor. He could see the brothers were talking to each other. Because of the distance he was unable to make out what they were saying but what he did see was Patrick get into the back of the van and start cutting the support bars out on the inside panelling. Clearly, this would make the sides of the van much weaker, which to Tony didn't make any sense. Looking around, Tony saw that next to the van was a rusty 50-gallon drum; alongside that, was a smaller drum with what looked like a tube coming out of it.

Declan had made his way to a long table that had an

assortment of wires on it and began to sift through them, or so it appeared to Tony. That's when he noticed that underneath the table were several large flat bags about 4ft long, 2ft wide and four or five inches thick.

He watched as Sean come out of the office carrying what looked like quite a heavy box. Walking over to the table where Declan was, he dropped the box on top of half a dozen other similar boxes. Tony had no idea what was in the bags or the boxes but clearly, they were all needed. Trying to breathe slowly, he could feel his heart pounding in his chest, and he decided that he been there long enough. Carefully turning around, he made the short distance back to the window and started to climb out onto the fire escape. He was hoping that the metal steps of the fire escape were okay and not broken. He started to walk down them trying to make as little sound as possible.

Getting to the bottom, he turned and made his way back the way he had come heading towards the chain-linked fence. Walking quickly, and then with a bit of panic, he decided to run to the fence. Unfortunately, in the dim light, he crashed into a metal box that was lying in his way, and went flying onto the gravel, cursing as he landed. He'd managed to knock over the box and everything inside scattered across the gravel, the row was deafening. *Oh shit!* he thought. Picking himself up he ran at full tilt towards the fence.

Inside the warehouse, both Donny and Sean looked up and at each other and instantly ran towards the warehouse door. Bursting through the door they could hear Tony's footsteps on the gravel over to the left and gave chase. Tony hit the chain-link fence at full force and started to climb as he guessed, quite rightly, that the noise would have made its way through the yard and into the warehouse. Breathing heavily, he crawled his way up the fence and then felt someone grabbing his right leg. A second later, his other leg had been trapped as well and with that he was yanked off the chain link fence onto the gravel floor.

The pain in his side was excruciating. Sean kicked him in the ribs and delivered a blow to the side of his head; Tony saw stars. Another kick on his back and two more punches to the head and Tony almost lost consciousness. He had never felt so much pain in all his life and tried rolling up into a ball. He was pulled to his feet and a vice like grip held around this throat to the point where he could barely breathe. Donny grabbed his arm and the two of them half lifted, half dragged Tony into the warehouse and threw him on the floor. With another hammer punch to the head and his head spinning, Tony could hardly see.

'Who the fuck are you? What you doing here? Who do you work for?' *Smack!* Another blow to the head. 'Answer me you little shit,' bellowed Sean in his ear. A punch to the face and this time Tony felt as if his nose and whole side of his head were about to explode.

'Don't hurt me,' gurgled Tony blood filling his mouth and clogging his throat. 'I'm sorry, stop it please, stop.' Tears welling in his eyes, he curled up again. 'Don't hurt me, please.'

'What the fuck are you doing here? Answer me or you'll get another smack. What's your name? What do you want?'

The questions screamed through to his brain. Tony, trying to gain his senses, tried to answer but struggled to get the words out of his mouth.

He vaguely heard someone say, 'Leave him for a moment.'

Donny pushed Tony into a kneeling position. Declan leaned over him, 'Answer me, who are you?'

'My name's Dave. Dave Hartman,' Tony replied. The slap across the face took him by surprise and he rolled into the dirt. Donny grabbed him and again threw him on his knees. 'What you doing here?' said Declan. 'Don't fuck me about boy, tell me, tell me now before this gets worse!'

'I was looking for some MOT certificates,' blubbered Tony. 'Me and my mate thought you would have them and we could sell them.'

Sean punched him; Tony lost all hearing in his right ear and sprawled again across the floor. 'Fucking liar!' shouted Sean, kicking him in the thigh.

'I'm not, I'm not, we thought you'd have some, we didn't know you'd be here, honest,' blurted Tony.

'Where's your mate?' asked Declan.

'He's at home. We were going to meet up tomorrow down the pub. Listen, I'm sorry. I'm really sorry, I won't come here again,' said Tony, wiping his face with a trembling hand.

Declan stood up and walked over to Donny, 'You seen him before?'

'I might have done but I can't remember,' said Donny.

Sean walked over to Declan. 'Get rid of him, stick him in one of the cars and get it crushed. We don't know what he's seen.'

'Hang on a minute,' said Donny. 'That could cause problems. You're here until next Friday and the last thing we need is his mate asking around or worse reporting him missing and the Old Bill tipping up here.' 'He doesn't know anything, and I doubt he's seen anything, just a stupid asshole trying his luck.'

'Threaten the fuck out of him and give him a good hiding, then throw him out,' said Patrick.

Sean looked at Declan, not the way they normally did things when people got in their way but. . .

'Ok,' said Declan.

With that, Patrick and Donny grabbed Tony, hauled him up onto his feet and dragged him through the door to the main padlocked gate. Punching Tony on the side of the head as Patrick opened the gate. 'Don't you fucking dare come back here or let me see you ever again,' he shouted at Tony. Patrick pushed the gate open, turned and kicked Tony full force in the groin. Tony collapsed to the floor.

The two of them, one arm each, threw him out of the yard.

'Fuck off you little shit!'

The gate closed and the two men made their way back to the warehouse.

Tony could barely move: the ringing in his ears, the pain in his head, his stomach and his kidneys. The kick to the groin was agony and as he tried to stand, he threw up.

Sinking to his knees, his hand sank through his vomit to the ground. He crawled round the side of the yard and, exhausted, toppled onto the grass verge.

He couldn't move. Any movement was just agony. Every part of his body hurt. He thought he was deaf and blind in one eye; he thought his arm was broken. His face was bleeding and what was left of his nose was haemorrhaging blood, and his ears were the size of footballs. He tried to touch his mouth and nose, but the pain was too much.

Lie here for a while, he thought. *Stay still, don't move, the pain might go away.*

He had to move. He didn't know how long he had been lying on the grass; it seemed like hours. Trying to sit up, the pain stabbed straight through his left side across his stomach and down his right leg. 'Shit that hurts!' he said out loud. Rolling onto his side, he had more success pushing himself up onto his knees. Grabbing hold of the fence, he slowly managed to stand.

No longer feeling sick and deciding not to touch any part of his body, he hobbled out of the estate and onto the side road where he had left his car. Taking the keys out of his jacket pocket, he gently eased himself into the driving seat. Clenching his teeth, the pain in his side was like nothing he'd felt before.

At least they didn't break any fingers, he thought. Licking his lips, his tongue decided to join in the pain stakes, which was when he realised that one of the times he had suffered a punch to the head he had bitten his tongue.

Looking in the mirror, his left eye was half closed, and the right side of his head seemed to be swollen. His ear, he could make out, was very red, split and still oozing blood. Wiping it with his hand, he switched on the ignition.

What the fuck am I going to tell my mum? he thought.

Looking at his watch, it was about 3:15am, or that was all he could make out. Heading slowly down Oxford Street, he pulled into the Shell garage. It was all locked up for the night so he got out and walked about 50 yards out of the station to a phone box. He knew someone would answer and he needed to tell them quickly what he'd seen.

Dialling the number and waiting for the pips, he struggled to get a coin out of his pocket. The phone was answered. Pushing the coin into the slot, he said, 'It's Tony in Reading,' proceeding to explain what he had seen and briefly covering up the extent of the beating he had been given.

'You're an idiot,' came the voice. 'You were told in no circumstances were you to go near anyone or do anything at all that involved anything other than just look, not even get close to listen, just watch and report. Son, you are very lucky you're still alive. God knows why they let you go.'

'I thought you would want more information about what they are doing,' said Tony.

'That's not your job nor will it ever be. Go home and count yourself lucky,' and with that the line went dead.

Tony slid back into the driving seat. 'Thanks for your help Tony,' he said sarcastically.

Pulling into his driveway at home, he made his way inside and went straight to the kitchen, hunting for some painkillers. With four in his hand he put them in his mouth and found the water from the glass dribbling down his chin as any feeling he had in his lips had disappeared. Running a bath, Tony took off his clothes and put his foot into the hot water. The initial heat made him flinch, which hurt his side. Gradually though, he eased himself into the water. He watched as his skin turned red from the scalding hot water, momentarily thinking he looked like a lobster, the pain of the heat taking away from the agony he felt in his ribs and face. Tony relaxed as the water flooded over him. Twenty minutes later he crawled into bed, pulling the sheet over him, trying to lie very still. The pain came in waves.

It had been a long week, punctuated only by a constant stream of painkillers and a dubious reason for his injuries. He told his mother that he and Pete had had a few on Saturday night. Pete had gone home and he had fell down the concrete steps of the Top Rank club. It didn't seem much like she believed him but that was the story he was sticking to. Having five days off work didn't help either. Didn't work, didn't get paid.

Pete had come by on the Monday night, keeping the story more or less the same. Pete covered for him by phoning his work and agreed with his story whenever his mum asked.

Chapter 5

The Counter Terrorism Branch was located on the fifth floor of Scotland Yard and was staffed by 370 officers of various ranks, garnered from several different units and multiple police forces throughout the UK. Predominantly London-based officers, it did have a small presence in Manchester, Birmingham and Edinburgh. The unit came to prominence for its role in investigating the Post Office Tower bombing in 1971.

Its division's focus was on investigating the IRA within the UK and Northern Ireland. A separate group was centred in Belfast and reported directly to Assistant Commissioner Paul Lang. Since bombing by the IRA had increased during the early '70s, and continued to do so, he had monthly meeting with various branches of the intelligence and security services: MI5, MI6 etc.

Any raids, arrests or criminal proceedings against terrorists were led by the Met Police. The small division was growing weekly as more information was gathered, and with the increased activity on mainland Britain by the IRA it needed more officers to investigate. There had been more losses than successes over the years, but the information they were getting now had been of a higher standard and more credible than previously. Paul was confident that the division as a whole had a better handle on the situation than before.

The monthly meeting seemed more like a poker match than open sharing of information. He was aware that everyone acceded to the need for confidentiality, but there was still a long way to go before everyone trusted each other implicitly. 'Blood from a stone' was a phrase that resounded with him when he left some of the meetings. Never fully grasping why they didn't all get that they were on the same side.

Geoffrey was a regular attendee of the meetings and Paul knew that he was pushing ahead with surveillance, as he had provided some good intelligence over the last year or so which had enabled the Branch to arrest several individuals before they had become engaged in going through with a terrorist incident.

He, as did all the other men in the monthly meetings, had direct telephone contact with Detective Inspector Harry Roberts, who headed up the day to day operations in Scotland Yard, and whom he was listening to now. Geoffrey had contacted him in the early hours of Saturday night providing him with credible evidence of an IRA plot.

The meeting was being held in a secure room; both he and Geoffrey were present as they listened to Harry outline the situation to a specialist team.

'The information came in late last night,' DI Roberts started, to a group of some thirty men.

'Our target,' he said, turning and pointing to the large map attached to the white board behind him, is this yard. The yard is situated at the end of this road' – pointing at the map- 'and it appears that there is only one way in and one way out. The back of the yard has an earth mound which separates it from the river; around the other three sides is a chain-link fence approx. 8ft high. The main gate is pad-locked. The yard is full of scrap cars, and in the middle of the yard are two main warehouses and a Portacabin.'

'Our targets are the O'Dowd brothers and two other men who we believe make up the ASU (Active Service Unit of the IRA). We think they could be Sean Keating and Declan Cassidy; either way, we are assuming they will be well armed. Our information now is that they are preparing a car bomb.'

'Do we know which warehouse they are in?' asked Sgt. Pears.

'Not at the moment, and surveillance is limited and very difficult. We will hit all three at the same time. The plan will be to enter quietly, if we can break the padlock, and get to the warehouses and Portacabin before any alarm is raised. If the padlock is a problem then the lead vehicle will ram the gate open,' explained Harry.

'We are coordinating the raid with Thames Valley and a Sgt. Easeman, who knows the area and has provided the information on the site we currently have,' continued Harry.

'We leave here at 18:00. We have access to a secure compound in Thames Valley nick and I want the raid to be at 9am tomorrow morning.'

Paul nodded, he had been in touch with Chief Constable

Morgan at Thames Valley early and had secured the use of the six local police officers, the meagre information they had on the site and the secure use of a base within Reading station. He had emphasised the need for absolute secrecy and on a need to know basis.

Chief Constable Morgan, a veteran of thirty-five years, was more than forthcoming with his help and suggested the officers on his staff which, he trusted, knew the area well and could perform well under pressure if needed.

'Why so late?' enquired the sergeant again.

'We don't know if all of them are sleeping there or whether they are off site and then arrive in the morning each day. We will have put in our own surveillance from 4am onwards. It's important that we let them get into the site before we raid. We will not take them in the streets. We will have a further briefing and action plan when we get to Reading,' and with that he said,

'Right let's go.'

The unit made their way downstairs to the armoury and signed out a selection of weapons and ammunition. DI Roberts collected his equipment and with the others got into the waiting four transits and four unmarked Ford Granada's.

Making their way out of central London and onto the M4, DI Roberts ran through the raid in his mind, how the team would operate, who would go where and how they would breach the warehouses. At least now he had some decent equipment, he thought. The increased budget had allowed the Branch to purchase Heckler & Koch MP5's, which were far more reliable than the ones they had before. Their body armour had been upgraded as well, plus flash bang grenades, decent side-arms and new vehicles at their disposal. More than once, they had been on raids when one or more of the vans had packed up and the raid was cancelled because of a lack of men, or equipment failing at the designated moment.

Their training programme had been increased; they had spent time with the Special Air Service in Hereford. Most of that period had been on how to enter, search and recon buildings. Valuable lessons had been learnt. It was now an ongoing procedure so every six months they had a week to go over any issues they had faced and work through some of the problems they had encountered. It was proving very valuable as the SAS were constantly improving their own techniques.

The convoy of vehicles was staggered, leaving ten minutes apart so as not to attract too much attention and, more importantly, when they reached Reading they would be going in to the compound a couple of vehicles at a time and not in a convoy.

By 8pm, all the Met Police team and the six officers assigned to them by Chief Constable Morgan were in a large briefing room on the second floor of Reading Station. Sgt. Easeman had a larger map of the area attached to a briefing board and began to describe the yard's interior as he knew it, the location of the yard and the various roads leading up to it. DI Roberts picked four of his team and two of the local officers and the six men left to set up surveillance on the site.

In direct radio contact, they would report every activity in and around the yard and the industrial estate itself over the next few hours.

DI Roberts put the remaining men in teams of eight, each one with a specific task of either entering a warehouse or the Portacabin. The plan, if the padlock on the gate proved not to be a problem, was for the teams to drive straight up to each of the buildings and quickly gain entry into each one. Whilst the measure of surprise would be slightly lost, it meant that Harry could get all his men into and by the target locations in the fastest possible time. The other option was to enter the yard and then stealthily make their way to each of the buildings. This was, he thought, somewhat riskier as if the first of the men were spotted, it gave the four inside more of an opportunity to strike and it would then mean his men would have to try and get to the warehouses on foot from about 50 yards after they came around the bend in the driveway.

It was unlikely that the doors would be locked, but just in case he made sure that all three teams had designated a member who had a solid steel door ram. The Portacabin was the simplest to enter as they were typically all the same in design and structure. They had had experience in entering these before so, as they had done previously, four men would enter and the other four outside smash the windows. It would be unlikely that all the suspects would be in there, but if they were then the team entering would be offered protection by the group outside by the windows.

The warehouses would be a bit more difficult, some 8 to

10,000 sq. ft., they knew one had a mezzanine floor and an office, but the information did not specify which one. Both warehouses had been and possibly still were being used as a garage, so an unknown number of vehicles, bikes, workbenches etc. would more than likely be inside. The only saving grace for this raid was that it was in daylight so some light would be available, and the thought process was that the O'Dowd brothers and the other two would need light, either natural or otherwise, to assist in their preparations.

It was a possibility that the main roll doors to the warehouse would be open. If this was the case then access would be easier; however, the risk then was increased significantly as they could well be spotted before they got there.

If they were closed, then they would go through the main entrance doors. Again, the difficulty lay in whether or not these main doors went straight into the warehouse or, as with so many buildings like this, into a workroom/office and then onto the warehouse.

The risks were incredibly high, and Harry would have liked several more days of planning, but unfortunately, as with many tip offs like this, they did not know how long they had before the suspects moved on.

He stood down the team for two hours, allowing them to get a cup of tea, a short nap or go outside for a fag. He knew the adrenalin would be running, as it was with himself. The unknown was always the killer in situations like this; 'plan for the worst and hope for the best' crossed his mind. He rang Assistant Commissioner Paul Lang and filled him in with the plan, the options he had taken, the risks associated with the unknown and a disaster recovery plan.

The plan was with the approval of Chief Constable Morgan and Chief Inspector Deer, who were also at the briefing, and although they had no overall command of the events, the Chief Constable's approval was needed. Chief Inspector Deer would coordinate any activity at the station, and he would alert the ambulance service and put them on standby. The local hospital would not be informed unless the ambulances were deployed. In addition, the Chief Inspector would brief Inspector Johnson, the current commander of the local division, and in turn they would brief the duty sergeant and have on standby 20 local police officers whose role would be to take control of the area if the raid went pear-shaped.

At 6am, the vehicles left the compound and made their way to the designated waiting area. Sgt. Easeman was in the lead vehicle with Harry, who had been in constant radio contact with his surveillance team. They had reported that whilst they each had a decent vantage point, there was no movement at the yard yet.

They had selected a cul-de-sac at the other end of the industrial estate to park up and wait. The four transits and two unmarked cars made their way onto Cullen Lane then into Park Drive, which was about five minutes from the entrance to the yard. There was nothing left to do but wait.

Chapter 6

Donny was always an early riser, and at 5am he made his way downstairs and flicked the kettle on. Opening the fridge, he pulled out the milk and when the kettle boiled made himself a coffee and settled down at the kitchen table and lit a cigarette. He thought through the day's tasks: the van needed a few more adjustments and he needed to check the engine over to make sure it was in good nick. The last thing they needed was for it to break down on the way to London. The Cortina needed a look as well just to be on the safe side.

He and Declan would go up in the van with Sean and Patrick behind in the Cortina. The previous weekend they had been up to London and around the Leicester Square area. They were going to leave the vehicle in Bear Street, just off Leicester Square itself. It was a very busy thoroughfare on a Friday night and the chaos it would cause would be enormous. At 6pm on a Friday evening you had thousands of tourists milling around, along with the early evening theatre goers, and on a Friday night, a great many office workers made their way into the area for drinks at the many bars and pubs.

They would, as usual, give a three-minute warning, but Donny knew that that was a token gesture. It was highly unlikely that the area could be evacuated in three minutes. He also doubted that they would identify the vehicle that quickly either. He didn't see the point in any warning, he hated the British and they could all die as far as he was concerned. However, in some bizarre reference to keeping various interested parties on their side, and to keep the links open with funding options and suppliers, it was deemed that whilst they were at war with the British, they weren't terrorist who wanted to kill women and children indiscriminately, so to keep up this pretence they always gave a warning of some description.

At 6am, he could hear his bother Patrick walking around upstairs, so he put the kettle back on and dropped some more coffee into a couple of cups. Declan and Sean were staying at two different bed and breakfast houses in Reading. It was too much of a risk for all four of them to be in the same house, and whilst in was unlikely that either Declan or Sean would be recognised, it was far safer to be split up for most of the time.

Both the houses were run by sympathetic Irish related families, so they were comfortable that they were relatively secure in both places. At 6:30am, the brothers got into Donny's car and made their way to pick up first Declan and then Sean. At precisely 6:45am, Declan walked out of the house, Donny was just pulling up outside and Declan climbed into the back. At 6:55am, Donny pulled up outside the second bed and breakfast and Sean walked down the path; he too got into the car.

Apart from a perfunctory 'Morning', nothing was said between them and they arrived at the yard at 7:25am. Patrick got out, unlocked the padlock and Donny drove the car through and pulled up to the second warehouse. Patrick locked the gate and made his way into the Portacabin and then unlocked the first warehouse door.

'Activity on site,' crackled the radio.

'All targets have arrived and are in the yard; the gate is padlocked,' continued the update from one of Harry's team stationed close to but hidden from the main site near the yard.

Switching his radio on, DI Roberts spoke, 'Sparrow 1. We will go in at 07:40.'

The teams, to a man, checked their watches.

The two surveillance officers and Sgt. Easeman waited. They would keep watch and not move towards the yard until all the other teams were in. Their roles were to secure the gate and prevent anyone from entering.

The two unmarked vehicles and transit vans moved out of the cul-de-sac and drove slowly down and around the corner and along the street towards the yard entrance. Pulling up about 100 yards before the gate, two officers got out of the second vehicle and, staying close to the hedge, moved towards the gate. The second man locked his gun tight into his body and put his hand on the shoulder of the man in front. Carefully, they made their way to the gate.

Because of the number of scrap cars piled high they had no view of the Portacabin or warehouses, which made their task a little easier. The second man's eyes gazed past his colleague and focussed on the gravel path that went into the yard. His partner lifted the heavy bolt cutters and slipped the jaws onto the padlock link. Snapping the padlock, he lowered the cutters and unhooked it.

'Padlock off,' he said into his radio.

With that he lifted the right-hand side of the gate and his partner took hold of the left-hand gate.

'Go! Go! Go!' radioed DI Roberts.

The two men pushed the gates wide open as the lead vehicles and transits flew through the gate, down the drive, around the bend and came to a grinding halt outside of the warehouse and Portacabin. The teams poured out of the vehicles and ran towards their given targets.

Team one went straight to the Portacabin. The men leaped up the stairs and crashed into the door flinging it wide open. The windows were shattered and guns trained into the office. The two men burst into the room, with two more right behind them, searching left and right quickly looking for a target. The Portacabin was just one long 30ft room so hiding places were non-existent. Within a fraction of a second, the lead man signalled to his colleagues that the room was empty.

'Sparrow 14: Porta all clear,' he called into his radio.

Simultaneously, team two and three burst out of their vehicles and made their way to their respected targets. Team two, out of the van, ran towards the first warehouse. The main roller doors were down so they headed for the office door on the right-hand side. The lead man quickly tried the handle, which proved to be unlocked, swung the door open and saw that it led directly into the warehouse itself. Two of the team threw in flash bang grenades as far as they could. The blinding light and noise echoed throughout the huge warehouse, and with coordinated precision, the eight men made their way in. Splitting up, four took the left-hand side and the other four went straight over to the other side, searching and moving forwards as fast as they could. The warehouse housed several vehicles and bikes in a variety of stages of repair. Work benches were littered with spare parts, wires and old batteries.

The team worked its way down the warehouse, constantly on guard for any movement or sound. Within a few minutes, they had covered the whole of the area with the result that no one was there. No mezzanine floor, no office, no one was hiding under a work bench or in an old vehicle. They radioed through to Harry that the building was clear.

Team three hit the second warehouse within seconds of the van coming to a halt. The team of eight piled out and ran towards the entrance door. As with the first warehouse, the roller doors were down so the only way in was the battered red door in the warehouse wall.

Johnny Sturgess, an officer of 20 years, 12 with this unit, tried the handle of the door; it turned and he pushed it open. Mark Stephens, his partner, was on his shoulder and the two of them looked and stepped inside. The door opened into a small office, a single vacant desk with a telephone and a pile of paper were the only things in the room. Behind the desk was another door. Johnny, with his weapon at the ready and teammates behind him, moved quickly to the door.

Opening the door and pushing it open, both he and Mark crouched down; a hail of gunfire met them, the bullets tore into the door frame and door. Leaning back, Derek and Jeff. who were directly behind the lead pair, unpinned two flash bang grenades and launched them into the room.

The noise was deafening and the bolt of light blinding. The team had rehearsed this manoeuvre many times at their training ground and with the boys from Hereford. Their heads were covered with both a helmet, protective ear defenders and gas masks, which, though whilst cumbersome, gave them the edge when on an assault such as this.

With less than a second of the grenades going off, the first team rushed into the room, guns raised, looking for targets. Fractions of seconds later more gun fire was directed at them but this time it was more disorganised, the bullets ricocheting off the floor, the door and the ceiling. Pinpointing the direction of fire, Johnny and Mark opened fire in unison. The gun was silenced.

As Johnny and Mark had made their way into the warehouse, Derek and Jeff entered and took the left-hand side, working their way along the wall. The other four men came into the room and quickly took up positions protecting the lead men.

With the smoke clearing, the team could assess the site in front of them. Moving forward, Johnny and Mark stepped towards what appeared to be somebody with their hands in the air.

Derek and Jeff went around one of the work benches and found another of the target men kneeling and coughing uncontrollably. Pushing him roughly to the ground, and with two other team members protecting them, Derek quickly searched the man. Pulling his arms behind him with Jeff holding his weapon close, he strapped the man's hands together.

Johnny, as with Derek, pushed the man to the floor, and with Mark watching over him, searched all his pockets looking for any kind of firearm. None found, he too was strapped and left on the floor. Steve, along with his partner Andy, had come across a target who was lying motionless on the floor with blood oozing out of his mouth; a gun was in his left hand. Steve kicked the weapon away and checked his vital signs. 'Sparrow 11: Target down and out,' he radioed.

'Sparrow 6: Target down and cuffed,' said Johnny.

Continuing their search, they went through the cars that had their bonnets up and were waiting for spares, they then carefully moved on past the work benches, acutely aware that their fourth target was here somewhere.

'Sparrow 10: Target down and cuffed,' said Derek.

'Sparrow 1: One to go, careful everyone.'

Cautiously, all the team members made their way further into the warehouse. Martin and Clive, the seventh and eighth members of the group, started to climb the stairs to the mezzanine floor.

They got to the top of the staircase and very slowly inched forwards looking and listening for any movement or sound. Covering the floor in a few minutes, they were confident that no one was there.

'Sparrow 12: Mezzanine clear,' said Martin.

Clive walked to the rail of the mezzanine and looked into the warehouse. Quickly taking in the whole scene, he noticed what he thought was a door at the very back of the warehouse; a shaft of light was coming through it.

'Sparrow 11: Door open back of warehouse,' he called on his radio.

DI Roberts, on hearing the call, radioed team one, who had entered the Portacabin to go round the back of the warehouse. Running past several columns of scrap cars, the officers came to the back of the warehouse only to find their way blocked by more cars, and behind that, the huge mound of earth that had been piled up to prevent flooding.

'No access here,' called one of the men.

The other members of that team had gone the opposite way and again tried to make their way past dozens of scrap cars. Passing the back of the first warehouse, they too were hampered by more cars and bikes and on this side, bushes and thick tangled growth had grown up across the mound and blocked their way to the back.

'No access this side,' came the call to Harry.

Johnny, Derek, Jeff and Mark worked their way at a faster pace towards the back of the warehouse, on hearing the call from Clive. Getting to the door, they pushed it open and cautiously stepped outside.

The door opened onto a small grass patch, which ran the length of warehouse's back wall and was about 10 ft. to the huge mound of protective earth. Both sides to the warehouse were blocked. On reflection, Johnny first thought this had been done on purpose to stop anyone from breaking in.

Johnny moved towards the mound and on closer inspection he could clearly see footprints dug into the earth. He followed them up to the top, lots of loose earth where someone had lost their footing but a clear route to the top.

'Boss,' he called on the radio, 'I think one of them has gone over the top of this barrier. I'm going up.'

With that, both he and Jeff jumped at the loose earth and crawled their way to the top. Within a few moments, they were both looking over to where the water lapped up and onto the banks of the opposite field.

'Can't see anyone,' said Johnny on his radio.

Jumping down the other side, trying not to dig the barrels of theirs guns into the soft earth, the two of them made it to the bottom and scouted around.

It didn't take either of them very long to spot the footprints going into the river.

'He's got across the river and has gone through the field, best guess to those trees over to the left,' said Johnny to Jeff.

Johnny radioed to DI Roberts his thinking; DI Roberts immediately called base for a request to set up roadblocks.

Chapter 7

Sean was the first to react. Hearing the revved engines of vehicles outside and the unmistakeable crunch of gravel as they came to a halt, Sean dropped the cup of tea that Patrick had brought in and rushed over to the workbench. He grabbed his Widowmaker, the Armalite AR-18, which had a 40-round magazine already loaded. Spinning around, instinct and history had taught him that this was not going to be a social visit by anyone. Not knowing who it was did not occur to Sean, as in his experience, no one came knocking at the end of vehicles racing into an area that had been securely padlocked to stop unwarranted visitors. 'Raid!' he shouted at the top of his voice.

A fraction of a second later the door at the top of the warehouse swung open and Sean fired a burst of bullets straight at the door. Moving from the bench he jumped forward and tried to make it to one of the cars on his left-hand side, which would provide him with a defensive position, one he thought would give him a better line of sight to the door and whoever was going to come in. In the second that he made his way forward, an almighty blast and blinding light filled the room. Sean had been straight on to the grenade as he moved forward and caught the full force of the light straight into his eyes, blinding him instantly. The noise followed an instant later. Falling to the ground, on his knees he raised the weapon in the general direction of the noise and who-ever he thought would be following in, and he pulled the trigger. Only being able to hold the gun in his right hand, the bullets spewed from the magazine across the space in a haphazard fashion. Grabbing the gun properly, he swung to aim at the door.

Three bullets caught Sean: one is his upper arm, tearing his left-hand grip from the machine gun, one hit his chest, pushing him backwards, and the final lucky strike, which hit him straight in the face, disintegrated on hitting the bone of skull killing him instantly. As he fell to the floor, the blood, a lifetime of hate, poured out of his face and spread across the oil-soaked concrete in front of him.

Donny didn't hear the vehicles approaching, nor their skid to a halt on the gravel, as he was inside the back of the Simca van removing the last of the strengthening bars. He did, however, hear the bullets being fired by Sean. Scrambling out of the van, tripping and falling to the floor in his haste, he was caught by the light and noise, which disorientated him. He could not stop himself breathing in the acrid smoke, which slowly filled his lungs. Rising to his knees, he could no longer see properly or hear anything that was happening around him. He felt sick and was desper-ately trying to breathe as he felt himself being pushed to the floor, arms wrenched behind him. Feeling the straps closing tightly around his wrists, his vision began to come back to him. Still unable to hear, he just lay there and tried to breathe slowly.

Patrick was walking across the garage, sipping his tea. He had made cups for all of them and had just left Donny's on the inside of the van. Having seen that he was making good progress with the struts, he began to walk over to the workbench where the straps that would hold the drums in the van were. He wanted to make sure that each one would hold tightly, as any spillage or movement on their way to London would cause considerable damage, or even cause the explosion, neither of which he needed to happen.

Patrick looked upon hearing Sean's shout and watched him as he ran to the bench, grabbing his gun. Trying to relive what Sean had shouted and to be sure he had heard right, Patrick, like his brother, had never faced any form of threat, raid, or attack from anyone and was completely unprepared for what was about to take place. Whilst they had spoken about various scenarios, living them was a completely different thing.

Responding to threats of any sort required, at first, practice, if possible, in a training environment and even then, the real thing was always different to the training programme. In the main, this was because of the unexpected ability of the enemy you faced. In a stand-up fight you can at times second guess the moves that someone will make. When it is an unpredictable event, and in a setting that is in the open arena, then anything can and pretty much will happen. For Sean and Declan, however, preparing for a raid, or attack was something that they had gone through, both spoken and practised.

All four men were at war with the British Government; Declan and Sean were on the front line, so they were far more aware of the dangers that they faced. A raid was a high probability, and it was how they reacted to it that would define the outcome and their futures.

Being prepared, however, would not have helped Patrick in the slightest, as neither he nor Donny were on the front line nor had had any form of training, so as Patrick watched in what he thought later was slow motion as Sean fired a burst towards the door, he looked at the door and then his world came to a halt. His eyes filled with white light and his head exploded in an unbelievably loud noise. Completely disorientated, he fell to his knees and put his right hand over his mouth and nose, the cups of tea falling to the floor and smashing as they hit the ground. His brain trying to catch up with what had just happened, not being a fighting man, he put his left hand in the air. What seemed like an age but was in fact only 30 seconds or so, he too was pushed to the floor and both wrists strapped together.

Declan was at the back of the warehouse; he was filing down a metal bar that would brace the two drums together and secure them to the side of the van. Whilst both would be strapped to stop any movement, the drums had to be tight together to allow the feed pipe and wires to link each other together.

Concentrating on the task at hand, in the back of his mind he heard the vehicles and the noise they made when they came to stop outside. Knowing, or second guessing like Sean, that this was a raid, he swung around from the bench and began to run up the warehouse to the door.

His weapon was on the same bench as Sean's. He cursed under his breath as he realised that he would not make it in time to get it and support Sean. He'd put it there early and was, at that time, in two minds whether to take it with him down to the end of the warehouse and put it on the bench by him as he worked. However, he had chosen not to as the metal brace he was fashioning needed two hands to carry it back to the van to install, so he thought the better of it and left it with Sean's. Knowing he'd made a mistake, he stopped running and swiftly turned around.

His thought process had already advanced on the scenarios that were about to play out in front of him. Run, get the weapon and support Sean, killing anyone who came into the building. They had plenty of ammunition for both weapons, and Donny and Patrick also had guns with which they too could keep the police at bay. That would lead to a stand-off at some point, with the eventuality of getting killed or surrendering to the police. Getting killed was not a problem but surrendering would lead to incarceration and many futile years spent behind bars.

The other option was to evade capture if he could. Spinning around, he ran down the warehouse, and as he heard the bullets come out of Sean's gun, he kicked the metal bar of the fire exit door on the back wall of the warehouse. It flew open and he ran outside. He heard the noise the grenade made but was not disabled by the light. He launched himself at the earth mound and clawed his way as fast as he could to the top. In the background, the sounds of gunfire drifted to him as he half ran half fell down the 20ft high mound.

The mound fell away to a grass bank that was alongside a small tributary; it hadn't flooded in years. Approximately 30ft wide and at its deepest point about 6ft, it flowed peaceably into the Thames. Winding its way along the back edge of the industrial park and then carrying on through several fields, it was home to a variety of fish and provided a safe landing place for hundreds of migrating birds. There was no path along this part of the stream and no boats ever came this far. It didn't lead to anywhere in particular and just meandered as it had done for hundreds of years across farmlands and through the occasional clump of trees.

Declan ran straight at the stream and began wading into the middle. Within a few seconds, he dived in and made a few swimming strokes to get across as fast as he could. He swam as close as he could to the other side, as stepping into water-filled earth would hamper his ability to get out.

Fortunately, because the stream wasn't deep there was no embankment to climb up so he just had to crawl out and get his footing as soon as he could on the dry field. Swimming in a river fully clothed creates enormous problems for the swimmer but looks easy enough when you are on the bank looking down. When you are in the river and trying to get up and out it's an incredibly difficult activity. With a huge effort spurred on by adrenalin Declan heaved himself onto the edge of the field.

Standing up and running to his left, he headed towards a group of trees that were on the opposite side of the field. The stream ran along the edge and the back of the yard, past the boundary of Donny's property, and then ran for about hundred yards, making its way west towards the Thames. He ran ignoring the squelching in his shoes and the drag his wet clothes made on his progress. He knew that if the police had scaled the mound as he had they would not open fire on him. Apart from the distance, they would have to shoot, and as far as he knew, it was not the policy of the British police to start shooting at an unarmed man racing away from them.

Crashing into the first few trees, he'd made the distance without hearing any shouts in the background. Panting heavily, he tore off his sweater and looked around back at the mound. No one was there, or in the field, it looked, he thought, as if he'd got away, well, at least this far for now. Squeezing as much water out of his sweater as he could, he put it back on. Taking each shoe off and wringing out his socks, he quickly put those back on and made his way through the small copse.

Not knowing where he was or how far the trees extended, he ran through and jumped over fallen branches and pushed through some overgrown shrubs. Within a few minutes, he hit a road. Looking up and down, it looked like a main road on another industrial estate; this one was made up mainly of offices with a few big industrial units. Careful not to run, he walked quickly up the road looking into a couple of car parks for a car. It was still early, and people were just starting to arrive at work. There were several people around, but they were distracted by their own thoughts about this Monday morning and the tasks ahead at work rather than watching a walking man.

About 200 yards up from where he had broken through the trees onto the road, he came across a small car park belonging to a manufacturing company, with an assortment of cars. He surmised that most of them had started at 7am with some of the office workers turning up at 8:30/9:00. The car park was empty of people. Scouting the cars he saw a brown Cortina parked near the bottom of the car park. Walking straight up to it and picking up a brick from the edge of the kerb he smashed the passenger window. Looking around, no one had heard, and he unlocked the car door, slid over to the driver's side and kicked the central console under the steering wheel several times until it broke.

Hot wiring cars had been a fun pastime and a way to spend a Saturday afternoon when he was a kid back home. A car like this proved no problem to Declan and within seconds the car burst into life. Selecting reverse, he pulled out of the car parking slot and then onto the main road. Driving away from the way he had come he was hoping that this road led onto a main road. A few moments later, he came to a T junction. 'All routes' 'M4' said the sign, so Declan turned and made his towards the motorway.

Less than ten minutes later he was on the M4 heading towards Bristol. Keeping the car at about 65mph, and mostly in the nearside lane, he'd attract little if no attention from any police cars. He doubted that the car would be reported stolen until midday anyway or, if he was very lucky, at the end of the worker's shift, which was probably around 4pm. The local police, even if it had been reported by the squad who had raided them that someone had got away, would be very unlikely to block the M4, more likely, they would be searching on foot with dogs somewhere where he had been.

It wouldn't be long before they suspected that he'd taken a car but finding him and finding which car had been stolen would take some time, at least enough time for him to get to Bristol. As he drove he thought about the recent events, and wondering how the others had fared, he guessed that Sean would make a fight of it. They had never discussed a plan if they were to be raided but it was an unspoken rule that they would fight if they could, escape if an option presented itself, and worst case scenario, to give in and get arrested.

He reasoned that with the amount of bomb making equipment in the warehouse, the three of them would fight for as long as they could. Anyway, once he got to O'Connor's, over the course of the next few days he would find out.

So, how did they know we were there? he thought.

The options that presented themselves were firstly, the two brothers had let slip they were coming over and someone had informed the police. Declan ran through this with a fine-tooth comb but decided that if the police knew they were coming they would have raided Saturday or Sunday morning and the brothers were not the sort to run away with their mouths, which was one of the reasons that they were there in the first place.

Another option was that someone back home had leaked

the plan. There were only four other people who knew what they were planning and two of them were him and Sean. The other two, one was the quartermaster and the other was Seamus, who ran the ASUs, a dedicated IRA man through and through, so again not really an option.

Which left the bloke who was snooping around on Saturday night, 'What was his name? Dave, Dave Hartman,' he said out loud.

He came up with some cock and bull story about MOT certificates. *Bullshit!* thought Declan. *Coincidental, I don't think so. I don't believe in coincidences never have. Not sure how he got word to the right police or what he saw but it's got to be him who tipped them off.*

The longer the drive lasted, on his way past Hungerford, past Swindon, he thought about Dave. By the time he made the motorway services he was convinced that Dave was the man who had informed on them.

'I'll kill the little shit,' he said through gritted teeth.

Pulling into Leigh Delamere services he parked to the side of the main block with a few other vehicles to avoid any unnecessary attention. Quickly looking through the pockets in the car and the central cup holder, he found a few coins. Enough, he thought, to make a phone call. Walking to the phone boxes on the outside of the service station, he rang the Bristol number. On answering, he pressed the coins in and asked for O'Connor.

'O'Conner.'

'It's Declan, I'm at Delamere services. I need somewhere to stay immediately.'

'Head onto the M32 and take the very first exit A4174 and pull up at the first layby on your left, you can't miss it. I'll be there,' and with that both men hung up.

Declan walked back to the car, started it up and got back onto the M4. Within twenty-five minutes he drove onto the M32 and pulled off at the first junction as instructed and looked out for the layby. Spotting Brendan O'Conner he pulled in. Brendan walked over as Declan came to a stop. Another man got out of the vehicle that Brendan was in and he too made his way towards Declan. For a moment, Declan was caught by surprise and for a brief second, he thought that he was going to have trouble.

'Hi Declan,' said Brendan.

'This is Alan, my cousin. He'll take yours, you get in mine.'

'Don't worry about Alan, as I said he's my cousin and he's going to get rid of the car. I was guessing that it needs to be lost.'

'Thanks,' said Declan.

Declan got in beside Brendan, who pulled out and made his way into Bristol through Temple Meads and up to Bedminster. As they drove, Declan outlined briefly what had happened in Reading. Leaving Bedminster, Brendan drove for about 20 minutes and then pulled off the main road. After about a mile he came to a small dirt track on his left-hand side. Driving down the track through the gate he pulled up outside a small farmhouse. The area was secluded, surrounded by tress and extremely difficult to access if you didn't know your way.

'Come in,' said Brendan, 'stay here for as long as you want. Is there anything you need?'

'I have to think,' said Declan, 'and to make a few phone calls.'

'Help yourself, phone's over there and the kitchen's through here,' said Brendan. 'I'll be out on the farm. No one is coming here today so you won't be disturbed. I'll be back in a couple of hours. If you need me, just toot the car horn.'

With that, Brendan walked out and left Declan to his thoughts.

As night drew in Brendan walked back into his house and found Declan sitting next to the fireplace, coffee in hand, deep in thought.

'I'm making some food. Do you want some?' asked Brendan.

Turning around, Declan looked at Brendan and said, 'Yes, I will.'

Following Brendan into the kitchen and placing his cup into the sink,

'What do you want to do?' said Brendan to Declan.

'They are either dead or at the station in Reading. We need to find out tomorrow what happened. I've rang Seamus and told him. He'll wait for a call from the O'Dowd's solicitor before he does anything. We should know tomorrow what the next move will be,' said Declan.

With that, he watched Brendan cook some sausages and potatoes. Wandering back into the lounge, he switched on the TV in time for the 6 o'clock news. Nothing on the BBC mentioned the raid, not that he thought it would do at this early point.

Finishing off their meal, Brendan told Declan where he would be sleeping, and with that Declan closed the bedroom door, lit a cigarette and contemplated the day's events.

I'll know more tomorrow, he thought

At 8 o'clock the next morning Brendan gave Declan a lift into the centre of Bristol. Parking up, Brendan made his way towards a café for some breakfast and Declan opened the door of one of the phone boxes situated in the main street just down from the Hippodrome.

Piling coins into the box he listened to Seamus.

'I've got some bad news for you,' said Seamus.

'Sean's dead, they shot him in the raid, and he died at the warehouse. Patrick and his brother Donny are in custody, they are in Reading nick at the moment. Mike Jefferson, their solicitor, is being told that they will be transferred to London today. Obviously, he will be there at their interviews.'

'Oh shit! Sean's dead! Those bastards are going to pay for this,' said Declan

'They'll pay, don't worry about that,' said Seamus in his deep, heavy Irish accent.

'It appears they knew there were four of you but Mike doesn't seem to think that they know who you are. The brothers aren't talking and they won't. Stay at Brendan's, end of the week I'll arrange for you go up to Birmingham. You will stay there for a couple of weeks and then we will set another target up,' said Seamus.

They will have your prints, but as you have never been fingerprinted, you won't be on their system. When you get to Birmingham, I'll get another passport to you.'

He could hear Declan breathing heavily, knowing that it was the loss of Sean. The two of them had known each for some time and it was always difficult when you lost a brother in arms.

'You listening to me?' said Seamus.

After a second or two, 'Yes, I hear you,' said Declan.

'Have you any idea how they caught onto you?' asked Seamus.

'I think it might have been some kid we caught trying to break into the place on Saturday night. It's a long shot but I can't think of anything else, unless they were following the O'Dowd's or there was a leak over by you,' said Declan.

'I'll look into it over here. I'll talk to the QM, see if he has heard anything. We'll find out,' said Seamus

With that Seamus put the phone down. Declan walked over to the café where Brendan was eating a bacon roll.

'Tea and bacon roll,' said Declan to the assistant.

Sitting down opposite Brendan he said, 'We'll talk on the way back.'

On the drive back to Brendan's, Declan told him of the conversation he had had with Seamus and aired his thoughts about the event.

'Sorry about Sean,' said Brendan. 'Never met him.'

'I can't think it would be a leak from over home. They would have either arrested both of us as we had got into the country, or at the very least Sean. I doubt that the brothers have been followed. They haven't done anything for a couple of years, nor would they tell anyone about what they were up to anyway. Why would they, no benefit to them at all. If they had been followed and saw the four of us together, they would have raided Saturday or even Sunday. Why wait until Monday morning? Doesn't make sense,' said Declan.

'Also,' continued Declan, 'the solicitor said that Donny told him when he taken out of the warehouse, there were about 30 or 40 of them, several vans, most of them armed, and all the buildings had been hit, which means they didn't know which building we were in,' said Declan.

'They weren't watching the yard then. Ok, so what's left?' asked Brendan.

'Some guy tried to break into the yard on Saturday night. We caught him and gave him a beating. He said that him and his mate were after MOT certificates and they were going to sell them. We thought about getting rid of him but changed our minds and let him go. Monday morning, we are raided,' said Declan.

'But why would a kid report you to the police and, secondly, why the level of raid they did? What did he see when he was in there? Does he work for the Old Bill?' asked Brendan.

'He wouldn't have seen anything apart from the van, couple of drums and some bags, but drums are what you see in garages and how would he know what was in the bags? As for working for them, he was too young, about 18-19, 20,' said Declan.

'Too young for anything decent in the police,' said Brendan.

'Yes, but I don't believe in coincidences,' replied Declan.

Pulling up at the farmyard, they both got out, walked

around the back of the house and sat at the iron table in the garden overlooking several acres of grazing land.

Lighting up a cigarette, Declan said,

'It has to be the kid called Dave. He said his name was Dave Hartman. Maybe it was because we threatened to kill him – we are Irish – beat him up, and he thought he would get his own back. Maybe he rang the police, the O'Dowd's were flagged up somewhere and someone in the Met decided that four Irish blokes in a yard were a threat. Bit thin but that's all I've got at the moment.'

'So what do you want to do?' asked Brendan.

'I want you or whoever to go to Reading and find this bloke and his mate.'

'That's a needle in a haystack. Where would we start?' said Brendan.

'The only time the four of us were out was on the Friday night at a pub in the centre of Reading called The Railway, start there. I do care how long this takes but I want that guy. Just tell whoever it is that's doing the looking that he only has to find him. I don't want him touched at all. I'll do that. Understood?' said Declan.

'Leave it with me, we'll find him,' said Brendan.

Chapter 8

Most of the pain had gone by Friday and so on the Saturday he decided to get up fully and get out of the house for a bit. Looking in the mirror, his face was bruised, red and his ear was still very swollen. He could see out of both eyes and the pain in his leg had gone. The ribs and groin, on the other hand, still delivered sporadic lightning bolts of pain that made him wince and sit. He knew his mother knew he was lying, as the injuries to his face were not the sort you would get by falling down steps, but he stuck to his story and that was that. She would lose interest now he was up and about.

Driving out of Reading onto the M4 he headed towards Slough. Twenty minutes later, pulling into the town centre, he made the short walk to the High Street and into the Wimpey. It was 11:30am and the place was empty. The smell as he entered the shop was just mouth-watering. Him and Pete regularly used this place before work and at weekends, pretty much any time they could really. Freshly made burgers on the hob sizzled and chips, giving off their distinctive aroma, were cooking away next to them. Ordering a cheeseburger, chips and Coke, the guy behind the counter told him to take a seat and he would bring it over when ready.

Sliding into a small chair behind a plastic covered table, with his back to the wall halfway down the shop, he picked up *The Sun* newspaper. From where he sat, he could see everyone who came and went without really looking.

Ten minutes later, the food arrived, and he bit into the best burger in the world, or so he thought. Reading didn't have a Wimpey; the best they could do was a Little Chef and he didn't fancy one of those. *Wish they would open one soon*, he thought, *they'd make a fortune in Reading.*

With the burger finished and with a few chips left, Geoffrey sat down in front of Tony. Tony had seen him come in but had chosen to ignore him as he did now.

'You're a complete idiot,' started Geoffrey. 'Look at you, and for what? You didn't need to go anywhere near that place. We had it all under control.'

'How am I supposed to know that?' said Tony.

'You're not, it's not what we want you to do. Which bit of "do not go anywhere near the suspect" did you miss at your meetings last year?'

'I gave you information that you didn't have, and by the way what have you done with it?'

'Not that I have to tell you anything, but we went in, during the week, and all four have been arrested and will be charged under the Terrorism Act for bomb making.' He didn't mention and felt that it was not in the best interests of Tony to tell him that one of the men had escaped.

'Good.'

'Are you in pain?' asked Geoffrey.

'Yes.'

'Serves you right, because, let this be a lesson, I really don't care. We will not now or ever come to your rescue, do you understand? Let's be very, very clear, moving forward. It's not your job, it never was your job and it never will be your job to get close to, talk to or even go on a snooping spree with a suspect. Your job is only to watch and report, that's it. Understand?'

'Well that's it for me anyway,' said Tony. 'Me and Pete, we are off to Germany, getting out of here. Sick to death of the weather and sick to death of you.'

'What are you going to do over there, you don't speak German, either of you?'

'The guy I work for now has asked us to go sell life assurance to the British troops over there. Captive market, young, all got jobs, all got money and you never know what might happen to them. Anyway, that old bag Ester Rantzen has pretty much screwed up the door to door selling over here.'

Geoffrey just looked at him.

'Don't know what you're looking at. As you say, it's my life, you don't own me, you don't pay me and I've got to make a living, so fuck you!'

'Where are you going?' asked Geoffrey.

'I dunno, Padda something. We're off end of next week,' and with that Tony got up, grabbed his Coke and made his way out onto the High Street.

Wonder if Pete's up for a beer, he thought.

Geoffrey watched him go. He didn't try to stop him or convince him to stay. *Let him go*, he thought, *been a bit of a shock and a wakeup call for the lad. He'd been lucky though,*

70

if this had been Ireland, he would be dead. He's just the sort of bloke we need on the outside, quick thinking, resilient and calm under pressure. He began to remember the first time he'd met Tony. They were in a hotel just outside of Farnborough, and Tony had been sent a solicitor's letter asking him to attend a meeting, as a follow up in relation to the event at Greenham Common the year before. Tony had rung the solicitors. Did he need a solicitor and who exactly was he meeting? They had fed Tony the line, as directed, that it was a general chat. They had been given the report from Lieutenant General Scott Mckinny USAF and wanted to make sure that the events of the day were as correct as detailed. There was nothing to worry about, he wasn't in any trouble, they wanted to close off the file on the UK side.

'Come in,' said Geoffrey to Tony.

'Sorry to keep you waiting,' it was 11am. A test of patience.

'No problem,' said Tony, and he sat down on the chair offered.

'You know why you are here,' said Geoffrey, 'it's a sensitive subject, and I know that you are probably surprised and possibly a bit worried to be asked here. Let me say straightaway that you are not in trouble. You can leave at any time and nothing in the future will affect anything you may do. This is just an informal chat, so relax. Ok. Tea?'

'Ok yes thanks,' said Tony.

'Tell me in your own words what happened last year,' said Geoffrey as he poured Tony a cup of tea.

Chapter 9

'Right let's go, get in the van!' shouted Greg to the group coming out of the paint shed. Greg Adams was the foreman in charge of the painting team who were sprucing up the barrack blocks for the United States Air Force's young men who were stationed at Greenham Common Airbase, near Newbury in Berkshire. They had been there about eight weeks now and had finished four of the eight blocks that needed doing. Each unit was the same and housed approximately 50 men in a variety of dorms and single rooms.

The base had seen increased activity over the summer due to the placement of the Cruise missiles now being stored on the base. The security had been tightened up, especially with Greenpeace and CND, amongst others, making camp and protesting at the entrance into the base. Rumours were that at some point they were going to try and break into the base and cause havoc. Greg, along with most other people, didn't really care too much, a job was a job and also, they enjoyed the same privileges as the guys on site: their food hall and canteen were brilliant.

Every day, him and his guys would go in for breakfast and be overwhelmed by the amount of food that was available to eat free of charge. Again, at lunch time and on some weekends, some of them would come back onto the base and play pool and ten pin bowling with the air force men who were off duty that weekend. It was a great job, would last most of the summer, so he knew his blokes had been dragging it out a bit.

'Common let's go!' he shouted again. 'It's Friday night, time for a few beers.'

The four men got into the back of the van. Greg was driving and next to him was Sailor, a long-serving painter who always sat in the front.

Tony lit a cigarette up in the back of the van. 'Doing much this weekend Mark?' he asked.

'Usual, pub, the bookies tomorrow. I might do a bit of fishing Sunday', replied Mark. 'What about you?'

The conversation between the four of them was idle banter for the next 20 minutes until Mark got out in Newbury and then Tony was dropped off a bit further on for the short walk home.

Walking up the path to his home, Tony searched his pockets for his keys and then realised with panic that he'd left his coat up at the base. His keys, and more importantly, his week's wages, were left behind in his coat pocket. He swore repeatedly, trying to think about what he could do.

With dejection, he sat down on the doorstep and waited for someone to come home. *So much for getting home early on a Friday*, he thought.

About 5pm his sister drove onto the path, got out and walked up towards the front door.

'What you doing?' she asked.

'Waiting for you, left my keys in my coat.'

Opening the door, Tony went to the phone and rang Greg.

'Hello mate, I've left my keys and wallet up the base. Can you come back and give me a lift back up there?' asked Tony.

'No!' said Greg.

'Oh, come on. Everything I have is in my coat and I will be screwed this weekend if I don't get it back, just this once, please.'

'No chance, I'm not coming all the way back there, up to the base and then driving back to Hungerford in the rush hour. it will take me ages. Anyway, I'm getting changed, me and the missus are going out, you'll have to wait 'til Monday,' said Greg, and with that he hung up.

'Prick!' said Tony out loud.

I have to get my money, thought Tony, *how the fuck am I going to get in the base?* His pass was in his coat pocket and without driving there in the company van with Greg, he wouldn't get in on his own. The staff at the base on the weekend who were on guard duty didn't want to be there, and he'd seen before that they would be awkward and just be a bunch of pencil pushers and sticklers for the rules.

Running upstairs, he pushed open his sister's door, 'Give me a lift up the base will you. I've left my coat, keys and money up there.'

'No, I'm busy,' said his sister.

'Come on, I've done loads of things for you and it won't take you more than 15 minutes.'

'Can't remember you doing anything for me,' she said.

'I'll pay your petrol, get you some drinks and I'll get you into Valbonnes for free,' said Tony.

Thinking about it, his sister said, 'And my mates?'

'Yes, all of them,' said Tony in desperation.

'I'm not waiting for you. I'll drop you off and then you can make your own way back.'

'That's fine,' said Tony, 'let's go.' Anything to get his stuff back.

On the way up to the base, Tony said 'Don't go to the front gate, take Parsons Road and then there's a small road just off it, you can pull in there. I'll go in the back way, it's easier on a Friday,' he lied.

'Also, I can catch the bus back, there's a stop halfway along Parsons,' he said.

After being dropped off, Tony made his way down the small single gravel track towards the base.

From Parsons Road, the fence surrounding the base was about 500 yards down the gravel track. It was hidden, for the most part, by trees that covered the edge of the fence around the enormous air force base.

Getting to the fence, Tony turned right and walked along the edge towards some gates. The double gates were pad-locked, unmanned and a camera and light were fitted to catch any intruders. Passing this, Tony kept walking for about another 100 yards and came to a single gate. This gate was chained and then padlocked. Except the padlock wasn't locked, it just appeared locked. Tony went through the gate and onto the air base.

The paint shed was the other side of one of the runways, and although it was still daylight, he knew that it would only take him a few minutes to get there. He walked across, the temptation to run was great but running, he thought, might attract attention whereas someone just walking, he surmised, would be less of a risk.

Getting to the paint shed, he walked around the back and climbed in through the window: the shed was locked. Greg had the key, but him and a couple of others had got into the shed before. Climbing down he saw his coat on the chair. Breathing a sigh of relief, he picked it up and checked the pockets. Badge, money and keys were there. *Thank goodness for that,* he thought. Slipping the coat on, he looked at his watch: a bus would be along in about 20 minutes.

Lighting up a cigarette, he sat down on the chair and smiled. *Going to be a good weekend*, he thought.

Tony climbed back out of the window and walked around the front of the shed.

'Oh shit! Fuck me!' he exclaimed.

'Put your hands in the air, don't move. Put your hands in the air,' the voice bellowed.

Tony just stared at the sight in front of him.

Four police vehicles were lined up, blue lights on, and half a dozen police officers were behind their vehicles. Tony could clearly see each one had a gun in their hands. Each one, scarily, was pointed at Tony.

'Put your hands in the air!' came the shout again.

Tony put his hands in the air.

'Kneel down, don't move, do it now!' came the shout.

Tony chose not to make a smart-ass comment about 'kneeling down was moving' but given that he thought he might get shot, he thought the better of it and knelt with his hands in the air.

An officer approached him with his gun pointed directly at Tony. 'Are you on your own? Is there anyone else in the building?' he asked.

'No, just me, I've come to get my coat,' said Tony nervously.

'Put your hands behind your back, stay still!' said the officer.

Tony saw two other police officers move towards him and then go past and try the door handle.

'It's locked!' shouted Tony. 'I went in through the back window, there's only me. I came to get my coat, I'm a painter. We are doing your barracks and I left my coat here,' said Tony quickly, trying to explain.

The officer locked the handcuffs on Tony, and he was hauled up and put into the back of one of the police cars.

'You can explain everything when we get back,' said the police officer driving the car.

The short distance to the offices on the base was a journey made in silence. Tony sighed with relief that they hadn't started shooting at him.

Escorting Tony through the building to a small room, they uncuffed and searched him. Putting the contents on the table in front of him, they sat him down.

'Name!'

Tony told the officer his name, who he worked for and

what he was doing there. He showed him his badge and apologised several times for causing a problem.

'I don't think an apology will cut it,' drawled the American police officer.

Picking up Tony's wallet and his badge, 'Stay here and don't move, you're in enough trouble,' he said

'Can I smoke?' said Tony.

'Yes, Ok,' said the officer. 'I'll be back in minute.'

Tony lit up a cigarette and waited.

About half an hour and three fags later, the door opened and an American Air Force sergeant entered the room.

'Come with me,' he said.

Tony followed the master sergeant down several corridors to an outer office.

'Wait here!' he was told.

The sergeant knocked on a door waited for the command to enter and went in.

A minute later he came out.

'Come in here!' he said.

Tony entered the room. Sat at the desk was Lieutenant General Scott McKinney, a 35-year veteran. He had served in Vietnam, had won a medal of honour and was now in charge of RAF Greenham Common, overseeing the safe keeping of the newly arrived cruise missile.

Looking up, he introduced himself and told Tony to sit down and explain what he was doing.

Tony ran through the events of the last hour or so, apologising several times as he went. There was a knock on the door.

'Enter!' said Scott.

Tony breathed a sigh of relief. Buck Sergeant Michael Weinstein walked in.

Saluting the lieutenant general, he looked at Tony and shook his head.

'You know him then,' said Scott to Michael.

'Yes Sir, very well,' replied Michael.

Michael and Tony had known each other since Tony had first come onto the base. They played pool together in the canteen, and on many occasions, Tony had taken Michael down to Pete's place to play snooker.

Michael confirmed to Scott who Tony was and what he did on the base.

'You are a lucky man,' said Scott.

'Unfortunately, this is not the end of it. My men have to file a report which I will then pass onto base command in Brize Norton. Probably nothing will come of it, but you may be getting a call from your local police and a potential reprimand or fine. I'm not sure what sort of punishment they will give you, but suffice to say, do not ever, and I repeat, ever, do this again,' said Scott to Tony.

Tony, looking suitably chastised and inwardly relieved, apologised and confirmed that he would not be doing anything like this again.

'The sergeant will escort you out. By the way, before you go, how did you get in?'

Trying not to look at Michael. 'There's a gate on the other side of the base,' said Tony.

'I thought all our gates were locked,' said Scott.

Standing up, he turned to the large base map on the wall and said, 'Come here and show me.'

Tony walked over to the map and pointed.

'You see these double gates here, padlocked and with the camera, lights etc., well if you walk along here. . .' Tony drew his finger along the perimeter of the fence, 'this single gate here is where I got in,' he said

'But that's locked and checked,' said Scott.

Deliberately not looking at Michael. 'Well. . .' said Tony slowly,

'not really. It looks chained and padlocked but the lock is not fully fastened.'

'Why not, explain, and tell me the truth,' said Scott calmly looking at Tony.

'Most of the base is secure, you have some cameras, lights etc. at the main points, but we all know that we can get in and out if we need too. The gate is used by your guys to get back into the base late at night or on weekends instead of going through the main gate. The perimeter is checked by the same people, so people like you, no disrespect, but officers etc. don't go around checking things. So it's easy enough to get in and out,' said Tony.

Scott looked at him in disbelief.

'Good grief, what do you mean by "we all know"?'

'The base has been here a long time; local people know stuff. They walk their dogs around here, you know. Your guys are in and out, sometimes they get lifts back up here. There's no cameras or lights. No one tells anyone as such, just everyone knows. No real harm done. Sorry,' said Tony.

'So, who specifically knows on this base?'

'Oh, I don't know anyone,' said Tony. 'Just heard that's all.'

Scott looked at him, thought better of it and said,

'Ok, you'd better go. Sergeant take him home please and then report back here, we need to have a chat.'

'Yes Sir,' replied Michael.

'Thank you and sorry again,' said Tony. 'By the way, may I ask how you spotted me?'

Scott smiled and replied, 'One of your local dog walkers saw someone walking across the field and go around the back of the paint shed, called the local police, who rang us.'

'Oh right,' said Tony and with that turned and walked out of the office.

Walking down the corridor, Michael looked at Tony.

'What was I supposed to say? I'm in the shit anyway and he would have kept on and on if I hadn't told him. I don't need any more trouble,' said Tony.

'We'll just have to find another way out then,' said Michael.

'Easy, the base is big enough,' laughed Tony.

Chapter 10

Geoffrey watched Tony closely as he relayed the story of how he had gotten into the base and his encounter with the police and Scott McKinney. The file in front of him had given him the details of the encounter. Scott had written it up that day and passed it across to their command centre at Brize Norton. As with all breaches of American bases, the report itself had been copied a few times, set over to the CIA, a copy to the Met Police, local Newbury Constabulary and one over to his office in Counter Terrorism.

What had intrigued Geoffrey was Scott's impression of Tony that he was apologetic, calm under pressure, and it appeared to Scott, that Tony possessed an intelligent grasp of what could have been a very dire situation. Many young men of his age would have either crumbled or got aggressive being faced with armed police officers. Tony, on the other hand, had been clear, passive and confident, without arrogance.

The event, whilst a high-level breach of security, was deemed a misdemeanour and no further action would be taken. He had spoken to Scott and with Scott's permission also Michael. Michael at first was protective of his friend but had given a few insights into Tony's behaviour when the two of them had met up on the occasional weekend to go clubbing or playing snooker in Tony's friend Pete's place in Reading.

There had been an incident in one of the nightclubs when Michael, a black American, had been talking to a girl and some of the local lads had confronted him about being an American and abusing the UK with what they were doing at Greenham Common. Tony had stepped between them and talked the men down, without the resulting fight that Michael had expected. Michael, apart from being relieved facing off four or five locals, said that Tony's ability to quell a potentially volatile situation very quickly was a testament to, in his words, 'the coolness he had in him'.

Geoffrey had requested further information about Tony, his background, parents, work, and having read the report thought that Tony was a possible candidate for his inclusion in the surveillance project that he was creating.

Born in the late '50s, Tony had spent his first few years growing up in small industrial towns along the M6 corridor. His mother had divorced, and they moved several times over the next ten years until settling in the Reading area. By this time, his mother was on her third marriage and Tony and his sister had attended five different schools. His school reports indicated a bright child, but he was often caught daydreaming. With no close friends at school, he had not excelled in any subject, although he had passed his 11+ and had gone to a decent boy's grammar school. At the age of 16, with a clutch of CSEs, he had started as an apprentice painter and decorator.

His current stepfather had been a police office and had retired a few years earlier, his sister worked as a trainee solicitor in a practice in Reading and his mother worked in the local supermarket. Other than a few speeding tickets, Tony had no convictions and as far as the report could go, did not associate with any known criminals. By and large just an ordinary young man indicative of the day.

Geoffrey opened the file on the table in front of him as Tony drew his tale to an end.

'I've read the report that Lieutenant General Scott McKinney wrote about your escapade on the base and I've also spoken with Michael,' said Geoffrey.

'Have you seen Michael recently?' he continued.

Tony glanced at the report and saw that written on one side were his age, address and a short description of his job and where he was currently working, his parents' names and what they did, plus his sister's details. On the other side, he saw a sheet with the heading 'Official Secrets Act'.

Geoffrey glanced up and saw Tony reading the file, so he closed it.

'No, not seen Michael for a couple of weeks,' said Tony. 'I think he will be around at the end of the month; they work odd days, so I'll possibly bump into him in a week or so.'

'I'm quite happy with what you have told me, it matches the report, no harm done, but I have to say that it raised a few eyebrows with the Americans that you could get into their base so easily. I expect they have tightened up their security. This time, both you and they have been very lucky,' said Geoffrey.

'As I said, I'm sorry for creating a problem. I didn't really think it would matter that much but also, I thought I'd be in and out without anyone seeing,' said Tony shrugging.

'More tea?' asked Geoffrey, rising and pouring himself another cup and offering one to Tony.

'Thanks.'

Settling back into the chair, Geoffrey looked at Tony and said, 'That's about it, but before you go, tell me about yourself.'

Tony smiled, 'Ok, but surely you have everything you need to know in your file,' pointing at the closed loose-leaf folder on the table between them.

Geoffrey laughed, 'Yes I do, but I'd like to know a bit more. You can read upside down I take it.'

'Yes, something I learnt at school,' said Tony grinning.

'Not much to tell really,' started Tony going on to give a brief synopsis of his background, where he grew up and what he was doing now.

'What do you think about the cruise missiles being brought to this country?' asked Geoffrey.

'Not much, haven't really given it any thought. I know they may be used overseas but we have our own problems here so that's more in the news than the Americans,' said Tony.

'Yes, one of the reasons why your incident got put across to me is that you never know who is doing what and what their intentions are,' said Geoffrey

'Well, we don't seem to be doing much, still get the bombing. I take it you are more than just a follow up person,' said Tony.

'What makes you say that?' replied Geoffrey.

'Well, bit obvious now, you have a file that wouldn't be given to just a run of the mill solicitor nor would it have details of me and my family in it, or probably be given to a solicitor in the first place. Plus, we are meeting in a hotel so I guess you don't work for the solicitors I spoke to, if you did, we would be meeting at their offices,' said Tony.

Geoffrey smiled, 'You're right, I don't work for the solicitors, they arranged the meeting for me. I work for Her Majesty's Government in a department that looks into terrorism, hence the reason why I have your file, 'said Geoffrey.

'Why me? I'm not a terrorist, which that should tell you,' Tony said pointing at the file. 'Shouldn't you be catching the IRA? They seem to be all over the place the last few years bombing the hell out of us,' said Tony bitterly.

'The IRA are a big concern for us, but the trouble is we can't be everywhere. We catch more than you think but the public don't get to hear about that.'

'Well, they ruined one of my mate's lives, so the quicker you can get them the better as far as I'm concerned,' said Tony.

'What happened to your friend?' asked Geoffrey.

'When he left school, my mate Phil went straight into the army, and then last year he got posted to Ireland. Apparently, he was doing a routine car check, something they had done many times before and in the same place. When it rained, there was this small concrete bus shelter they would wait in; when a car came along, they would walk out, stop, and do the check etc. Anyway, one day, it was raining, and he stood in the shelter and a bomb went off. There was a traffic cone on top of the shelter, it had been there for weeks, this time, however, they'd put a bomb under it, waited for someone to stand in the shelter and it went off. He's not dead, but he can't hear anymore and he's got a few scars, but the noise just blew his eardrums out They're fucking shits,' said Tony

'That's dreadful,' said Geoffrey.

'I know a couple of others through Phil as well; they've also been attacked, mainly in riots in the streets. Pity we can't end it,' said Tony.

'We need information,' said Geoffrey, 'that's our biggest problem, in England, knowing who's about, where, what they are doing. If we knew more, then we could catch them and stop them quicker,' said Geoffrey.

'Well best of luck with that,' said Tony. 'I don't know any Irish, the one or two pubs me and Pete go in they are there, but we don't mix with them.'

'Would you consider telling us if you saw or heard something that wasn't, in your opinion, quite right?' asked Geoffrey.

'Yeah, suppose so. I would but that's unlikely,' said Tony.

'Ok, but what if I gave you some photos of people to look out for, you could keep an eye out for me.'

'Yes sure,' shrugged Tony. *No skin off my nose*, he thought. Him and Pete went to a lot of pubs, but the odds of some IRA guy wandering in was, in his opinion, highly unlikely, also Reading and the surrounding area had never been bombed nor, thought Tony, would it be.

'Alright, then I think we may be able to work together.

I'm not offering you a job Tony and you wouldn't get paid, it's purely an observational role. In other words, from time to time I can show you some photos of some people and if, in your weekly routine, you come across someone who's familiar then you let me know. It's that simple and nothing else. How's that sound?' asked Geoffrey.

'Yes, that's fine. Glad to be of help.'

'I need you to come up to London in the next week or so. We will need to take your photo and brief you on the sort of things you could look out for. I do need you, however, to keep this to yourself, no one must know. Ever. Are you Ok with that?'

Tony thought for a moment, he wasn't in any trouble and it seemed that it might make for an interesting couple of months.

'I'm changing my job shortly, me and Pete have been offered a job selling life assurance around where we live. It's more money and for me, smarter work. You ok with that?' said Tony.

That's interesting and more ideal, thought Geoffrey, it presented an opportunity for the lad to get around the place.

'You can do whatever you like, you need to earn your own money. I/we don't control you as such, you do what you want. What you do for us won't take up much of your time and it's mainly keeping an eye out, so that's fine,' said Geoffrey.

'So where do you want me to go and when?'

Opening the file, 'I need you to sign this, take a moment to read it through.'

Picking up a piece of paper, he passed it across to Tony, stood up and went over to the table and poured himself another cup of tea as Tony read the document.

Tony scanned the words, not really paying much attention other than to the heading which was titled 'Official Secret Act 1939'.

He wasn't going to tell anyone what he was doing anyway, so Tony signed and dated the bottom of the sheet of paper and handed it back to Geoffrey.

Sliding it back into the file, Geoffrey took out another small piece of paper and handed this to Tony.

'This is the address in London. Are you familiar with London?' asked Geoffrey.

'Sort of, been up a few times with Pete.'

'Come up by train and take the tube from Paddington to Gloucester Road, from there to Green Park. It's a short walk from there. Buy yourself a small map of London. It's straightforward enough. How about week Monday at 11am?'

'Ok, sounds good. I'll be there.'

Standing, Geoffrey shook Tony's hand and walked him out of the hotel. 'Look forward to seeing you again,' said Geoffrey.

Tony smiled, turned, walked to where his car was parked and made his way home.

Chapter 11

Brendan pulled up to The Coach and Horses in Tilehurst, locked the car and walked inside. Making his way to the bar, he ordered a Guinness. Looking around, he saw a small table in the corner near the door that was empty. It was early: 12 o'clock on a Saturday lunchtime. The pub was a bit of a dive, located in the run-down area of the town, and it attracted only the locals for custom. No one would come here on the off chance of a decent night out or drink.

It housed the obligatory dart board, juke box, pool table and, of course, fruit machine. The seats were threadbare and the floor was sticky underfoot. The landlord was pushing 70, grey-haired, and as Brendan watched, he poured himself a half of cider, which he sipped and slid under the bar. With dandruff evident on his shoulders, the shaky hands and the lick of the lips, Brendan surmised that this man was an alcoholic.

A few minutes and a couple of locals pushed their way into the bar and ordered their first drinks of the day. Picking up a newspaper, Brendan busied himself with the headlines whilst keeping an eye on the door and watching each one as they came in.

After about 45 minutes, he recognised Eugene as he walked in. Eugene glanced causally in Brendan's direction, ordered a Guinness and, picking it up, walked over to where he was sitting. 'Is that you Brendan?' asked Eugene in a thick Irish accent. 'Been a while.'

Brendan nodded and pointed towards the seat next to him, which Eugene took.

'Guinness not too bad in here,' said Brendan.

'It's the only place me and the lads drink. What brings you here?'

Looking around, Brendan nodded towards the bar. 'We Ok to talk in here?'

'It's our pub so that's not a problem,' replied Eugene.

'We need you to do something for us.'

Brendan ran through what he knew and what Declan wanted.

'I know the O'Dowd brothers,' said Eugene, 'good pair of lads, shame that they are banged up. I'll take a look at their yard to make sure it's looked after.'

'What does this Dave Hartman look like and did Declan say anything about his mate?'

'Other than that, they were going to sell bent MOT certificates, no idea what his mate looks like, but my guess is that they are always together. The only place that Declan seems to think he was spotted was in The Railway. Do you know it?'

'Yes, we've been in there a few times. Me and the boys will start there.'

'Once you find them, don't touch them, ring me on

this number,' said Brendan, passing Eugene his telephone number.

'Declan wants them for himself and only him, you know what I'm saying?' said Brendan.

'It might take some time.'

'We want them both.'

Brendan finished his drink, nodded towards Eugene and left the pub.

Eugene sat in thought, a brute of a man, well versed in metering out punishment on a Saturday night in the pubs himself. Working on the M4 was gruelling work, but he made good money even if he did spend most of it on Guinness.

Standing up, he walked over to the pool table where Liam, Enda and Finbarr were playing. When they came in, they saw Eugene talking to Brendan, and although they didn't know who it was, it was clear they knew enough not to interrupt.

'We have some work to do,' said Eugene.

'You two!' pointing at Enda and Finbarr. 'Go over to the O'Dowd's place and make sure it's all locked up. Any mess, clear it up and then come back over here.'

Without asking, the two left.

Eugene looked at Liam, they had known each other for over 40 years, school together, Army together and now working the black treacle together.

Eugene ran through the conversation he'd had with Brendan.

'We'll start at The Railway,' he said, 'someone will know

something. My guess is that they will turn up in the next week or so. Brendan said Declan had given the kid a good hiding so anyone with a broken face will make people talk about them,' said Eugene.

'What do we do when we get them?' asked Liam.

'We are not taking them, just let Brendan know; he'll take it from there.'

Can I borrow your phone book?' Eugene shouted across the bar to the barmaid.

Collecting the book, he opened it up.

'Heartman, Hartman,' he said. Scanning through the pages, he saw there were about 15 Heartmans listed and a further 20 or so Hartmans. Tearing the pages out, he gave Liam the list of Heartmans and kept Hartman for himself.

'We'll start with these. Keep the story simple, looking for Dave, he had a couple of tyres we wanted to buy from him etc. Nothing complicated. If you find him just say you were mistaken, looking for an old garage worker or something,' he said to Liam.

'Ok.'

'Tonight, we will do the pubs and then every Thursday, Friday and Saturday until he crops up. No need for the nightclubs as there will be too many people in them and no one remembers anyone in those sorts of places,' carried on Eugene.

When Enda and Finbarr came back into the pub, Eugene ran through what they were going to do.

'Tonight, you two split up and start going round the pubs. Enda, if you start up by the Woking area and work your way in. Fin, go out to Theale and come in that way. I'll go Pangbourne way and you,' pointing at Liam, 'go out on the Maidenhead road after we've been to The Railway.'

'There must be 100 pubs or more,' said Enda.

'Doesn't matter, just keep looking and asking the same story. And be nice. Also, wear some clean clothes, jeans, white shirt, no scruffy kit. No one will talk to you if you look like a fucking pikey.'

All four left the pub. That evening, Eugene and Liam walked into The Railway, ordered a couple of pints of Guinness and casually asked the bartender if he'd seen Dave.

'Dave who?'

'Dave Hartman, normally comes in here with his mate, young bloke. He's selling some tyres and we need a few.'

'No, don't know who you mean. Don't think I've heard anybody selling tyres,' said the barman.

'Might have a couple of bruises on his face, looked as if he's been in a fight.'

'No, if he comes in, I'll tell him you're looking for him.'

'Ok' said Eugene. 'Don't worry about it. I'll probably catch up with in The Chequers.'

Moving away from the bar, Eugene said to Liam, 'Have to be careful with that. Don't want people to start telling him we are looking for him.'

'Brush it off then, play it down. Make it like you're not bothered and then they will forget.'

'Good idea,' said Eugene.

Over the course of the evening they went into another couple of pubs nearby, but the story was the same: no one knew Dave or had seen anyone like him. They split up and went off across Reading and started the long haul of visiting as many pubs as they could before closing.

On the Sunday afternoon, Eugene and Liam started to visit the houses of Heartman and Hartman. By the end of the day they had both covered about half of the houses, and when all four met up that night, the story was the same: no one knew, or no one recognised Dave Hartman.

'The Heartmans I've seen so far have either been old people, or 30, 40-year olds with kids. No close matches to Dave,' said Liam.

'Pretty much the same as me,' said Eugene.

'We'll keep at it, me and Liam. We will finish the houses by next week after work and then just keep looking in the pubs,' he said to the other two.

The following two weeks proved just as frustrating for the men: nobody had seen or knew a Dave Hartman or any two blokes who were mates selling anything. They had covered all the pubs, and on the third weekend, which was a bank holiday, Eugene had them go through the pubs again. The plan was, after this weekend, that they would concentrate on the pubs they had seen that seemed to be the favourites of the younger people who were meeting up on a Friday and Saturday night before they went into the clubs.

Visiting pubs in the villages and small towns surrounding Reading was a slim option, as far as Eugene was concerned. So the eight or ten pubs in close proximity to the town centre were where he had decided to keep the four of them. Brendan had said that it might take a while, but everyone was prepared to wait. Dave would show up at some point, he was convinced of it.

With the thoughts still fine tuning his plan to find Dave and his mate he pulled his car into the car park of The Mayfellow. A big sprawling pub on the Maidenhead road about three miles outside of Reading, he'd been in there a couple of times and it was somewhere Liam had said might be worth going to on a regular basis as it was a trendy bar, had a DJ on a Saturday night and attracted a lot of the 20-30 year olds before they went into Reading itself.

It was about 7:30 and the bar was beginning to fill up, the girls wearing the latest dresses and the young men with the flares, wide collars and brightly coloured shirts. Ordering a lager, he looked around. He spotted a table with a couple of girls sat at it and made his way over.

'Mind if I just sit here?' he asked.

'Yeah, sure mate,' said one of the girls eyeing him up. Eugene knew better than to directly look at the girls, they were much younger than him and he wanted to talk to them not date them.

The girls were chatting about makeup and how one of their friends was supposed to be going out with Freddy. 'He's got a new car,' said one of the girls.

'Won't get me in it, he stinks,' replied her mate.

After a few minutes, nearly finishing his pint, Eugene said out loud enough for the girls to hear, 'Oh well, he's not here.'

Smiling at the girls, 'Looking for Dave, thought he would be in but he's not. Don't suppose you know him or have seen him have you girls?'

'Dave who?'

'Dave Hartman and his mate. Heard they had some tyres they wanted to sell. Couple young guys, your age, told they would be in here, but looks like I've missed them.'

'I don't know a Dave Hartman. What do they look like?' asked Susan.

'Young blokes, your age; Dave has a few bruises on his face, apparently, he fell over at work. Don't know what his mate looks like, only Dave. They are always together though.'

'No, don't know, sorry,' said Susan.

'Hang on,' Susan said, looking past Eugene to the bar.

'Claire!' she shouted. 'Claire!'

A young girl holding a drink turned and looked across. She smiled and waved at Susan. Beckoning her over, Claire wandered over to the table.

'This chap's looking for Dave and his mate. Do you know him?'

'Dave who? I know a couple of Daves,' she said.

'Dave Hartman and his mate, always together,' replied Eugene. 'He's got some tyres I was going to buy off him. He's got a few bruises on his face. Looked as if he's been in a fight or something.'

'Don't know a Dave Hartman, sorry,' she said.

'You off to Valbonnes tonight?' Claire said to Susan.

'Yes, will be, should be good night.'

Smiling, 'See you later then.' Claire turned and started to walk back to the bar.

Stopping suddenly, she walked back the few paces to the table and said to Eugene.

'You sure his name's Dave?'

'That's what I was told,' said Eugene.

'He's a dick,' said Claire. 'Bruises on his face you say?'

Eugene nodded

'That's Tony, Tony and Pete. I saw Tony last Saturday night in The Rank, said he'd fell over at work that's why he got the bruises. Didn't look like it to me, more as if he'd been in a fight. Him and Pete are always together. It's probably him you are looking for.'

'Oh, really, thanks. Where can I find him? Will he be here tonight or in Reading somewhere?' said Eugene.

'Bit late now,' said Claire, 'you've missed him.'

'What do mean?'

'Him and Pete left this week to go work in Germany.'

The journey down to Dover was uneventful. Passing through customs, they boarded the hovercraft to France. Tony had the map, and as they passed through customs at Calais, he saw a sign that said 'Brugge'. 'That'll do, follow that,' said Tony.

'Why am I driving?' said Pete.

'Because you used to drive your dad's left-hand drive car around the field when you were learning to drive.'

'Yes, but that was at home and this is a right-hand drive car,' said Pete.

'Yeah, but it's more or less the same as you are on the wrong side of the road, so it's just easier for you,' shrugged Tony.

Pete rolled his eyes, 'Well I'm not driving fast and I'm not overtaking.'

'You're dead right you're not overtaking,' said Tony. 'It's scary enough as it is with cars coming straight at me, so make sure you keep in.'

'How far is it anyway?' asked Pete.

'Not far, I don't think,' he said, turning the radio station knob trying to find a music channel, 'Couple hundred miles I think. Nobby said when we come out of Calais turn left and just keep going. We will see signs, and I've got me dad's map. We'll be alright.'

'At least we'll have decent weather when we get there,' said Pete.

'How do you know?' asked Tony.

'Well, every time Nobby comes back he's got a decent suntan.'

'He's a fucking bricklayer, bound to have a tan isn't he?'

'I also asked Nobby about the food and stuff, 'cause he doesn't speak German either,' said Pete. 'He reckons most people there speak English anyway, and he said, just hold out your hand with money in it, point and shout if we need anything.'

'Oh, that'll work,' said Tony, sarcastically. 'We don't need to worry about that anyway. The blokes we are working with are English. We're selling to the English Army guys so language won't be a problem.'

Only managing to get lost twice, three days later, they drove into the centre of Paderborn. The instructions they had were to park next to the Imperial Palace and the cathedral; they were reliably informed that they couldn't miss it. Spotting the cathedral, they parked up and made their way to a local phone box. Having a selection of coins, which Ross, their old boss, had given them before they left, they dialled the number as instructed. The phone answered, they piled in the coins and spoke to Dave Pent.

About ten minutes later Dave arrived. Tony was smoking as Dave arrived; he spotted him straight away. *Why do the English look the same?* he thought. Dave was 6ft 2in, well-built; he walked towards them. Tony noticed the slight limp as he approached. 'Hi, I'm Tony; this is Pete,' he said, offering his hand.

Dave nodded 'Hi', but instead of shaking Tony's hand he put out his left hand instead. Slightly taken aback, Tony took his left hand and noted that his right hand was strangely bent.

'No, I wasn't in the Army,' said Dave. 'Before you ask, I was in a car accident and lost my right arm to the elbow and busted my leg up. It's OK now, been a couple of years.'

'Oh, right, sorry,' said Tony.

'That's fine, it's easy for me here as well. The Germans don't care much about us Brits and they rarely check for car insurance etc. In the UK it's a pain in the arse. Anyway, you hungry?'

'Yes, we are.'

'OK, let's go. You follow me. We'll get you in the house and then grab some lunch and meet the other guys.'

Tony and Pete jumped back in their car and followed Dave through a few streets until they came across a small car park where Dave parked up and went inside a pub. Following Dave, they entered a large tavern and watched

Dave walk over to a table where three other men were sat eating lunch. Dave introduced them.

'New team members,' he announced. 'This is Tony and Pete. Introduce yourself guys and I'll get the beers.'

The next afternoon Tony and Pete were dropped off at the top of a housing estate with the instructions just to go knocking as every house housed a soldier's family. They would be picked up in five hours from the same spot. In a couple of weeks, said Dave, they would go out on their own once they got the hang of the district etc.

Pete tossed a coin. 'Heads left, tails right.'

'Heads!' called Tony.

'Tails you go over that side,' and with that they approached the first doors on the estate.

Each house was by and large the same: three bed semis, small gated garden with a few toys outside. Tony knew that this was going to be easy. *Prey on death*, he thought, *make the women cry about losing their loving husband by being shot dead, get the deal.*

Tony knocked; a minute or so later a woman answered.

'Good afternoon, my name is Tony from Acorn Life and I have been asked to call by and run through some options for you to protect your future income. Is your husband home and if he is could you spare us a couple of minutes?'

'Brian!' shouted the woman. 'There's a bloke at the door.'

Brian came into the hallway, bare chested with the obligatory tattoos on both arms. 'What do you want mate?'

'Hi, my name's Tony and I've been asked to call and run

through a few options regarding your future income. Can I pop in for a few minutes and explain?'

'What you selling?'

Tony smiled his reassuring smile at Brian. 'I expect you get a few salespeople around. It's Ok, I'm not selling anything. I've been given your address and asked to call in and speak with you and your wife about some options that you might want to take advantage of. Do you have a couple of minutes?'

Brian shrugged.

'Yeah sure, why not,' he said. 'Come in.'

'Would you like a cup of tea?' said Brian's wife as Tony stepped into the hallway.

'That would be lovely,' said Tony, 'not had one all day.'

Chapter 12

On the Wednesday morning following the raid DI Roberts walked into the briefing room, made his way to the head of the table and sat down; as he did so, the talk in the room faded and everyone brought their gaze to rest on him.

'Before we start, I would like to say that I think we did a good job on the raid, and at short notice we achieved most of our objectives. Naturally, there are areas where we need to improve and I have asked Johnny Sturgess to write up where we could do better,' Harry began.

'I've been in touch with Reading and they have not had any complaints or any reporters asking questions about what we were doing, so, apart from those involved, the situation is that it's not been reported so we can hopefully use that to our advantage over the next few days,' Harry continued.

Twelve counter terrorism officers were seated at the table. They were the main members of the team that raided the yard in Reading, part of a larger force numbering some 60 officers. The 60 were split into teams each one concentrating on the numerous leads and operations that had either been undertaken or were about to be. The unit had grown considerably and there were rumours amongst the group that a further 30 or 40 new officers would be joining, in response to the increased activity of the IRA over the last couple of years.

'Round the table then please. It's been three days since the operation and I have reports from all of you as to progress, but it's a priority that everyone is in the loop and any piece of information or intel is passed between us. Also, any information I get from MI5 will be passed around. So, Malcom, where are we with the known suspects?'

DS Malcom Pears was Harry's number two. They had worked together for six years in the division and had a mutual bond of respect for each other.

'As we know, the two brothers Patrick and Donny are in custody. They have been interviewed on three separate occasions and are, predictably, denying any involvement with the bomb-making equipment. Other than admitting that two other people were onsite at the yard, they are saying nothing. They deny that they know the other two; however, we have their fingerprints on the weapons and of course the van and other equipment. They will be charged with bomb making and eight other charges, possession of firearms etc. If you look in the notes the charge details are there. They will be kept at Reading nick for the time being before being brought here for trial. With regard to the other two, Sean Keating died at the scene.'

Passing out the autopsy report to the others around the table, it confirmed that he was killed by three bullets from the team's weapons. 'These,' passing around a further document, 'are the details of what we know about him and Declan Cassidy.

Fingerprints were found on the weapons recovered from the yard, both vans and the other equipment in the warehouse. We have searched the bed and breakfast places they were staying at and other than clothes, there is nothing else there.'

Standing and walking up to the main whiteboard in the room, he pointed towards one of the pictures pinned to the board, showing a photograph of a vehicle taken from a CCTV camera in a car park. Pointing, 'This is the brown Cortina we believe was taken by Declan. We also think that he has made his way to Bristol: a similar car is seen travelling along the M4.' Pointing at another grainy photograph taken from one of the many traffic cameras on the M4, 'Not long after the raid. We are currently looking for the vehicle in Bristol but nothing so far.'

Moving his hand to highlight the weapons found on site he said, 'I am also working with forensics and we are waiting on ballistic reports to see if that throws up if these weapons have been used before. Both of the machine guns had the prints of Sean and Patrick on them, plus one other. We know it's not Donny, so it has to be Declan. We recovered about two hundred rounds of ammunition, so I suspect that they were not expecting to use them other than maybe in quick bursts if they needed to get away. The ammunition is of a standard make, available from the usual suspects, along with the Armalite AR-18s. We also recovered two handguns.' Pointing at two more pictures, 'Small amount of ammunition for these, one was in the office the other in the Portacabin; both had only the prints of the O'Dowd brothers on them. We are currently looking through the files in the Portacabin, which hopefully will give us an indication as to where the fertiliser and other equipment was purchased.'

The photographs of the known suspects had been labelled and put into an organisational tree as they were known at the time and pinned on the board.

'With any operation, they are obviously not working alone. Who gave the orders? What was the target? Funding for the operation came out of Ireland. We don't believe that the O'Dowd brothers have been involved in any other operations here, as an extensive search of their yard has not revealed anything other than the current equipment for this one. I have asked Reading to provide us with as much information about the background of the yard and the brothers as they can. They have said so far that nothing in the past has required any further investigation, from their point of view, so I suspect that, as with many sympathisers of the IRA, they have been available to act as and when called upon.'

'Thanks Malcom, Mark?'

'Both men entered the country a week ago. Declan came in on his own passport via Fishguard. The van we recovered at the yard has his prints on it; nothing else has been found. Sean came into England via Liverpool on a ferry from Dublin. Neither men were on a watch list as they have not been actively associated with any recent IRA activity; however, there have been many rumours that Declan has progressed to being a proficient bomb maker and it has been suggested that he is the current go to man when they need something made. It is, however, only speculation at this point, but given we have now found him in an active plot with bomb making equipment it seems likely that the presumptions were accurate. Whilst both men are known, no red flags came up as they came in, so neither were stopped. We are trying to trace Sean's family, but as usual, very little progress is being made. We are going through the CCTV images from the station in Liverpool and Reading and hopefully we might see him being picked up by one of the O'Dowd brothers at Reading. This will tie the two men together significantly.'

'Martin?' said Harry.

'We are working with BT and colleagues over in the Belfast office. No increased activity as far as we can tell. We are monitoring all the numbers we have; what we are hoping for is a call from England. However, that may not reveal where in England. We are getting a list of numbers that were called from the O'Dowd's yard plus any calls that were made from both the two bed and breakfast places and the brothers' home addresses. We are making enquiries locally for anyone who saw any activity at their houses or people that they had not seen before in the area; it's a long shot. If they were in contact with another person, it may be that is where Declan has run to.'

'Thanks Martin, Wayne? For those of you who don't know, Wayne has been working on an analysis of IRA targets, attacks, interviews. His role is to try and give an insight into where we could possibly look or what could be in the minds of any suspects we are tracing. Before. . .' he said loudly, 'any of you start it's an area that in the future we are going to develop. Its model is based loosely on what the Army do when trying to second guess the enemy. It's not exact, it doesn't always work, but it's an option we are going to pursue because any insight that gives us an edge against these buggers is worth it. So, Wayne, what do you have for us?'

Wayne Brooks looked exactly like anyone would think a boffin would look like: slightly dishevelled dress, glasses, which he constantly pushed back from the bridge of his nose, pale complexion, as if he'd never seen the sun, and an air of superiority. He had spent ten years in military intelligence and had worked closely with many of the intelligence services, and when the new commissioner for the Met Police had been given funding for a specialised psychological operations unit similar to the American model used in Vietnam, he had jumped at the chance to join.

Having spent over two years reading interview after interview of IRA suspects and convicted men, digging into the backgrounds of co-conspirators and accomplices, reading reports of released men and what they did, where they went and who they were friends with, as much as he could, gave, from time to time, an indication of what potentially someone like Declan might do or where he might go. He had helped the Belfast branch on several occasions when it had come to second-guessing activity. More failures than successes, but with the greater knowledge he could glean from the enemy, his bosses were convinced that, overall, it was better to have him on the team than just ignore the potential benefits he could bring.

'Yes Sir,' said Wayne. 'I've focussed mainly on Declan and where he would go, based on patterns from others in similar circumstances. He will have a fallback position; typically, these are contacts who do not know of any current operations, rather, their role is to support, at a moment's notice, and help when requested by a so called 'colleague.' If he has gone to Bristol it's unlikely that he will stop there. His contact can hide him there for a few days. Also, he will know that the car he took may well be traced. Assuming it's Bristol, I suspect that he will go to Birmingham. They, again, typically go with large numbers of their own. It's easier for them to be hidden and they can be moved from house to house quickly should the need arise. There is a large contingency of Irish in and around that area who can quite easily hide him for some time. It's unlikely that he will leave the UK. He would be running on his own passport and it will take four or five weeks for the IRA to get him a new one so he can return to Ireland. Manchester, Newcastle and further north are of no benefit to him. He can move from Birmingham quickly to any of the main ports as the need arises. Given what we know about his suggested expertise, I would suggest that they will keep him here and use him again in the next two months or so for another attack, revenge for the death of Sean. We don't know how close he and Sean were but history has shown that they mount a revenge attack as quickly as they can. We can also expect a more violent attack. My recommendation is we look at Birmingham. My other suggestion is that we revisit Reading.' Pausing, Wayne looked around.

'He won't stay in Reading,' said Harry. 'Too risky.'

'I agree,' said Wayne. 'However, based on previous activity, in my opinion, Declan will be looking for a focussed revenge, in other words, he will know or will have guessed that someone tipped us off so my guess is that he will want to know who that is. The best way to do that is to get some of his friends to visit the places he had been whilst he was here.'

'Ah, I might concur with that,' said Geoffrey.

The others looked around, past Harry was an elderly gentleman sat on his own at the back of the room.

Harry turned, nodded at Geoffrey and said, 'This is our liaison from MI5. He provided us with the initial tip off. What can you add?' he asked Geoffrey.

Geoffrey stood and walked towards the group.

'We also suspect that Declan will come looking for who-ever it was. Our initial source said he had been in contact briefly with Declan and my thinking is that, on reflection, Declan may well come to the same conclusion. I too don't think it will be Declan looking, more likely, as you say Wayne, some of his colleagues. It's a difficult scenario. If you go looking for someone and asking questions about someone who's been asking questions, then it could well alert Declan's friends to your presence; on the other hand, it could well throw up a few more sympathisers who may lead you back to Declan, not an easy call to make.'

'Ok guys,' said Harry. 'Concentrate on Bristol for now. See if we can locate the car and also dig up any known IRA sympathisers in the area. Mark, keep on at the Irish side. See if anyone crawls out of the woodwork other than his next of kin, assuming we can find any. Peter. . .' looking at Peter Johnson, a long-term member of the team, 'lean on some of your contacts in Birmingham. We need to find this guy as soon as possible. We meet again tomorrow at 12. Any updates pass around, keep me informed.'

Standing up, meeting finished, he said to Geoffrey, 'Let's have a quick chat. Malcom,' he said turning, 'come and join us.'

The three men moved away from the table and entered DI Roberts' office. Closing the door behind them, Harry motioned the two men to take a seat in front of his desk.

'I'd like to speak with your informant,' said Harry to Geoffrey. 'He could provide us with some information as to the lead up to the raid.'

'That's not something that will happen,' said Geoffrey. 'As you can imagine, an informant would wish his cover to remain so, and I know. . .' said Geoffrey, holding up his hand to stop Harry from speaking, 'you would make every effort to ensure his anonymity; however, it's far too risky and not something I am willing to entertain.'

'Why were you watching Declan and Sean in the first place?' asked Harry.

'I'm pleased the raid went well, or as well as can be expected. Your men averted what was clearly going to be a major incident in one of our cities,' said Geoffrey, rising.

111

'I will do everything I can to keep you updated about any other activity we come across. It's imperative that we stop this and hopefully successes such as these will resonate with the IRA and bring home to them that they are never going to win. Nice to meet you again Malcolm,' said Geoffrey, offering his hand.

'You too,' said Malcom, rising and shaking hands.

'See you at the monthly briefing Harry,' and with that, Geoffrey opened the door and made his way out of Scotland Yard.

'Help but no help,' he sighed. 'We need to get Declan but it's going to be like looking for a needle in a haystack,' said Harry.

'My guess is that the car will be long gone. If he has gone to Bristol then finding him will be a stroke of luck, and if they do move him to Birmingham, then, other than actually having him sighted, the chances of finding him will be remote,' said Malcom.

'Follow up everything we have. Put together a case for the prosecutor and let's get what we do have on trial and behind bars,' concluded Harry.

Chapter 13

Stepping out of his bed and breakfast into the warm sunshine, Tony lit a cigarette and made his way down Grassenstrasse towards the pub where he had said he would meet up with Pete. Pete had, about a month or so ago, gone over to Munster where he was part of a new team.

He had rang the week before saying he was coming over the next weekend for a catch up and beer. Tony had detected in his voice that he wasn't too happy, but when he had pressed him, Pete had assured him everything was ok; he just wanted to get out of where he was for a day and grab a beer with him. Tony had missed Pete as the two of them had been good at bouncing off each other each night after they had been around the doors of many of the Army houses. They ended up most nights in the local pub where they enjoyed many glasses of lager together and the occasional strange meal: a Weiner Schnitzel.

It was not only the food that took some getting used to, it was also the beer. Small glasses of lager that the barmen would fill to over-following and then scrape off the excess froth. Relatively cheap, but not as good as the beer they had back in the UK.

They'd tried a couple of the beers in a Stein but found that by the time they had got to the end, the beer itself had warmed up and tasted crap so they stayed off them. Not one for spirits, they had tried what the Germans called 'Altbier', which was, in Tony's opinion, just dark, cloudy, barley tasting rubbish. So they stuck to lager.

It had gone well since they had arrived, and in the five months of being in Germany they had made good money. Pete had bought another car and was getting the hang of driving a left hooker. Tony wasn't sure he had insurance but no one seemed to check and, as Pete said, he would just plead ignorant if he ever got stopped.

They had taken a trip out onto one of the Autobahns. It was good fun; you could drive at whatever speed you liked. They thought they were going fast until, one day, they were belting along, and Pete looked in his mirror and a Porsche was pushing him.

Because they had done so well the boss had moved Pete, and although Tony was still making decent sales, the fun and novelty of the place was wearing off. Most of his time now before work he would just sit in his room and occasionally after work have a couple of beers. Living in the middle of the town, there weren't any English people, and at the weekends he avoided the main pubs and clubs as these were invariably full of soldiers.

One Friday evening he had wandered into what he thought was a regular bar, The Milleure, sat at the bar and had ordered a beer. Thinking about his current situation and what he should do next, if anything, after a couple of beers, he became aware more of his surroundings. The clientele had changed subtly, the place had become slightly darker and the bar had taken on a more glamourous aspect. Looking around, he took in the bar more closely: there were several cubicles all nicely decorated with padded furniture, and each one had its own small chandelier above it. The floor was nicely carpeted and over towards the back of the bar there was a small stage, none of which he had noticed when he had walked in.

The music was beginning to get a bit louder and the bar was filling up; however, it was only men. Ordering his fifth beer from what now seemed a very glamorous bar maid, it dawned on Tony what this place actually was. He laughed to himself. 'Fuck me!' he said out loud; the bar maid glanced at him. 'Sorry,' he said. 'Time for me to move on.' With that, Tony had finished his beer and walked out. 'Never paid for it, never will,' he said to himself as he had walked back to his bed and breakfast.

He hadn't wanted to buy a car as exploring wasn't really his thing, and he got picked up every day outside his bed and breakfast and then dropped back there in the evenings, so there wasn't really any point. The other guys in the team were married and they went home to their wives and kids, so he didn't really have much in common with them.

It would be good to catch up with Pete, he thought as he strolled down the road. It was towards the end of the summer months now and it was starting to get a bit colder.

Walking into the pub he spotted Pete sat at one of the many bench tables with a couple of beers in front of him.

'Hiya mate,' he said as he approached.

Smiling, Pete stood up and shook his hand. 'Been a while, got you a beer.'

'Cheers. Fag?' said Tony.

Offering Pete a cigarette, Pete looked at it. 'I know, I know, still can't find any Bensons but this is close, not too bad.'

'Thanks,' said Pete lighting it.

'What's been happening then?'

The two of them chatted for the next hour or so about work and where Pete was staying. Tony got another couple of beers, filled Pete in on the work, where he was and how he was getting a bit bored.

'Know what you mean,' said Pete. 'The guys I'm with are a bit old and don't really go out much, so I'm getting fed up with it. Let's go. There's a market round the corner. Want to get a new shirt and a couple of other bits.'

The two of them left the bar and walked towards the open-air market. The market consisted of about 100 stalls selling just about everything you want: beer, food, clothes, old and new. As they walked through looking at this and that Pete said, 'Billy has offered me my old job back in Reading.'

Tony looked at him, 'Oh right. Ok. You taking it?'

'Think I will, we're not together anymore and I've asked Bandit if I can come back here and work with you.' Tony laughed, 'Bandit' was the nickname they had given to Dave, one armed and all that. 'He said that I have to stay where I am, and he said that you were doing ok here so you couldn't move either.'

'I know, I asked him the other week and he said pretty much said the same thing to me.'

'Will you go back to being the manager of the snooker hall then?'

'Yes, the guy they got hasn't panned out so he's leaving,' said Pete, picking up a cane from one of the stalls.

'How much is this mate?' said Pete to the stallholder. The man leaned forward and took the cane out of Pete's hand and at the top showed him how to press a button and the cane came apart, transformed into a sword stick. '50 Deutsche,' said the stallholder.

Tony laughed, 'You can't buy that. That's illegal in England.'

'Is it? Oh well.' Looking at the man, Pete said, 'Sorry mate, too dear,' picking up a black belt with a large buckle. Again, the stallholder took it out of his hands, slipped the buckle around his fingers and pulled: a four-inch knife came out of the other half of the buckle. 'Thirty Deutsche,' the man said, smiling at Pete. 'Ha-ha, nice one,' laughed Pete and gave the man the money.

Collecting the bag, he gave it to Tony. 'I don't want that,' said Tony.

'Call it a leaving present,' said Pete laughing. 'Look, some shirts here,' as he walked over to the next stand.

'So, when are you going?' said Tony.

Pete, pulling a shirt off the hanger, said, 'Well, if you don't mind then it will be the end of next week. Gotta give Bandit a week's notice and to get my money.'

'I don't mind mate; you do whatever is good for you. I'm

getting a bit fed up anyway. Might give it another month or so and then come back. Not sure I want to spend Christmas here, better off at home. You buying that?'

The shirt was pale blue and fitted Pete. He also took another pale yellow one and asked for the price. Putting them into a bag, Pete paid the money and the two of them ambled through the rest of the market. Looking at bits and pieces, Tony thought he might buy a souvenir, but at the end of the market they drifted into another pub and the souvenir idea was forgotten.

As Pete got into his car that evening.

'It's been good. Made a few quid, different beer and food, but won't be sorry to go home though,' said Pete to Tony.

'I'll give it a couple more months, try and save a bit and then come back home myself.' Maybe back by November. Give us a ring when you get back and settled,' said Tony.

'Will do,' said Pete and slipped the car into gear and drove off out of the town and on to Munster.

Tony turned, a bit sad that his mate was leaving. *But life moves on,* he thought. They'd had a good time but now that he had been on his own for a while the fun was slipping away, and he too missed home. *Well I could always go back painting,* he thought.

Chapter 14

David Attcliffe threaded the last gold cufflink through and stepped back from the mirror, *not bad,* he thought. Adjusting his black tie slightly and peering closely at the mirror to make sure that there were no blemishes on the shirt, or his face, he picked up his dinner jacket off the back of the chair and slid it on.

'You ready darling?' said his wife.

'Yes, let's go.'

Walking down the main staircase, they entered the opulent lobby of the Dorchester Hotel and made their way into the dining room area. The room had been set out with some 40 odd tables each seating ten people. At the front, across the dance floor, there was a small podium alongside a beautifully decorated table with a selection of boxes, envelopes and other items neatly laid out.

The charity event was held once a year by the hotel to raise funds for their selected charity of that year. The event was attended by some of the wealthiest and most prominent people in London, and it also attracted a few Americans and Europeans who either had an influence or were wealthy enough to be invited to what was quite a prestigious event.

The small band at the side of the floor were quietly tuning up, and there was a distinct buzz in the air.

Walking through to the room next to the dining room where the bar was situated, David escorted his wife to a seat on a table that was occupied by the head of Coutts Bank, Paul Fettle, who was there with his wife Claire. Also seated was Michael Harrington CEO of Goldman Sachs and his wife Sheila.

'Good evening everyone,' said David, greeting each man with a handshake and, for the ladies, a polite kiss on each cheek. Pleasantries done, Susan, his wife, sat down and David looked around for a waiter.

'Looking forward to a decent evening,' opened David, and with that, the next twenty minutes or so followed topics of conversation for the men on the market and business and for the ladies on how their children were getting on in their respected schools.

David was the chairman of British Telecom. He had joined what was the Post Office in 1965 and rose through the ranks. When the Post Office set up Post Office Telecommunications, he became a territory manager (London). During the early 1970s, he had made a name for himself by streamlining several departments and sectors within the organisation and became overall national manager in 1975. In 1980, when the company was renamed British Telecom, he joined the board as CEO and two years later became chairman. It had just been announced that British Telecom would become a private organisation, so much of his work these days was with city bankers and high level fund managers making them aware of the dominance the company had and its ability over the coming years to make vast sways of profits for investors. Education and awareness had been the order of the day for the last year, and for a couple of years to come. Throwing off the old image of the little yellow vans scurrying through the towns and cities of the UK, the plan was complete rebranding, new markets, new products and new divisions being set up to capitalise on the investments made and being made.

There were five main courses to choose from and he had chosen the venison, beautifully cooked, succulent, pink on the inside with a velvety port sauce to accompany it. Susan had gone with the chicken which, as David looked over, looked extremely enticing as well. The wine complemented the food, as you would expect from the Dorchester, and the meal was rounded off after desert with a selection of coffees and delicate chocolate biscuits.

'Excuse me for a moment. Need the men's room,' said David. 'And me,' said Paul. Rising from their seats, 'Did you bring any of those lovely cigars?' said Michael to Paul.

'I did.'

'I'll join you then in the lounge,' said Michael.

'We'll stay here for a bit,' said his wife.

The three men made their way out, and Michael settled into one of the comfy chairs waiting for them to return.

Paul exited the men's room and made his way over to where Michael was sitting. As David was walking through the door he almost bumped into Geoffrey.

'Good evening, Geoffrey,' he said, with a shake of the hand. 'Nice to see you.'

'Likewise,' said Geoffrey.

'How's the company? Heading towards privatisation nicely I trust?'

'Busy times ahead,' said David, as they moved out of the way to the door.

'Do you have a moment?' asked Geoffrey.

'Of course.'

Geoffrey guided David a few yards down the corridor and opened a door to an empty room.

'I understand that you are setting up a few new divisions, one of which is focussed on delivering voice and your new data technology to UK companies.'

'Yes, that's correct. We are starting to recruit about two to three hundred people in the next month or so.'

'I wonder if we could have lunch next week. There are a couple of things that I could do with a bit of help with,' said Geoffrey.

'Of course,' replied David. 'Get your secretary to call mine and we can set something up.'

'Many thanks, look forward to it. Enjoy the rest of your evening,' said Geoffrey.

With that, Geoffrey slipped away, and David made his way back to the dinner.

Enjoying a delightful cigar, spending £1000 on a vase for his wife, the event and evening passed pleasantly.

The following week, David saw in his diary he had a lunch appointment with Geoffrey at the club in St James.

That Thursday morning the meeting passed swiftly enough, and David set out for his lunch with Geoffrey. Walking along the embankment, which he always enjoyed, he had no real preconceptions as to what Geoffrey needed. Whilst the organisation had an obligation to assist the intelligence services, and he was provided with regular updates as to what the company was engaged with, he had had little or no involvement with any specific requests in that area. So he was a little intrigued as to what Geoffrey had in mind.

'Good morning, Sir,' said the doorman, opening the door to the member's only club on St James.

'Morning, Arnold,' said Geoffrey, as he made his way up the carpeted stairs to the elegant foyer. Housing only a porter's lodge and a grand staircase to the upper floors, the walls were resplendent in pictures depicting the Great War and the servants of the then King of England whom they had served, winning many battles and forging ahead with the United Kingdom's domination of almost all the lands that they had invaded.

Following the head porter, he was escorted towards the dining area. As he passed through the doors the quietness surrounded him. There were several diners already enjoying lunch, one or two in deep conversation. The tables were suitably placed to accommodate four comfortably if required but spaced far enough apart to allow conversations to be had in confidence.

Geoffrey rose as David approached.

'Good morning, David,' said Geoffrey, shaking his hand as the porter pulled out a dining chair.

'Good morning, Geoffrey. Lovely weather today,' he replied as he sat down.

'Very much so, in for a decent summer so I hear. How's your wife Gloria?'

'Marvellous as always. I bought her a 1920s Art Nouveau vase at that charity event last week, so she was more than delighted and it is now adorning our main entrance hall,' said David.

A few more pleasantries passed between them as they studied the lunchtime menu.

The waiter appeared and they ordered. Pheasant for David and steak and kidney pudding for Geoffrey.

As the waiter moved away, Geoffrey began the explanation of why he wanted to see him.

'As you know, we have had a very difficult ten years with the bombings on mainland UK, and we think that it's unlikely that it will recede anytime soon. We've always been active of course, but it's been a challenge to keep tabs on everything that's going on,' said

Geoffrey.

Geoffrey could talk frankly with David as they had known each other for several years. They had first met when David became overall National Manager for Telecoms in 1975, and they had kept in touch over the years as David had risen to his new position of Chairman. David had been briefed by several intelligence officers over the years, and Geoffrey had always been in on the meetings. He had looked at him for confirmation on several occasions as, although they had never spoken of Geoffrey's seniority, it was clear that most direction during the meetings had come from him. They had formed a decent relationship and so had their wives as coincidentally both of their sons attended the same school: Cheltenham Boy's College.

'We reviewed our approach on how we collect information as we needed people closer to the ground than we currently have,' continued Geoffrey. 'The Minister was acutely aware that we needed to make deeper inroads into getting more and more up to date information, and for the last couple of years we have worked on several different avenues, which has proved beneficial.'

Geoffrey paused as the waiter appeared with their food and placed it in front of them.

'Let's eat,' said Geoffrey.

Small talk over the quality of the lunch proceeded as David savoured his aromatic pheasant and Geoffrey tucked into his sumptuous steak and kidney pudding with lashings of gravy.

As both men retired to the sitting room, they made for the corner of the room and settled into two beautiful red Queen Anne leather chairs and sipped the coffee the waiter had brought. Geoffrey began again to expand on his request.

'It's a very delicate situation as I can't strictly ask you to help, as you are planning to become a private company and how your run it and what departments, people etc. you have is obviously down to you and the management team, and at some point, private investors, but I wonder if there is a small way that our two interests could be served. Whilst we have access to some telephony services, and from time to time we request various connections in and outside the UK, this is a bit more involved. I wonder if you could slide a couple of people into the organisation. I would like to have them on the ground, just observing occasionally, and I mean occasionally, the day to day activities of people that have been brought to our attention. Ninety-nine percent of the time they would be actively involved in the jobs you recruited them for, going about the routine business that they have been employed to do. They wouldn't work for us, they would be working for you and would be subject obviously to the same employment terms as other members of your staff but would have a degree of flexibility shall we say, for a brief period every now and again to work on their own without rigid reporting protocols. It is purely an observational role without any contact so they would not be in harm's way at all, ever,' said Geoffrey.

'Almost all of the time they would be gathering information out of hours so not impacting on work time at all, but it's the flexibility to move around, not only in the city but across many of the towns in England and Wales,' continued Geoffrey. 'Ideally, a semi-senior role that wouldn't attract too much attention. I understand that it may not be possible, but if it is, it has to stay between me and you', said Geoffrey.

David sat in thought for a moment or two, sipping his coffee. Geoffrey let him think. He'd had the same conversation with GWR two years ago and that had worked out quite well, as construction of the railway network was expanding, and with the advent of investment they were making on the new 125 high-speed trains, it enabled observation by a few of the teams of Irish who were coming into the country as labourers on these rail link projects.

'I can't see that is an issue. I'm sure I can accommodate you,' said David

'I'll give it some thought over the next few days and see what I can come up with. We are a big company, employing over 250K people and we are changing all the time. New people are always arriving, new departments created to take advantage of our strategic network advancement. New buildings and, of course, we have privatisation around the corner so big changes are afoot.'

'Appreciate that,' said Geoffrey.

'I'll keep it to myself,' said David. 'I don't see the need to involve anyone. Let me get back to you by, say, middle of next week.'

'Excellent, many thanks. I'll leave it in your capable hands.'

Rising, Geoffrey shook David's hand and left.

David sat back down. *Interesting*, he thought. *Novel idea but the amount of trouble those guys are causing we certainly need to do something to beat them.*

'More coffee, Sir?' asked the waiter.

'Thank you, Maurice, yes please.'

After phoning his secretary informing her that he wouldn't be in for the rest of the day, he sat back down and started to think through just how he could help Geoffrey.

Geoffrey had every confidence that David would come

up with something, the man had risen through the ranks for a reason, one of which was his ability to think laterally, his ability to see the whole picture and create a strategy that would see his company grow from strength to strength. It was not a surprise then that on Monday morning he saw in his dairy an appointment for Tuesday to meet with David in Hyde Park.

The bandstand in Hyde Park was an imposing structure built in the late 1800s and moved to Hyde Park in 1886. It symbolised a period of time of days gone by when families used to venture into the park with a picnic to listen to the concerts of the day.

It had fallen into disrepair over the last few years, but he had heard that there was a petition to get in spruced up. It was with the London City park's office at the moment, but with all the red tape there he expected that it would be a few years yet before the Labour run London Council would spend any money on it.

Next to the bandstand were several benches on one of which he saw David reading *The Times*. 'Morning, David,' he said. 'Fresh this morning.'

'Hello, Geoffrey,' catching his hand. 'Yes, bit brisk but nice later by all accounts.'

'So,' said Geoffrey taking up his seat next to David.

'I've given your idea some thought and I believe that we are in a position to help. The business is setting up several different departments over the coming months, as I mentioned to you when we met the other week at the charity event. We will be recruiting several hundred, as I said, so if you like the idea I'm about to talk about, getting your chaps in will not raise any suspicions at all.'

'Ok,' said Geoffrey.

'We are taking on these people predominantly to market a new brand of desktop computer to businesses across the UK, coupled with that, a data network that will then allow them to communicate with each other. In addition, we are making advancements in our voice technology so we will be actively promoting voice and data integration. You don't need to know the technical aspects of this other than it involves a considerable investment, around £100m to set up, and we believe it will enable us to corner the market in what is a very technological fast-moving industry,' continued David.

'Currently, the UK is split into nine territories; each one is run like a business in its own right. They are responsible for their part of the current voice network, support, new installations, training and maintenance; they only look after the local voice customers.

In addition to this, we have a national sales team, whose responsibility it is is to work with national and international companies like the banks, for instance, Barclays, or retail companies such as Sainsbury's. This new organisation that we are creating will sit on top of all this and promote data services to both local and national companies. This is where the new people come in. They will report directly to a new sales and marketing team, who report through to the Board and are not controlled by any of the territory managers. My thoughts are that in addition to this, I think we need to sell these integrated data services to these various territories. I'm going to suggest we create a specialised internal sales department of five or six people specifically detailed to this task. They would have a senior manager who reports to the overall sales director who sits on the Board. This way, the group will remain autonomous, have the seniority they need to get to the various territory managers, the authority of the Board too, if necessary, force the territories to use our own equipment instead of a third party, which they do now, and allow them a great deal of flexibility in the way they work and where they work,' said David.

'That sounds really positive,' said Geoffrey. 'Where would they be based?'

'Predominantly in London, either Newgate Street or I can get them into Gresham Street, if needed. Then we could arrange for them to have say, office space in Bristol or Manchester, wherever needed I imagine,' replied David.

'If you like this then I can get Arthur Kelly my current CFO to work out the details and get the ball rolling. He is good enough to know when and when not to ask questions and I trust him. I won't tell him the main reason but he's astute enough to close any doors firmly if anyone starts to ask,' said David.

'Thank you. How long will it take to set up?' said Geoffrey.

'About a month or so. Softly, softly, need to allocate cash etc. and formalise the structure,' said David.

'Excellent, really do appreciate your help,' said Geoffrey. Handing David a piece of paper, 'A couple of names that should come through your recruitment process in the next month or so. Any problems let me know.'

'My pleasure,' said David, standing and shaking Geoffrey's hand. 'Glad to be of help.'

Chapter 15

'Thank you very much. Pleasure to meet you both. You have made a good decision and secured your financial position should anything occur. The paperwork will come through over the next few days and, as of today, you are in the programme. I'm always around and about so if you need anything let me know,' smiling and shaking hands with Carol and Stephen, he waved as he closed the gate to their three-bed semi. Walking up the street, Tony smiled to himself: *Another £150 in the bank. This is too easy, and it's only 6:30pm.* One of the benefits of having an early appointment on a Friday night: close them quick and get out, you nor they want to spoil a Friday night. He would get £35 out of the £150 next Thursday if he made sure his paperwork was registered by Monday. Had to wait six weeks for another £35 just in case they cancelled and then on the anniversary of the sale the remainder of the money. He'd been doing this now for some time and was finally seeing the anniversary payments coming in from the sales he had made in England.

It was a bit annoying when someone cancelled, but there was so much scope that the half dozen who dropped out didn't really make that much difference. He mainly lived on the immediate payment and the six weekly ones, twice the amount of money he had earned as a painter and with food and beer over here quite cheap, apart from his rent, he had been saving a bit since Pete had gone and had bought a second-hand Capri from one of the squaddies.

He wasn't going to get a car but his hit ratio was one in one so instead of waiting now until after eight or nine o'clock at night for a pick-up with the other guys, he was able to set his own work times, which invariably meant he was back where he lived by 7:30pm during most of the week and 7pm on a Friday.

Getting into the Capri, he drove through the housing estate where up to 1,000 squaddies and their wives lived. He worked his way across Paderborn to the road near his bed and breakfast. Leaving the car, he walked down the road to his, sort of, favourite pub.

'Abends bitte Friedrich, ein Bier und ich kann Eier und Pommes, zwei Eier bestellen. Danke,' he said to the barman as he approached the counter.

He didn't really like the sausages they had. The chicken was ok but he didn't know enough German to ask for a decent piece of chicken and he was sick to death of flattened veal. So egg and chips seemed to be a staple. He didn't usually bother with lunch as he filled up most days at breakfast, which consisted of eggs and cheese with a variety of bread and cakes. Why they didn't just have bacon and eggs, beans and fried bread was beyond him.

He'd been into the Naaffi a couple of times on the base, having been invited in by one or two of the soldiers he had gotten to know well. Decent English food there and plenty of it; unfortunately, he wasn't allowed in all the time, and joining up just for the food wasn't really an option.

The bar he frequented was small and appeared old. The interior was oak beams adorned with a variety of flags and shields depicting, Tony thought, either old German royalty or battles. Having no German history knowledge, he had no real clue as to what they were and was certainly not going to ask. Not that he could speak German other than his opening phrase, which he varied between ordering or not ordering food. The barman, Friedrich, had allowed him to drink there. He had asked him the first day he and Pete had gone in if they were in the Army, if they had been they would have been barred. It seemed none of the locals wanted any soldiers in the place, and from what Tony had seen, on the few occasions he had been into the main town where they mostly drank it was like a war zone on a Friday and Saturday night. One of the main reasons they had steered clear. They had been happy to just eat the food and drink the lager in this pub.

He sat down at his usual table, overlooking the bar and not too far away from the door. The pub generally had 20 or 30 people in most nights and a few of them ate there as well. The place was clean and tidy, and the furniture was decent enough. Taking a drink from his glass, he lit up a cigarette and waited for his food. *Another Friday night*, he thought. This is getting boring, nowhere to go, no one to chat to. The few clubs him and Pete had been into were obviously full of German girls and the competition from the squaddies to be with them wasn't in him and Pete's favour. Most of them spoke some English but it was hard work. Not that he'd suffered from a lack of female company, he couldn't complain, he thought, there were a few army wives who he'd met and had a bit of fun with. They were typically bored as their husbands were away for several months on tour to some country or another and they were young and up for a bit of extracurricular marital excursions. It was a bit dangerous though as most of the women knew each other and word soon got back to the respective husbands if their wives had been cheating on them. He'd been lucky so far, but he supposed it was only a matter of time.

His food arrived: two eggs and a plate of chips. Ordering another beer, Tony settled down and ate his Friday meal.

Geoffrey walked through the pub doors and up to the bar. Ordering two beers, he pulled some money from his pocket and handed it to the barman. Turning around, with beers in hand, he walked over to where Tony was sitting and sat down next to him. Placing the beers on the table, Geoffrey said, 'Beer!'

Tony had seen him as soon as he had walked in, not really believing who he was looking at. He wondered if he should get up and say 'hello' or if Geoffrey had seen him as he had come through the doors. His questions were soon easily answered.

'Thanks,' said Tony. 'How did you find me?'

Geoffrey just looked at him, shook his head and said, 'Have you forgotten? I'm in military intelligence and I'm looking for a young Englishman selling insurance to

English soldiers near an English army base in a town called Paderborn in Germany. How long do you think it took me?' he said, sarcastically.

'Fair enough I suppose' said Tony. 'Well, nice to see you. What do you want? I said I was done with all that.'

'Thought you might be bored and fancy a change.'

'No, I like it here, it's good. Plenty to see and do, friends to drink with, making money and enjoying myself.'

'Really, so that's why you are here on Friday night drinking and eating alone, and my information is that this is pretty much what you do every night now that your mate Pete has gone.'

'It's just quiet tonight that's all. Anyway, what's it got to do with you? What do you want?' said Tony, annoyed. 'You didn't come all this way to buy me a beer and tell me my life is shit.'

'You're right, I didn't. I want you to come back to the UK. I've kept an eye on you from time to time and I know what you are like, now the fun is over, you can't speak the language, you are probably fed up with the food and, while you are making good money, Paderborn is not England and my guess is that you are missing home to some degree.'

'And . . .' said Tony.

'And I've no doubt you have kept up with events back home. The bombings are still happening and we, as ever, need information. We are doing well but we can do more and its with people like you who can give us, as I've said before, grass roots information.'

'Ok,' said Tony, 'but why me? It's a long way for you

to come, and I told you that I wanted out. You must have others so why bother with me?'

'We do have others and we are getting more all the time, but we've invested in you and it would be a shame to go to waste as you know what is needed and can get up and running quickly.'

'Invested in me,' said Tony. 'You're taking the piss. I don't think half a day in an office in London taking my prints and a picture, making me remember a telephone number and showing me some photos is called 'investing in me'.'

Ignoring the comment, Geoffrey said, 'I want you to work in London. It's a big area and will require a lot of effort from all of my team and as many as I can get onto the patch. Nothing is easy and we have a lot of work to do. There are a lot of people who have died unnecessarily, and we need to stem the flow as much as possible and as soon as possible.'

Tony nodded and said, 'I don't expect it will be easy but finding someone like last time was, I think, just lucky, and London is a far bigger place and I can't live there, I don't have a job. I can't afford it nor do I want live in some dodgy room, even if I did come back.'

'Think about it,' said Geoffrey, standing. 'Another beer?' Picking up the glasses, Geoffrey went over to the bar and ordered two more drinks. He was not going to tell Tony that it was easier for him to get Tony back to the UK than it was to try and recruit another person. Getting someone on board took time, and he had precious little of that.

Sitting back down and taking a drink, Geoffrey said, 'Thought about it?'

'No, not yet,' replied Tony.

'Well, you're doing it. This is a one-time offer. You are bored here, nothing is happening and nothing will. Time to come back. You've had your fun. I'll expect you back in London, week Monday.'

'Hang on a minute, I haven't thought about it. I can't get back that quick. I've got a job, commitments and I've got no money to get back.'

'You just said you were making money,' said Geoffrey.

'Yes, but I've just bought a car.'

'Fine, as a one off,' said Geoffrey. Pulling out his wallet, he took a mixture of English and German money and handed it to Tony. 'It's £120. That's enough to get you back and I want receipts for everything. And I want any money left over. As for your job, you are self-employed so you can leave when you like.'

'What about work?'

'When you get to the office, I'll go through all that with you. See you Monday.'

Rising, Geoffrey finished his beer and walked out of the pub leaving Tony to contemplate what had just happened.

'Bye then,' said Tony to himself.

Sitting and holding his glass, Tony went through the conversation. Geoffrey was right, he was bored, and this wasn't any fun anymore; maybe it was time for a change. Finishing his beer, he glanced at his watch: nearly 9 o'clock. *Might as well have another beer*, he thought. *Got a handful of cash. Geoffrey might as well pay for my meal.* Ordering another beer and paying his tab, Tony went and sat back down and ran through what he would do over the next day or so.

Might as well leave straightaway, he thought. *What's another week?* It would take him a couple of days to get back to Calais. He might have to wait a day before he got a boat; no point rushing. Saturday morning, he rang Bandit and explained that his mother wasn't well, and he had to go back to England. Dave was sorry that he was leaving and hoped his mother got better soon. He promised to ring him when she was better as he said that there would always be a job here for him.

Packing the few clothes he had, he said goodbye to his landlady, got into his car and headed off. The journey down to Calais took him two days. He stopped off at a roadside motel for one night, courtesy of Geoffrey, had something to eat and started to look forward to getting home. *First thing I'll do*, he thought to himself, *is get some decent fish and chips.* On his arrival in Calais the following evening, the next ferry was in the morning. Settling down in his car, Tony couldn't be bothered to go and find a B & B for the night. The following morning, he joined the queue, got on the ferry and sailed over to Dover.

His mother wasn't in when he got back, so he went down to his local and had a few beers. *Decent lager,* he thought, *good to be home.* The following Monday, Tony caught the train into London and made his way to Geoffrey's office. Having no ID on him, the security guard at the front desk asked him to wait while he called Geoffrey.

Collecting his badge, he was escorted up to the room he

had been in before, by what he presumed was Geoffrey's secretary. On opening the door, he saw Geoffrey was sat at the end of large boardroom table. 'Morning, Tony. Grab a cup of tea and sit down,' said Geoffrey.

Tony sat down at the table and began sipping his tea.

'Let me be very clear again, Tony,' said Geoffrey. 'Your role is very much just observation, you don't work for us so we won't be supporting you or there to help you. If you get mixed up in events like that stupid fiasco you got yourself into last time, you are on your own. Your safety is down to you, you are not nor will you ever be asked to speak to or engage with anyone we ask you to look at for us. Do I make myself clear?'

Tony nodded.

'I need you to say it,' said Geoffrey.

'It's clear, just observation,' said Tony.

'At a distance.'

'At a distance,' repeated Tony.

'Don't get me wrong,' continued Geoffrey. 'I appreciate what you will be doing. It's more eyes on the ground, which is invaluable to us, but I want you to be safe, so don't be stupid.'

'So,' said Tony, 'what and where am I going to be doing/ working?'

'Most of our activity is centred around London. Whilst it is not easy to cover, it is somewhat easier to manage than trying to spread ourselves all over the UK. That said, there will be occasions when you will need to look around different towns from time to time,' began Geoffrey.

'First off,' said Geoffrey, handing him a piece of paper, 'you need to apply for this job. This will get you based in London. It should be in a couple of months after you've had the company training etc. This,' said Geoffrey, handing Tony another piece of paper, 'is the new telephone number and also, a Post Office box number in Farringdon where we will drop off any information you need. For anything urgent, this is the location of a drop off point on the embankment,' showing Tony a small hand drawn map of Vauxhall bridge and the location of a box. 'There will be photos, names, addresses etc., like last time, of individuals who we/I would like you to observe and report back on. As before, burn the photos straight away. Go there every Wednesday. Don't be surprised if there isn't anything there, there won't always be. When you call in, Sheila will answer and take any information you have. If, in an emergency, we need to contact you then it will be Sheila calling you at your office. If you need to speak to me, then just ask. It's unlikely that we will need to meet or for you to come here again. Is that all clear?' asked Geoffrey. 'Any questions?'

'Salesman,' said Tony, looking at the paper. 'BT, and a car, nice. No, no questions.'

'OK, have a look at these,' said Geoffrey, handing Tony two photographs. 'It's unlikely that you will spot them, but we think they are in London, so just in case, if you do see either, call Sheila.'

'Ok,' said Tony, committing the photos to memory.

'I've arranged a small training course for you for the rest of the day. It's a few hours covering behaviour patterns, simple things to look out for when you are watching people. There will be other courses, some of which we will send you on and some that BT will arrange. With regard to BT, you work for them and abide by their employment rules etc. The department you will be working in will give you a degree of flexibility; however, no one there will know of our liaison so just do your day to day job as normal. OK?'

'Sure,' said Tony.

Rising, Geoffrey walked over to the table. He picked up the phone, spoke briefly into it, collected a tea and sat down.

'Sheila will show you to the training room. Any problems, let me know. Oh and Tony. . .' Tony looked at him, 'get married!'

There was a knock on the door and Sheila entered the room. Tony stood and made his way towards the door. As he was leaving, Geoffrey said, 'By the way, do I have any change?'

'No, it all went,' said Tony.

Receipts?'

'Sorry, forgot to bring them,' smiled Tony and followed Sheila out of the room.

Chapter 16

It had been a busy night; all 14 tables had been on the go since he'd opened at lunchtime. *Tomorrow would just be as busy*, thought Pete, as he collected the snooker ball set from one of the customers and laid the balls on the shelf at the back of the counter. Looking around the hall, there were two tables left; both were almost at the end of their games. *Another half an hour,* thought Pete, *then over to the club and have a couple of beers.* Watching the last two tables, they were playing properly and were concentrating on the game. A few years ago, he'd been robbed and was now wary at the end of the night especially when he was on his own and it was the weekend. More often than not it would be a Saturday night or late on a Sunday if he was going to get turned over. He had to keep all the money in the safe over the weekend as he had no way of banking any money until Monday morning. The safe contained about £400 for a Friday, so not a bad day.

After the last raid he now had help on a Saturday and Sunday night. The boss had decided that it was too much aggravation getting the money back from the insurance companies so it was easier to employ an extra person for a few hours at the weekend. It also relieved the boredom for Pete: someone else to chat to. *I'll leave the tables tonight*, thought Pete, *I'll come in early tomorrow morning to brush them down.* There wasn't a pro match until next weekend so the pro table was covered and didn't need doing. That always took him an hour to prepare, but when there was a match on, he made a few quid for himself selling the cheese and ham rolls he'd made. The boss turned a blind to this venture as for him it wasn't worth any serious money, but for Pete it was always an extra £20 or £30 and certainly worth the effort.

As the final balls were potted the two men from table eight came up to the counter. He knew them both, been regulars for years. Mike and Paul, nice blokes, always have a bit of a laugh and chat. 'How'd you get on?' Pete asked Mike.

'Lost again, 4–5. I'll have him next week,' Mike said, laughing and looking at his mate Paul.

'In your dreams,' said Paul. 'You've only ever beaten me once. Hah, once in four years. Give me my money, sucker,' said Paul punching Mike's arm.

'You going over the club?' asked Mike to Pete.

'Yes, just a couple tonight, early start tomorrow. I'll come over when these guys have finished,' said Pete, looking over to the other table.

The two men on table four had now finished and were at the counter. 'Be with you in a minute mate,' said Pete to one of them.

'You glad to be back now?' asked Mike.

'Yes, Germany is good fun. Made a few quid but it's not England. I miss the beer and decent food.'

'Is Tony still there then?' asked Paul.

Looking at Paul, Pete said, 'No he stayed on for a bit then came back about four weeks ago. He's got another job, so I won't see him for a month or two.'

'Used to enjoy our nights at the club, the four of us,' said Mike. It will be good if Tony gets back into town.'

'Yeah, been a while, right,' said Pete. 'Here's your change. See you in a bit.'

'Do you want us to wait for you?' asked Mike.

'No, that's ok. I'll just lock up and then come over. See you there.'

Pete turned to the other two men who had been waiting at the counter. 'Got you down for two hours 15 mins. Call it two hours as it's a Friday. That ok with you?'

'That's good, thanks,' said one of the men in a broad Irish accent.

Paying the fee, the two Irishmen made their way down the stairs and out into the cold Friday night air in the centre of Reading.

Pete deposited the money in the safe, along with the till roll and his notepad, which contained the hours each table had been used.

Flicking the bank of light switches on, the whole hall lit up. Pete made his usual walk around each of the tables, checking the pockets and picking up any obvious litter. Covering all 14 tables and checking the fire escape doors at the back of the hall, Pete made his way back up to the main counter. With one last look around he brushed all the light switches to off, apart from the last one, which covered the staircase down to the main road. Locking the top door, Pete walked down the stairs and entered the main road. Slamming the door shut, locking it and switching the alarm on, he glanced at his watch: 12.30. *Not bad*, he thought. He lit a cigarette and walked towards the centre of the town. Shaking the hand of Winston, the doorman, he entered one of the many night clubs opposite the train station.

'O'Connor.'

'It's Eugene. Got something interesting for you. Me and Liam were playing snooker last night.'

Brendan listened intently to Eugene's story of last night's events as he described the conversation he had overhead between Pete and the other two snooker players Mike and Paul.

'That's good enough,' said Brendan. 'Don't go back in there this week. Wait for me. I'll be over, probably next Friday. I'll meet you in The Coach and Horses,' and with that he put the phone down.

Picking up the phone, Brendan dialled a Birmingham number.

'Are you sure?' asked Declan.

'Sure enough. They talked about Tony in Germany coming back and his mate Pete was there with him and is now running the hall,' said Brendan.

'Ok, I'll be down next week on Friday,' said Declan, placing the phone down.

Bastard, thought Declan, *got you*.

The following Friday Declan climbed into his car in the Aston area of Birmingham and made his way onto to the M6 and then down the M5 towards Bristol. For him, this was the easiest route to get to Reading, and he was meeting Brendan at the services just outside of Swindon.

It was 7pm when he pulled into Membury Services. Parking up and walking into the entrance, he saw Brendan in the self-service area drinking a coffee. Nodding to him, he paid for a can of Coke and sat down opposite Brendan on one of the plastic uncomfortable chairs. There was no rush, Brendan would lead the way to The Coach and Horses where they would pick up Eugene and Liam; from there they would go to the club where Pete worked.

Brendan had told Eugene that he and Liam needed to be sober and ready to go when they got there.

Small talk passed between the two men, nothing, mainly focussing on the Irish rugby team and their successes in the last few games. At 8pm, both men left the services and drove the 30 miles or so through Reading to The Coach and Horses.

Brendan went inside and collected Eugene and Liam.

With Declan following, Brendan drove through the streets of Reading and parked up just off the King's Road. Eugene and Liam left and walked up to the snooker club where Pete was working. The plan was that, come closing time at 11pm, Declan and Brendan would come to the club and wait for Eugene to come outside and tell them that it was empty.

Looking at his watch, Pete sighed, only another hour and

then he could close and go for a pint. Looking around the hall it was very quiet tonight, only three tables left, one of which was about to finish and the other two probably only had about another 45 minutes left as well. *Might be able to get out early*, thought Pete.

Table 12 finished up, paid their money and bid Pete goodnight. Pete walked the floor early, passing each table, a cursory look at the cloth to make sure there were no marks or scratches that had damaged the green baize, checking the pockets for rubbish and picking up the odd paper cup and depositing it in the various bins around the walls of the hall. The second to last table had finished, so he made his way to the counter, collected the snooker balls from them and gave them their change. Looking up, he saw the final table were nearly at an end as well.

One of the men left the table and walked towards the counter and shouted to Pete, 'Back in a second mate, just want to see if my taxi is outside.'

Pete recognised him from the other week and just nodded as Liam made his way down the stairs to the front door.

Watching Eugene pot the last ball and begin to collect the snooker balls from the pockets, Pete turned as he heard the door open. Two men entered the hall with Liam behind them.

'Sorry fellas, we are closed for the night,' Pete said, walking towards the men climbing the steps to the counter.

The pain in his back took his breath away.

Eugene had come up behind him and swung the snooker cue like a baseball bat and smacked it into Pete's right side, causing him to stagger forwards.

Brendan and Liam jumped on Pete, wrenched his arms behind him, pulled him down onto the snooker floor and smashed him face down onto one of the snooker tables. Pete's nose broke and blood flew all over the green baize. Dazed and confused, he was held down and felt a punishing blow to his kidneys.

Tearing him round, he was thrown onto a chair with Liam holding his arms behind his back. Through glazed eyes Pete saw the punch to his face coming from Brendan, but before he could dodge it, the powerful right hook cut across his jaw sending Pete's head into a spin.

Eugene pulled some rope out of his pocket and tied Pete's hands together, securing the rope to the underside strut of the chair rendering it impossible for him to move either arm.

Declan walked up to Pete and punched him in the face. Without speaking, he turned and picked up a snooker cue from the table, spun it round in his hand, so that the bulbous end became a weapon, and cracked it with full force on Pete's knee.

Pete screamed in agony.

'Do you remember me?' asked Declan.

With blood still dripping from his nose into his mouth, 'What?' spat Pete.

Declan stood back and took another swing at the other knee. With a resounding crack, the kneecap broke causing an immense lightning bolt of pain to shoot through Pete's body. Pete, fighting to remain conscious, thrashed around on the chair and tipped over onto the floor.

Liam and Brendan picked him back up; Declan stepped forward and peered straight into Pete's face.

'I said, do you remember me?'

Shaking his head vigorously, 'I've no idea who you are mate. What do you want? The money's in the till over there. Take it, it's all yours.'

Taking a step back, Declan swung the cue onto Pete's left arm. *Pain is relative. That was not as painful as the knee, but maybe the knee pain is just now covering up for the arm;* the crazy thought flashed through Pete's head.

'Who are you working for?' shouted Declan.

'I work for Bill Wilson; he owns this place. I have done for ages.' struggled Pete. 'What the fuck do you want?'

With that, another two blows from the cue reigned down, the first on the broken knee, the second on his other arm.

Pete screamed with pain.

'I don't fucking believe you,' said Declan. 'Who do you work for?'

'I don't know who you are mate. I've never seen you before and I work for Bill. Who else would I be working for, you fucking dick?' Peter said, coughing up blood.,

'Are you and Tony working together?' shouted Declan in Pete's face.

'What?' said Pete. 'Not anymore. We did for a while in Germany, but I didn't like it out there, so I came back, left Tony there, but now Tony is back over here,' blurted out Pete.

'So, who did you report to? Who did you tell about me?'

After having had a moment to breathe, Pete said, 'We reported to the sales manager out there who took the details of the insurance we sold and passed those details onto the insurance company who paid us. I don't know what you mean about me telling someone about you. I've never seen you before mate, honest.'

Declan turned and looked at Brendan.

Brendan stepped in front of Pete and swung a blow to the side of his head knocking him to the ground. Liam dragged him up by the neck back into the sitting position and Brendan, with massive punching power, struck Pete several times in the chest, stomach, and then for good measure, a left hook this time, straight onto Pete's ear, exploding the membrane on the inner ear. Pete reeled from side to side trying to duck and swerve the blows in a vain attempt to lessen the pain he was suffering.

Dazed and barely conscious, he looked at Declan. He knew he was saying something, but he couldn't hear him.

Declan stepped away and turned and looked at Pete. *Maybe it was Tony. With this amount of pain and the beating he had taken it was unlikely*, thought Declan, *that Pete, at this stage, would be lying. Maybe they were just mates and Tony was the one who was the informant.*

Allowing him to recover for a minute, he then said, 'Where's Tony?'

'I don't know,' said Pete.

Declan swung the cue and this time it struck Pete's neck causing him to gasp violently for breath.

'Don't fucking lie to me you little shit. Where's Tony?'

'He's in Bournemouth. I don't know where. He's got a job with BT and they have sent him on a training course in

Bournemouth somewhere. I haven't seen him for a while. He's down there for another four or five weeks, I think,' said Pete quickly, drawing deep breaths trying to fight the pain and remain conscious, hoping that this would be over very soon.

'Where in Bournemouth?'

'I don't know, some hotel near the front. That's all I know,' said Pete.

Leaning forward, Declan pressed the snooker cue tip into Pete's broken knee and said, 'What's Tony's surname?'

Pete screamed in agony. The pain swept through his thigh, into his stomach, through his chest and into his head like a dagger.

'Blackreach. Tony Blackreach,' cried Pete.

Declan looked at him, thinking.

After a moment or two, Declan said,

'Don't think you can tell me anything else can you?'

'No, no I can't,' said Pete. The pain was now becoming unbearable in his leg and chest.

'No, I don't think you can either,' replied Declan darkly.

Pulling the gun from his waistband, he swiftly placed the barrel of the gun against Pete's forehead and pulled the trigger.

The noise was deafening in the great hall. The bullet tore through Pete's skull and out the back of his head. The force of the bullet pushed Pete backwards and, before the blood cascaded out of the back of his head to ooze across the polished wooden floor, Pete bounced onto the hard surface, dead.

The action startled Liam. He wasn't expecting that but knowing enough not to say anything, he looked at Eugene. Eugene was also taken by surprise; this was the first time either of them had been in the presence of a cold-blooded killing. Breathing out, he put the snooker cue he had been holding down on the table.

'Clean this shit up,' said Declan to Brendan, and with that he holstered his gun and walked across the hall, up past the counter and out of the doors, down the stairs and onto the main street. Walking over to his car, Declan started the engine and made his way back to the M4 and then the long journey back to Birmingham.

'Fucking hell!' said Eugene. 'Ok.' Gathering his thoughts quickly and looking at Brendan. 'What do you want to do? How do you want to play this? We can make it look like a robbery gone wrong or lock up and make this guy disappear.'

'Clean the place up, take the money out of the till, leave the safe alone, turn off the lights and lock up,' said Brendan. 'It will be next week sometime before anyone raises any sort of alarm,' continued Brendan. 'Make sure the blood is gone and wipe your prints off the till.'

With that, Brendan left the building and drove back to Bristol. Eugene picked up the phone and called Enda telling him to bring Finbarr in the pickup. 'Park round the back of the hall by the fire escape,' said Eugene to Enda.

On Wednesday morning, Sergeant Easeman was on patrol on the outskirts of Reading when the call came through that a someone had seen what they thought was a body floating in the river near Foundry Brook. Flicking on the blues and twos, Easeman powered the Rover easily through the early morning traffic coming off the M5 into Reading. Foundry Brook was on the south side of Reading near the Madejski Stadium, an area of Reading that was beginning to be redeveloped. Access to the brook was on the opposite side to the stadium and Easeman made the journey there in about ten minutes.

A patrol car was also on the scene as he approached. Getting out of his vehicle, he walked over to PC Dave Jenkins, who was the first to arrive on hearing the report.

'What do we have Dave?' asked Sgt. Easeman.

'I haven't seen it yet, but the bloke who called it in said that he was convinced he saw a body along the bank over here,' PC Jenkins said, pointing to a spot about 20 yards in front of him.

'He was over the other side and saw it; he then went and called us.'

'What makes him so sure it's a body?'

'Said he saw a face,' replied PC Jenkins.

'OK, let's go and have a look.'

The two men, ill-equipped to walk alongside a muddy bank, gradually worked their way along, looking over the small bank to see if they could find a body.

'Over here!' shouted Dave Jenkins, after about ten minutes of searching.

Sgt. Easeman came alongside Jenkins and kneeled down and tried to grasp what looked like a bloated coat. Almost falling in, the Sergeant at last managed to grab the grey cloth and pulled it towards him. With the help of Dave, they struggled and slipped on the muddy surface. With both feet in the water now, both men heaved what was clearly a body onto the embankment.

Breathing heavily, Sgt Easeman rolled the figure over.

PC Jenkins took one look at the face, spun round and threw up his bacon roll he'd had for breakfast.

Dave Easeman rolled his eyes He was made of sterner stuff, having seen several dead bodies before. Whilst an unpleasant sight, he was less inclined to react in such a way. The face was bloated and scarred, but as Easeman peered closer, he could see that this was no accidental drowning: there was a bullet hole in the centre of the man's forehead.

Pete's mother had reported him missing to the local police the week before. It wasn't unusual for Pete to stay out for a couple of days, but after a week of not hearing from him, and then having had the third call from his boss asking if she knew where he was, she had called into the local police station and gave them his description and a recent photograph, taken at her 65th birthday party.

Within hours of the body being taken to the local morgue, they had established with almost a 90 percent certainty that it was Pete who lay in front of them. The following day his mother had been called in, and with her other son Ian, they had had confirmed that it was Pete.

The slackness of the local newspaper reporting that a body had been found in the nearby river made it on the third page, but it wasn't followed up by the more experienced reporter for the Reading News, as he was still on holiday. The police had assured the editor that if and when they had more information, they would let the paper know. No information as to how he died was given other than a suspected drowning after a possible drinking session.

By Wednesday that week the report landed on Geoffrey's desk. Any unusual activity across the UK was reported, and although most of it took time and wasn't relevant, a murder was out of the ordinary, and in this case, given the Met had raided in Reading early that year, this report took precedent above others, just in case.

Geoffrey sighed, closed the report and picked up the phone to the Assistant Commissioner, Paul Lang. Explaining the situation in the briefest way possible, he asked if the murder could be made to look like an accidental drowning, with no mention of the bullet wound. Having a murder splashed all over the papers would alert the perpetrator to the fact that Pete had been found and they were looking for his killer. Which if it was the IRA, which Geoffrey suspected, in his view, would drive them further underground, and as difficult as it was now to find any active IRA, it would be even harder if this was made public. In addition, privately, he didn't want to let Tony know that his best friend had been murdered. Easier to keep it simple.

He knew that the family would have only been in the room identifying Pete for a few seconds and grief would have overcome his mother, so any wound on him would either be forgotten or put down to his fall into the river and him banging his head. Once cleaned up, a bullet hole is remarkably small at the front and would not disfigure the face too much, as in this case it was a single shot to the forehead. The back of his head was a different matter of course.

It was agreed that it would pass as a drowning. It was something the forces had done before, mostly in the national interest. Dreadful as it was and disturbing for the officers on the scene, they would be assured that it would not be swept under the carpet and justice would be served, even if it meant that it would take some time.

Chapter 17

Johnny Sturgess had spent the morning pushing his grand-daughter in her pram along the promenade. His son, daughter-in-law and wife had wandered onto the sand, enjoying the last of the sun. He had been happy to push Susan, occasionally picking her up and waving at mum and dad making cooing noises as all new grandads do. They all had had ice cream and laughed at the faces Susan had pulled when first licking such an ice-cold treat, not wanting it but then wanting it as the sweet sensation tantalised her tongue and taste buds. Fish and chips had been the order of the day and this stroll in the afternoon was a great way to finish off four days of peace, all of them away from work and an opportunity for Dawn, his son's wife, to have a break from the constant nappy changing and feeding duties of a new mum. Everyone had taken turns at looking after Susan, all enjoying the squeals of delight Susan was prone to let out every now and again.

They all met up at the end of the promenade. Coming off the beach and shaking the sand out of their shoes, Mum picked up Susan. His son Paul took ownership of the pram and he and his wife walked on behind them as they made their way back to the hotel just past the crazy golf course next to the Winter Gardens. Not really paying much attention to anything, Johnny caught sight of a man who was on the opposite side of the road heading back towards the prom.

Johnny instantly became alert: a face, he knew that face. As the man came closer, Johnny racked his memory; it came to him within a matter of seconds. Declan Cassidy. Johnny breathed out, he couldn't believe he was actually looking at Declan Cassidy. Cassidy wasn't paying any attention to the holidaymakers walking up and down the promenade, he was concentrating mainly on his plan as to how he would deal with Tony.

He'd been in town for a day, had booked into a local B&B and started to walk around the town. His plan was to get a sense of the town, streets that would serve him in the darkness and his best way of escaping once he had killed Tony.

His phone calls to Bournemouth hotels had revealed that Tony was staying at the Moat House Hotel at the end of the long promenade. With easy access to the main centre of Bournemouth, it was a large hotel of some 100 rooms and mainly serviced corporate clients. British Telecom had taken almost all the rooms for the next six months to accommodate the vast numbers of recruits they were taking on board.

It was also an ideal location in the town, as it was only a 30-minute walk along the sea front, then across into the main town of Bournemouth and onto Commercial Road, up Poole Hill over the roundabout to a purpose-built office block that had been refurbished as the British Telecom training centre.

Leaning towards his wife, Johnny held her hand and whispered in her ear, 'Don't say anything and just keep walking normally.' She turned and looked at him.

'I've seen someone we are after. There's no danger, but I need to keep track of him. Get everyone to the hotel and ring DCI Harry Roberts for me. Tell him I've seen Declan Cassidy and I'm following him and get him to get down here. When I leave you, don't turn back, just catch up with the kids and tell them I've gone back to get some souvenirs. Get Harry to come to the hotel. I'll ring there later as soon as I can. Don't worry, everything is fine, just act normally,' He said, kissing her on the cheek.

Cathy nodded, 'Be careful, please be careful,' she said to her husband.

'Always,' and with that he turned around and slowly walked back the way he had come, keeping an eye on Declan who was now halfway down, on the other side of the road.

Cathy knew what her husband did and that he had faced danger on several occasions but never dwelt on the fact that he may get hurt. Living in a state of fear was not the way any marriage should be, and he had been up front with her 22 years ago when they got married that his career would be a challenge from time to time. She knew he had moved over to the division that centred its activity on the IRA but never questioned what he did and knew her husband well enough to know now that whoever Johnny had seen it was important enough for him to follow up and get Harry down here.

Catching up with Declan on the opposite side of the road, Johnny knew his best option was to keep him in sight as much as possible, hoping that they would stay in the populated areas. If Declan walked off into some side streets then the chances of him being spotted increased dangerously. Johnny assumed that the man was more than likely carrying a gun, and as he wasn't armed he was in no position to safely arrest Declan. He also wouldn't put it past him, if he spotted Johnny, to start shooting in the crowded streets, which would cause panic and inevitably, possible injury to some civilians.

At a safe distance, Johnny followed as Declan made his way through town and across into the more commercial area. Johnny ducked into a newsagent as Declan stopped, paused for a moment or two and then turned around and started to make his way back the way he had come. Johnny looked up the road to where Declan had come to a halt, but there was nothing obvious as far as he could see that would be of interest, unless, of course, he thought, he'd made a mistake and gone up the wrong road. The area they were in had a few shops, a couple of high-rise offices, and at this time of the day, office workers were beginning to leave the various offices scattered along the street. *No target of high value*, thought Johnny.

As Declan retraced his steps, the thought that he'd gone the wrong way was quickly discounted by Johnny as he now was walking back down Commercial Road, onto Exeter

Road leading to the promenade where Johnny had first seen him. Declan slowed down as he approached a gap between the Post Office and WH Smiths. Watching Declan as he casually looked into the window of WH Smiths, at first, Johnny thought he had been spotted, then, walking past Declan on the opposite side of the road, he could see that the gap between the two shops was an alleyway that looked like it gave way to a car park at the rear of the shops. Having studied the area for a moment or two, Declan then walked off at a pace down towards the prom. Johnny was about 100 yards in front of him and pausing every now and again to look into the shop windows to make sure where Declan was. They continued along the road, passed the Pavilion and headed towards Boscombe. Veering off into one of the side streets, Jonny saw Declan run up the steps and enter a small bed and breakfast. Glancing at his watch, 6:30pm, Johnny looked around for a telephone box.

Tony stared around the classroom, they had just finished a role play exercise on objection handling. 'Just fucking buy it, you twat,' Mark had said in exasperation at the end of his session. With that, the room full of budding salesman dissolved into laughter.

'Ok guys, homework tonight is to build an argument on selling an intangible to a financial director who is over budget for the year. The brief is over on the table, take one before you go,' said Marcus, the BT trainer.

Marcus was a good guy. Approaching forty, he had spent ten years in the States and then had come over to the UK and had set up a business as a sales trainer. He had landed the contract with BT and was now into his fourth month of training, with two of his colleagues and over a hundred new salesmen and women.

The room that Tony occupied was filled with a variety of people from all walks of life. Their joint experience ranged from a fully blown IT salesperson to one guy who was a steel fabricator of 30 years who had worked at the docks on Teesside and having been laid off, needed a change of career. All were subjected to the basic training of six weeks, starting from simple telephone calling, introductions to presentations, proposal creating and training for public speaking at conferences. Every day someone learnt something new.

Tony was enjoying the course: it was rounding the rough edges he had developed when selling insurance door to door. No more hard, aggressive selling, much more subtle manipulation.

Two more weeks to go and then he would be sent to the main office, either in Gresham Street or Newgate Street depending on where his bosses needed him. All the others were spread around the country. *A hundred salesmen is quite a lot*, thought Tony, *but once you cover the country with a few in each city a hundred doesn't really go that far.*

Friday tomorrow, then back home. *Wonder what the new place is like*, pondered Tony. His parents had moved from Thatcham down to Somerset and had bought a pub. Sounded fun but from what he could gather it seemed a long way from anywhere, and he'd never heard of Chard. He'd looked on the map he kept in his new car and it seemed to be about a two-hour journey from Bournemouth, no motorways, all across country. Well he'd find out soon enough.

The previous weekends he had spent in the hotel. There was quite a lot of work to do and many of the others had also stayed, as travelling back for some of them to the North of England, Midlands etc. on either a Friday night or Saturday morning to then return again on the Sunday ready for the Monday really wasn't worth the effort. BT didn't mind and neither did the hotel; although Tony suspected that they rented out a few of the rooms when the BT people weren't there, which they shouldn't have done as BT had block booked every room, every day for six months. *Probably a way for the manager to complement his earnings*, thought Tony.

Following the others out of the room and down the stairs, about a dozen of them made their way out onto the main street and headed, as always, to The Crown, which was a couple of hundred yards from the training centre. This had become a habit. He, like all the others, was well paid and had very little outgoings, so having a few drinks each night before a meal not only relieved the boredom of staying away it was also a good laugh and he'd got to know everyone, many of whom he thought he would stay in touch with once they had gone their separate ways.

As he had approached the bar to order his pint he had rubbed up against Linda, who had backed into him. She stood firm as he pushed his crotch harder against her. Leaning past and pulling his arm around her unnecessarily to get through, he said, 'Sorry.' 'Am I in your way?' she replied, drifting her free hand across his front and onto the top of his thigh. They smiled at each other as she walked away from the bar and went to sit at the table with three others from the team.

He would see her later; they had hit it off within a matter of days of them first attending the course and had pretty much spent every night since then either in his room or hers. She had the softest of skin he'd ever felt, and images of her went through his mind as he ordered his pint of lager. Linda was his latest squeeze, a good player but not a keeper, Tony judged.

Collecting his drink and lighting a cigarette, he wandered over to the pool table along with Jeff and Billy. Clark would join them once he'd got his drink. They would play pool for about an hour and then go to one of the restaurants in town for a meal. The last four weeks on a Thursday they went out as group to eat. The food in the Hotel was ok and free but it became very repetitive, and after a while everyone just wanted a pizza or a cheeseburger.

Finishing their second drinks, the consensus of opinion was that they would go back to the Italian just down the road from The Crown. Everyone had enjoyed it there last week; freshly made pizza and pasta was the order of the day. They bundled out of The Crown and walked the few yards to the restaurant. It was ideally situated on the same side of the road and whilst no one was really lazy, it was easy, close and decent. There were other Italians in town but this one had ticked all the boxes for everyone so there they went.

Declan checked his watch: 5pm. Walking over to the table he picked up one of the magazines he had loaded earlier, slipped it into the Czech Phantom and snapped it into place. Pushing on the safety, he put it into the side pocket of his leather jacket and pulled up the zip. He would transfer it to his belt when he was out of the car and had seen Tony. He preferred the 9mm Czech pistol. Carrying 15 rounds in the magazine, it was lightweight and had never jammed on him

Early that day he had disassembled the gun, cleaned it thoroughly and loaded each magazine. Once complete and reassembled he had checked each magazine fitted easily into the Phantom and ejected smoothly. He then practised ejecting and loading the magazines, taking the new ones from his jacket pocket. He had seen it in the past when people had tried to reload and had either dropped the new magazine or it had got tangled in their clothing, which had cost them dearly. This was not, as far as Declan was concerned, going to happen to him. He was planning on using no more than two bullets to kill Tony. Fast and simple was his plan but planning for the worst was always a basic training exercise.

He picked up the other two magazines and put those in the inside breast pocket of his jacket. Gathering his bag, he left the B&B and approached his car. Looking up and down the street for anything that was unusual, he opened the car door. He wasn't expecting anything, but old habits die hard and he'd survived this long by being cautious. Throwing his bag on the back seat he set out on the short journey to the car park he had found at the bottom of the alley between WH Smiths and the Post Office.

Leaving the car, Declan walked up through the alley and made his way towards the building that he knew Tony was in. It hadn't taken him long to find out from the hotel exactly where the training centre was. At 6pm, he waited in the doorway of Giffords, the opticians directly opposite the training centre, waiting for Tony to appear. He didn't have long to wait. He spotted Tony in the middle of a group of people coming out of the centre. He watched them walk back along the expected path he had hoped they would take, reasoning that they would walk back to the Hotel. Declan hadn't expected Tony to be with so many people and quickly decided that he would get ahead of them and when they walked past the alley he would just walk out and shoot him there. That would panic the people he was with, and he doubted that any of them, judging by the look of them, would try and either stop him or chase after him. Quick and simple. Then down the alley into his car and away.

Turning out of the entrance of the opticians, he began to gain on the group on the opposite side of the road. There were quite a few people around and it was extremely unlikely that Tony, chatting to someone as he was, would turn around and see him. Catching them up, he began walking at a decent pace towards the alley, keeping an eye on the group as he did so. Catching him by surprise, he watched as they all went into The Crown pub. 'Fuck!' he muttered.

Waiting for a few minutes, he crossed the road and looked into the pub window. He caught sight of Tony at the bar getting a drink along with the others. The bar itself was very busy and Declan contemplated going into the pub and finishing Tony off there and then. It was something he'd done before back home so it could be a good option. However, there were too many in the pub and he thought he might struggle to get out, especially if someone in there decided to be a hero. Letting the thought slide, Declan turned and carried on walking down the road. Spotting a bench opposite the entrance to some war memorial, he sat down and decided to wait. Patience was the order of the day.

About an hour later he watched as the group came out of the pub and start to head in his direction. About to stand and move on towards the end of the road and near the alley, Declan then rolled his eyes as they walked into the Italian restaurant, chatting and laughing as they did so.

'Does this bloke not want to be shot?' he said to himself. 'Patience!' Declan lit a cigarette and waited. He decided that he would give them about 45 minutes and then go and have a look to see how far they had got with their meal. He hoped he would be able to spot them quickly through the restaurant window. The alley was literally 200 yards from the restaurant. 'Patience!' Declan told himself again.

It was approaching 8 o'clock when Declan made it to the entrance of the alley. He had seen the group were almost finished so he had walked the 200 yards or so, stepped inside and waited. It was dark, and as he rested in the shadows he looked up and down the street. From where he was stood it would be extremely difficult for anyone to see him clearly. The summer had gone and the nights were drawing in. There was quite a cool breeze coming off the sea and into the town, less people walking around, and Declan suspected that on this, a normal Thursday night, at this time of year the place would be very quiet. *It won't be quiet for much longer,* he thought.

He could see the restaurant from where he was, and he could watch the progress of the group as they got nearer to him. His plan now was simple: whether Tony was alone or in a group, Declan would wait until they were less than ten yards from the entrance, walk out, pick him out and kill him. If they came out of the restaurant and went a different way, then he wasn't going to waste any more time. He would follow them, catch them up and then just shoot Tony. He would chance running back to the car. If anyone chased him then that was their problem as he would just keep firing at them to keep them down. By the time the police got here he would be long gone.

Tony finished his drink. The pizza he had had was lovely, soft melted mozzarella on top of a picante tomato sauce, pepperoni adorned the top of the pizza and he had had some cheesy garlic bread to go with it. Two glasses of Chianti had, in his opinion, enhanced the flavours of the pizza immeasurably. Pulling his wallet from his pocket, the waiter had produced individual bills for everyone. Whilst it was a bit tedious for the waiter to do so it was the only way to stop any arguing over who had had what. Sliding a ten pound note out of his wallet, he picked up the receipt and handed that and the money to the waiter. As he did so, he caught sight of a flashing blue light passing the window of the restaurant at speed.

'Go! Go! Go!' came the call over the radio.

Simultaneously, two unmarked Land Rovers raced

from opposite directions towards the entrance of the alley. Covering the distance in under a minute and approaching from two different directions, they screeched to a halt, blue lights now ablaze and sirens penetrating the quietness of the Bournemouth road. Three armed offices from each vehicle piled out of the Land Rovers, and with masks on, guns aimed, they ran shouting 'Armed police, armed police, stand still,' to the man standing at the corner of the alley.

Caught by surprise, Declan saw the first of the Land Rovers approaching from the restaurant end of the road first. It was travelling quickly and it wasn't until the last minute that the sirens and light came on. Declan looked to his right and saw another approaching just as fast. Turning swiftly, he started to run back down the alley towards his car.

Johnny Sturgess leapt out of the vehicle. Along with his partner, they ran around the car and swept up to the rear of the alley shouting, 'Armed police, armed police. Stand still.'

Behind them four other offices of the tactical team had exited their vehicles and covered Johnny and his partner as they ran up the alley towards Declan.

Declan had nowhere to go. He contemplated, for a second, pulling his weapon and engaging in a gun fight. He was heavily outnumbered and was sure he would die if he attempted it. 'Fucking bastard!' he said in his heavy Irish accent.

He put his hands in the air and knelt down. Johnny was on him in a second, he pushed him against the wall and roughly searched him. Mark stood over him breathing heavily and watching for any sudden movement from

Declan. They knew from the briefing that Declan would be almost certainly be armed and was extremely dangerous. Covering Johnny as he found the weapon, which he handed to Steve, one of the other first officers who had come in from the front of the alley, he then found the two spare magazines; these too he handed to Steve. Steve withdrew and went to the lead police vehicle where DI Harry Roberts was waiting.

The street now had four other Police vehicles in it, all of whom had come from the local division. They had blocked the road and also had blocked the entrance to the car park. Harry grimaced as he took the weapons and magazines, putting them in a couple of plastic evidence bags. Tying them tightly, he put them in the secure box in the back of the Land Rover. He looked around, up and down the street, but couldn't see anything that warranted the appearance of Declan. Why was he waiting here? Obviously for someone, but who, they might never know. But it was a fact that whoever it was he was waiting for, they were going to go home alive tonight, he thought.

Declan pulled up roughly so he could stand, was read his rights and bundled into the police Land Rover. Not saying anything other than cursing under his breath, the door slammed shut. The officers returned to their vehicles. Harry got in the lead car and they sped off out of Bournemouth with their prize. It had taken less than five minutes, no casualties and an excellent result for the team.

Tony stood up; having paid his bill he stepped out into the street. The cool breeze licked around him, and as he lit a cigarette he looked down the road and saw a flurry of activity of police vehicles, lights on. The smoke from his cigarette as he exhaled curled up and drifted up into the night sky. The police, he noted, had now started to drive away. *Maybe a break in at the Post Office,* thought Tony. Linda joined him outside querying the police presence. 'Break in possibly,' said Tony. As the cars drove away, 'False alarm by the looks of it,' he said, taking Linda's hand, giving her a kiss. Sharing the cigarette, they walked slowly back down to the hotel.

Chapter 18

It had been a busy nine months for Tony. Heading down the A40 into London from Cheltenham, the journey taking about two hours, he cast his mind back over the events since he had left the training centre at British Telecom in Bournemouth. He remembered the day when he got the call telling him that Pete had died and his funeral was the following week. He didn't really question his death. He and Pete had, on many occasions, been out on the town and had consumed their fair share of alcohol. Too drunk to drive home, they had often walked across from the night club they had been in to Pete's workplace and fallen asleep on one of the many snooker tables. The police had said that he had probably fallen into the stream in the early hours having been out drinking that night.

He'd left the training centre in Bournemouth and drove up to Woodcote on that Thursday morning, arriving in the small village where he went to Pete's house where his mum and brother were. Giving her a hug and shaking hands with Ian, Pete's older brother, he collected a cup of tea and lit a cigarette. Silence. As Tony looked around for probably the first time he thought the room looked drab, which was unfair, everything was grey and old. Pete's mother sat on an old tattered settee and was being comforted by her sister Gloria. Pete's father had died about ten years ago. Pete's mum, Ellen, had married her first husband Stanley before the war and she had had two children by him: Ian and Carl. Carl had died of pneumonia in 1951. Stanley had been killed in the war and she had remarried in the late fifties to Pete Senior. He had worked at the car factory in Cowley after the war but had suffered dreadfully from an injury he had sustained in Palestine in 1946. Never really recovering, he died at home one Sunday afternoon.

The funeral was, as every funeral is a sombre affair. Tony sat at the back of the church. The coffin was carried out and they all stood around the grave as he was lowered into it. Tears flowed from the women who were there and as Tony looked, Ian too looked incredibly saddened that he had now lost his second brother. Once the service was completed, the 20 or so people who were there drifted away towards their cars. They had all been invited back to the house for something to eat and drink. Tony had declined, citing he had to get back to Bournemouth and promising that he would call in and see Pete's mum again soon.

Standing at the side of the grave, Tony lit a cigarette, inhaling and exhaling and looking into the distance. Taking one last look at where Pete lay, he flicked his cigarette on top of the brown casket and with no emotion in his voice said,

'See you on the ice mate,' pausing for a moment and then turned and walked back to his car.

He'd met Paula in Chard. After finishing the training in

Bournemouth, he'd gone to live with a friend in Basingstoke and that Christmas, as he visited his parent's pub, he'd met and started dating Paula. They got married in the February. It was a low-key affair with about 30 people attending. They then had moved to Cheltenham. Paula didn't want to leave the area as she was very much a homely girl. All her family lived in Chard but Tony had said that if they were getting married or had any future together then she would have to leave and go with him to Cheltenham. It seemed an odd choice of town for Paula. As far as she knew, Tony didn't know anyone there and neither did she; in fact, she'd never heard of the place and if the truth were told, neither had Tony. Cheltenham was the suggestion of Geoffrey. Tony wasn't bothered, he could live anywhere.

Initially, Tony had taken the train from Cheltenham into London every morning. It left at 6am and was the first train out; it got into Paddington at 8 o'clock. He then caught the tube across town from Paddington to Oxford Street and then jumped onto the central line to St Paul's. A short walk took him around St Paul's cathedral and onto Eastgate Street where the British Telecom headquarters were based.

The team he had been allocated to consisted of six people, including himself. They were an autonomous unit within British Telecom. There were four salesmen, one sales manager, and a senior manager who reported to the sales director who sat on the Board. Tony didn't know if any of them knew Geoffrey and he wasn't going to ask. His role was to promote BT's own computer products to the myriad of departments. Concentrating on London initially, his boss had said that they would include corporate clients later in the year. Because he lived in Cheltenham, Tony had access to the Bristol office where he had a desk, and he also had one in the Birmingham office. To cover London, he had set up in Gresham Street and now latterly in Ealing. Their seniority within the company allowed all of them to access any part of the organisation. The territory managers had been informed that new units had been set up but were not under their control so they had no interest in them at all.

British Telecom's money came from voice services, and the territory managers, many of them in their 50s, had no interest in computer technology. The bulk of the new salesmen employed in the new computer division were housed in the territories alongside the traditional voice salespeople. Tony's team had very little contact with them and, as far as he could see, very little reporting was required by him about where he went. He didn't know how much influence Geoffrey had had on his workload but it allowed Tony a considerable amount of freedom. Freedom in so much as non-BT work. About six weeks ago he had picked up a couple of photographs from his drop off point that Geoffrey needed information on. They had been seen in the Feather and Firkin in Ealing and he was tasked to observe any activity in this area.

Pulling off the A40 at the Hanger Lane junction, he drove the short distance south and turned onto The Mall leading to Ealing Broadway. Passing Lloyds Bank, he followed the road left onto the High Street and then, with 100 yards, steered his car into a small alley way which housed car parking space for four cars, one of which was allocated to him. Making his way up the fire escape to the run-down British Telecom offices that were situated above several shops, he entered the office and began to access emails on his computer.

At midday, he left the office and walked through Walpole Park to the Feather and Firkin. He had been going to the pub regularly for four weeks, Thursday and Friday nights, and this weekend he would go in on a Saturday night. He stayed at a local B&B and put the bill on expenses. They were never checked thoroughly and if anyone did ask, he would say it was either a training course or entertaining a client and had to work late etc. He visited this pub and three others in the area. He had chatted to the landlords on a regular basis and they all knew he worked for BT and he had given the impression that he lived in the area. Quickly establishing a routine, chatting to the locals and playing pool with some, he had become a regular. It was easier to be in plain sight rather than sneak around and attract people's attention.

The bombing in the UK had not abated, and there was more and more talk in the press about the IRA's activity not reducing in any way and calls were being made to the Government to do more. No one actually said how they could do more but that was the nature of the press, easy to criticise those in power but not offering any sustainable solutions. Tony wasn't bothered about the talk, as he knew that any information he could provide was hopefully in some small way helpful.

Walking into the pub, Tony greeted the landlord and ordered a shandy. 'Shandy?' said Dave the landlord.

'Yes. Got fed up behind the desk. Thought I'd pop out for a quick one. Can't have too much, got to work this afternoon,' said Tony. 'Are you in later?' asked Dave 'We've got a pool match, so the table won't be available.'

'I will be. That's ok. I'll just watch,' said Tony.

Looking around the bar, there were a couple of regulars. They were on the dole. *Familiar faces only today,* thought Tony. Sitting at the bar, he lit a cigarette and chatted to Dave for a bit about the up and coming football at the weekend. Not really interested in football, Tony made a habit of catching the headlines in the sports pages each week just to keep a few topics to talk about. After about an hour, with a few more coming in but nothing of interest, Tony left and walked the half mile or so to The Cross Hands. Similar exchanges with the landlord, another shandy and a cheese roll this time. Tony watched the coming and goings of the clientele for a while. Finishing his pint, Tony waved to the landlord and made his way to his final call of the lunch hour to The Lion.

The Lion was an old pub and still had the charm of low ceilings with oak beams, an open fireplace and antique furniture. Robin, the landlord, had took over the place in the mid '70s. He had come from Northern Ireland to escape, as he kept telling people, 'The Troubles'. The pub was never as busy as the others and Tony suspected it was because of the incessant talking done by Robin. Once he latched onto you he wouldn't let you go; pleasant as it was to begin with, it became increasingly irritating for some who were there to enjoy their own company and not his. For Tony, however, Robin was a good source of local gossip, some of which Tony knew he made up, but every now and again a snippet of information surfaced. Tony endured Robin, and as he entered the pub, Robin began pouring him his regular pint of lager, before Tony had time to stop him. *Oh well*, thought Tony. *One pint should be ok. I can always grab a quick kip later.*

The only reason he had come in here was to broaden his circle of locations in which he thought he might spot either of the two blokes he was looking for. When he found out that the landlord was Irish and hated what was happening in Northern Ireland he doubted that his guys would be coming in here, but as a gossip, Robin might drop something unknowingly, so Tony kept coming in.

'Afternoon,' came the greeting.

Tony smiled, 'Afternoon, thought I'd drop in for a quick one.'

'Good on you, me fine friend,' said Robin. Tony wasn't sure if that's how they spoke, but Robin seemed to like accentuating his accent from time to time.

It was 1:30pm. Tony looked around, nothing happening in here, Thursday lunchtime, a couple of regulars finishing up getting ready to go back to work.

Lighting a cigarette and sitting at the bar, Tony took a swig of his lager, took a deep breath and asked Robin, 'How you doing then, been busy?'

Forty minutes later, with earache, Tony left the pub and made his way back to the Ealing office.

The routine continued, August drifted into September and then October. Tony fluctuated between the pubs and had added another two to his rounds. He filed his weekly reports to Geoffrey, which contained nothing of interest, and towards the end of October, he began to start thinking about Christmas.

He hadn't been in The Lion for a couple of weeks. With work getting busy and two other pubs to visit he thought The Lion was not worth a visit every week. As he approached the pub on this Saturday night it had just gone 8 o'clock. Wandering in, he made his way to the bar.

'Hi Tony, usual?' asked Robin.

'Yes please,' said Tony.

'Not seen you for a couple of weeks.'

'No, I've been busy, work mainly, had to install some stuff at a customer's, usual crap,' replied Tony. Fortunately, thought Tony, Robin was being kept busy by the thirsty drinkers so didn't have time to chat to him.

Paying for his pint, Tony looked around the bar. It was quite busy for a Saturday but then there were a few football supporters in. Good banter between the rival teams, it sounded like to Tony.

The bar was a bit crowded, so he picked his pint up and walked towards the fruit machine, nodding and saying 'Hi' to a couple of the locals he'd got to know.

Sliding in a few coins and hitting the buttons, Tony looked around. The pub was an L shape. It used to be two bars but had been knocked through and was now one bar. The fruit machine was in a sort of alcove, which used to be the entrance to the lounge. It was still classed as the lounge bar, determined by the carpet that stopped at what was now the non-existent wall separating the two bars. Most of the tables were empty. The men in the bar preferred standing in groups or surrounding the bar itself, making it difficult to get a drink, which wasn't untypical of a drinking pub.

Placing his pint on top of the fruit machine, Tony took out his cigarettes and lit one up. As he did so he saw the door to the gent's open, and a man walked out and sat down next to another who had occupied one of the small tables near the window of the lounge bar. 'Fuck me,' thought Tony. Martin Dempsey.

Martin Dempsey was not one of the men he had been asked to look out for by Geoffrey, he was one of the approximately 30 faces he had committed to memory when he had visited the offices of Geoffrey last year. A known IRA member, there was absolutely no reason for him to be in England other than to cause trouble.

Not quite believing who he was looking at, Tony walked towards the toilet. The bar was too noisy for him to hear anything, so without losing his stride, he continued into the toilet thinking about what to do next.

He couldn't leave the pub and ring Geoffrey like last time as the nearest phone box was about half a mile away and by the time he'd done that they may well have left the pub and disappeared.

Coming back out of the toilet, Tony ignored them and walked straight back and picked his pint up. Finishing his drink, he went outside and made his way towards his car. Starting the engine, he moved it closer to the pub and reversed into the road opposite the pub, giving him a clear view of the entrance. Not sure whether to follow them on foot or by car he decided to decide that when they came out.

Chapter 19

At about 10:30pm both men emerged from the pub and began to walk, hands in pockets, away from the pub towards a small section of shops that housed a few takeaways, most of whom were getting busier as the pubs were beginning to empty. Tony decided that they were within walking distance of their base as he doubted that either of them now were going to get into a car. Following the two men at a distance, he watched as they made their way into one of the chip shops. Tony mingled with a crowd on the opposite side of the road who were in and out of a kebab house. Joining the queue in the kebab house, as he ordered he saw that Martin and his mate were also at the counter of the chip shop.

Seconds later, all three of them were emerging with food in their hands. Tony paused as he unwrapped his food, waiting to see which way they walked.

Turning left, away from the direction of the pub, they walked along the street eating the food they had purchased. Tony, similarly, started on his. Having taken a mouthful, he looked down at what he was eating: the kebab contained what Tony could only describe as shrapnel. As he walked, following Martin at a distance, he off-loaded the green and yellow things and the lettuce that was piled into the pitta bread. Looking underneath, he eventually spied the meat with some sort of red sauce on it.

The two men came to the end of the street, crossed the road and entered a town house. Some four floors high it was either a B & B or a set of flats, thought Tony, as he walked past still eating his kebab. Noting the number, he carried on walking, slowly eating his food. At the bottom of the road he spotted a phone box. Dumping the remnants of his kebab, casually stopping and turning to light a cigarette, making sure that no one had followed him he placed a call to the number Geoffrey had given him.

The following morning Tony arrived back at Martin's house at 6am. He looked around and found a space not far from the entrance to the house. Settling down to watch, he picked up his camera and checked to make sure the tele-photo lens that was attached to the camera was capable of zooming in onto the front of the property. Pressing the button a couple of times and winding on the roll, he was satisfied that if he had the opportunity, he would be able to snap either one or both men he had seen last night. It wasn't an expensive camera, he had planned to use it on holiday but had never gotten around to going on one so it had been gathering dust in his bedroom for a couple of years. The film was new, so he hoped that whatever pictures he took would come out ok.

On making the call to Geoffrey's office he had been told to report back in later that day. He'd also rang Paula, getting her out of bed, and told her that the car had broken down and he would be staying in London for the weekend but should be home either Monday or Tuesday.

It wasn't until about 9:30am that both men emerged from the house; Tony immediately started taking pictures. He had zoomed in on the man he didn't know, and as luck would have it, both men turned in his direction when leaving and made their way along the opposite side of the road towards him. After taking a couple of shots, he quickly ducked down hoping that he wouldn't be spotted, and counting to ten, he waited for them to pass on by.

Looking in his mirror he saw the two men walking towards the tube. Jumping out of his car, Tony opened the boot and put the camera inside. Not wanting to appear like a tourist, he thought it better to just walk and follow. The two men entered the tube and with Tony now close on their heels they caught the first train, city bound on the District line. Tony joined the train two cars down and waited. South Kensington was the exit for both men, and they walked up and out of the tube onto the Brompton Road. London was, as always, busy, so Tony kept to the opposite side of the road as the two men walked at a steady pace. It appeared to Tony that they were obviously going somewhere as neither man was interested in looking in any shop windows or stopping for breakfast at one of the many cafés en route.

Along Brompton Road, their paced slowed as they came towards Harrods. It could be, thought Tony, that because of the number of people who were always on the streets in this busy part of London, their progress was being hampered by the sheer volume of shoppers. Harrods was a massive store, well known throughout the world, and what with Madame Tussauds opposite, and many high-end boutiques, the area was a magnate for wealthy Londoners and tourists alike. It appeared to Tony that they were taking a great deal of interest in the shop itself, and as they passed by, they slowed down even more and looked at the street both next to and adjacent to Harrods. Without stopping completely, the pair crossed the road and continued their journey. Tony followed suit and he too walked over to the opposite thoroughfare keeping an eye out to make sure that neither of the men, he hoped, had spotted a tail. The pace went back to a normal walking pattern as the two men walked over the junction of Knightsbridge, along Knightsbridge itself and around Hyde Park corner, at which point, Tony wondered whether they were going to cut through Green Park towards Westminster; however, both men headed up Piccadilly and along into Leicester Square. Tony decided to forget the guessing game. There were way too many potential targets in London, many of which they had passed and many, many more within half a mile of where they were. That is, of course, Tony thought, if they were looking for something. Or maybe, it then occurred to Tony, they were going to meet up with someone.

Through Leicester Square the two men again slowed their pace and walked up into Covent Garden, the centre of which housed the Jubilee Market Hall. Tony slowed, knowing the area quite well, he was confident that he could still follow Martin and his companion without compromise. The two men, followed by Tony, walked around the square. Both of them were clearly talking to each other and looking at every street that opened up into Covent Garden itself. Walking around for a second-time, Martin headed into a small café in the centre where he purchased a couple of drinks and both men then sat on one of the many benches and went into a deep conversation.

Tony hid behind one of the many pillars supporting the structure on the outside of the shops that surrounded the area. Keeping an eye on the men via the reflection in one of the shop windows, no one took any notice of him as he lit up a cigarette and waited. After a few minutes, Martin stood up and they made their way out of Covent Garden and onto the tube network. Tony followed as they changed from the Piccadilly line they had caught at Covent Garden to the District line at South Kensington and then back into Chiswick where all three of them headed up onto the main road. Tony watched as they headed back towards their house. He retrieved the camera from his car boot, slid into the driver's seat and made his way to the drop off point at Millbank, just by Vauxhall Bridge. He deposited the film with a few notes and returned to his hotel.

Tony decided that there was little else for him to do that night, so he made up a more comprehensive set of notes on the journey they had all taken that day. First thing on Monday morning he also put this into his normal drop box at Farringdon and then went round to Millbank, where he noted that the camera roll had now gone.

Calling in sick that morning, he made his way back and parked up a few hundred yards from where Martin and his companion were housed. Not knowing if they were inside, he sat and waited. After several hours, Martin appeared, alone. Getting out of his car, Tony followed at a distance. Martin walked back to where they had had fish and chips at the weekend and went into a grocery store. Tony walked past the shop and waited, half hidden in a doorway about 100 yards away. After a few minutes, he saw Martin leave and head back towards his house with a bag in his hand. Tony followed. Watching Martin climb the steps and close the door to his house, Tony went back to his car and waited.

The following day he moved his car to a different position and again sat and waited. This time he had brought with him some food and a flask of tea. Preparing for a long wait, he didn't want to go hungry or risk missing either of the men if they left the house. He had also collected an empty milk bottle in case he got caught short. Not ideal, but at this moment in time he thought it necessary. The hours passed with no activity as such. The street jostled into life with a flurry of activity in the early morning with children going to school and then quiet until the time when again the street was bustling with children and mothers on their way home. No movement from Martin's house. To break the boredom, Tony had walked to the end of the street to see if there were any back entrances to the property. There was a small walkway along the back of the houses, but in most parts it was overgrown and had its fair share of rubbish dumped along it making it highly unlikely that Martin, or anyone in fact, would try and use the back entrance of their houses. Bins were placed at the front of each house in a small courtyard, which for many was the entrance to what was most likely a flat in the basement.

By the end of the week he had followed Martin once more to the shop and back. No sign of his mate. Tony called in to Sheila and requested a meeting with Geoffrey. 'Ring me back in an hour,' said Sheila.

Walking through the gates at Hyde Park corner, Tony made his way along the track alongside the Serpentine. It was 10am and the park was still relatively quiet, just a few gardeners tending the endless grass areas of the park, and as he walked, he saw a few ducks preening themselves in the early morning sunlight. Cold but pleasant, a typical November day. He spotted Geoffrey at one of the park benches and sat down next to him.

'Morning,' said Tony.

'What do you want?' replied Geoffrey.

'Why haven't you arrested Martin and his mate? I've been watching them all week and you haven't been anywhere near them. What are you waiting for?'

'They haven't done anything wrong, so we have no reason to arrest them,' said Geoffrey.

'He's a known IRA member in London with someone. What more do you need?'

Geoffrey turned and looked at Tony.

'Doesn't work like that. We suspect he's an IRA member but there is no arrest warrant out for him in Northern Ireland nor has he been officially linked to any particular crime and neither has the person who he is with, who by the way, we don't know.'

'But he's been eyeing up targets in Convent Garden,' said Tony.

'You mean he's walked from his house through London to Covent Garden sight-seeing and then back to his flat,' said Geoffrey.

'Have you seen him do anything unusual or take anything into his flat? Or the man he is with, have you seen him do anything or take anything that you would deem strange into his house apart from shopping?' continued Geoffrey.

'No,' replied Tony.

'Have you seen them drive anywhere?'

'No.'

'Do you know if they actually have a car?'

'No, but that doesn't mean they aren't planning something,' said Tony.

'That may be true but unless we have at least something to warrant an arrest or raid we can't just go around bringing people in on the notion that we think they may be planning something. We have hundreds of people on our watch list, as you have seen from some of the photographs. Everyone is a priority and everyone deserves a closer look, but we don't have the manpower nor can we ask the Met to allocate hundreds of police officers to watch potential suspects around the clock. The best we can do is follow up any leads we get and push our resources towards those. Whilst Martin is probably up to no good, we've heard absolutely nothing about him and you have not reported anything out of the ordinary, so we need to focus our efforts, your efforts, on looking for the people who we have been made aware of and may be up to something,' said Geoffrey.

'For fuck's sake,' said Tony. 'That's just all bollocks.'

'That's just life I'm afraid,' said Geoffrey.

'Look,' said Geoffrey, turning to look at Tony. 'You've watched them for more than a week. We have a photo of someone new, but at the moment nothing is happening with these two guys, so I want you to get back to your normal work and leave these alone unless or until I hear something. We know where they are and if anything transpires, I will let you know, but don't spend any more time on them. Carry on with your usual routine. As you know, we have other priorities. It's difficult, I know, but we've said before that patience, observation and information gathering is important, which is exactly what you are doing. Not everyone you spot will be an active suspect. A suspect they may be but not one who requires a massive amount of attention. It's just as important to us to know where they are even if they are not doing anything. I grant you that these two are probably not just sight-seeing, but I can't have you all day every day watching someone. Especially as you have had a week at seeing if these two are up to something, which on the face of it, they're not.'

'I hear you,' said Tony dejectedly.

'Good man, you're doing a good job. Swing by them every week or so, but that's it. We'll have another briefing session in the New Year. Keep the reports coming in and keep covering all the ground you can,' said Geoffrey.

Standing and patting Tony on the shoulder, Geoffrey

walked off and out of the park leaving Tony to watch the ducks.

Tony sighed, watching the ducks jump into the lake and head off to where an old lady had stopped by to feed the birds. There was quite a crowd gathering as the ducks, swans and a few gulls all fought for the scraps of bread. One enterprising gull had swept in and caught a piece of bread in mid-flight, much to the consternation of the waiting brood. Gathering himself together, Tony was disappointed that nothing had come from the information he had given to Geoffrey but, as he argued in his mind that unless there was actually something for them to go on there was very little that they could do, he settled on the thought that maybe Geoffrey was right. The police just can't arrest people for walking around London. More's the pity.

Chapter 20

Wormwood Scrubs prison has an imposing entrance. Built just before the turn of the century, it was like many others constructed at that time: strong, intimidating and basic. Whether you were on remand or serving a sentence, the place was overcrowded and a melting pot for impending violence. The inmates were locked up for most of the day and he had very little freedom to associate with the other inmates. The staff were under pressure all the time to keep a lock on the tension. Nevertheless, this was Declan's new home for the foreseeable future. A category B prison with five main wings, holding an assortment of prisoners, Declan was in A wing. There were several other convicted IRA members serving a variety of terms in the prison none of whom were serving less than ten years. one on remand like himself. There were also others, although at this time he wasn't allowed to associate with them, but he knew them and messages were easily passed between them. Once convicted it was highly likely that he would be on the same wing as the others. There was a slim chance he would be moved but this was the most secure prison in the country at this time. The prison was at full capacity and mostly it was two to a cell on remand, whereas in the main prison some cells were overcrowded with three to a cell. He had been there for just over a month. His solicitor had said that his trial would be anywhere up to a year away. Whilst the offences he was charged with were of a serious nature, his solicitor had told him that the more serious alleged offences of bomb making and intent to endanger lives would be highly contentious and in his opinion would be dropped before the trial started.

Thomas Godwin of Godwin, Clarke and Hillmont, barristers based in the Holmes Chambers in Central London just down from the Old Bailey, had been engaged by his solicitor, Owen Dawson. As the trial would be at the Old Bailey he needed proper and high level representation. They had been recommended to Owen on the nod from Declan's counterparts in Southern Ireland.

The door clanged open. 'Cassidy, your visitor is here,' said the guard. Stepping back, he let Declan walk past him, along the gantry, where he could hear the shouting of other inmates about nothing in particular, down the steep iron framed stairs and along the side of the wing to the main door, which once unlocked allowed him to pass through to another small extension with another locked door. Once locked inside this small area the outer door opened and he was led along a corridor to one of the interview rooms. As he was on remand, he was allowed several visits from his solicitor as and when required. Once convicted, however, it would be different; visitors would be a privilege that he would have to earn.

Owen was sat at the table as Declan came in. Sitting down opposite, Declan said, 'Well?'

'The charges relating to bomb making have been dropped,' said Owen. The other offences will stand at this time but the bomb making is all circumstantial and easily rebutted. There is no positive ID of you being there, all they have is fingerprints on the machine gun, the vehicle and one of the drums. The story from Godwin is that you were asked to deliver the drums from Ireland to the yard in Reading. When you got there you had a drink, explaining the prints in the Portacabin, and then helped Patrick move the drums into the warehouse. You had no idea what, if anything, was in the drums; it was a cash in hand job as far as you were concerned. All you knew was that they wanted the drums and the van, and you had to find your own way back home. With regard to the gun, it was on one of the benches under a blanket, and while you were in the warehouse, Patrick boasted to you that he had it, picked it up and gave it to you. You then put it back on the bench and left. Patrick gave you a lift into town but didn't see where you went. We will say that being unfamiliar with the area you caught a bus to London and not the train. While you were in the yard you didn't see anyone else there other than Patrick; you didn't see his brother Donny at any time. Patrick has confirmed that was what had happened, and he and his brother have denied that you were there on the day of the raid. Without an actual visual of you on site and no one coming forward to confirm they saw you then there is nowhere really for them to go with that. They didn't like the story, as you can imagine, but they want you convicted so an easy conviction using the hand gun is better than a long drawn out trial with the hope that they may secure a conviction, but Thomas is good and they know it,' continued Owen.

'Good,' said Declan, 'and the rest?'

'Well, they still have you on possession of a deadly weapon, carrying it in an open space, threat to public life etc. etc. but that carries a lesser sentence. They will push hard but we think you are looking at about eight years. By the time the trial comes around you will have at least eighteen months knocked off, having been served in remand. Patrick and his brother, on the other hand, are set to get up to twenty years.'

'What do we know about why they raided the yard, what have they come up with or have they admitted that there was an informer?'

'They deny all knowledge of an informer and are saying that it was reported by some local people who said they had seen some unusual activity at the yard. Which is clearly bullshit but it's hard to disprove. They say they sent a local bobby to investigate who reported back that he suspected he had seen Sean in the yard, hence the call to the Met, as they are not equipped in Reading for a terrorist raid nor have a unit investigating suspected IRA activity. They are lying through their teeth but, as it proved to be a correct assumption, the raid gave them the results they needed so I expect that part will be overlooked by the judge,' said Owen.

'How did they know I was in Bournemouth?'

'Apparently, one of their officers, Sturgess, was on holiday down there. He works for the Met and was on the initial raid in Reading so was familiar with your face. Unfortunately, and bad luck from your point of view, being in the right place at the wrong time, he saw you walking along the prom, followed you and called in his colleagues That part seems to hang together quite well as his wife has made a statement to confirm that they were in Bournemouth at the time and she rang his DCI on his request, and of course the rest you know.'

Pushing the cigarettes across the table, Declan picked up the packet and lit one, putting the rest of the packet in his pocket. 'Do you need anything else?' asked Owen.

'I've been thinking,' said Declan.

'I'm convinced that it's this Tony Blackreach who set us up. I nearly had the bastard in Bournemouth but I'm not prepared to wait for another eight years, or whatever it will be, until I get to see that little shit again, so I want him done. Do you hear me? I want him done and gone.'

'I can pass a few messages on but that's the limit as to what I can do for you,' said Owen.

'I'm not fucking stupid. I know that. I want you to get my sister Siobhan here. I'm allowed a visitor so pay for her to come over.'

'Ok,' said Owen, 'Anything else?'

'No.'

'Ok,' said Owen, collecting his briefcase and standing. 'I'll be back in a few weeks when I know about your arraignment. If you need me or anything in the meantime give me a ring,' said Owen.

Two weeks later, Declan was again escorted through the remand block into the visitor's room. The room was filled with an assortment of tables and chairs with around fifteen inmates talking with their loved ones: some with kids, some women crying, some who were just sat in silence.

Siobhan was waiting, and having been searched, made to leave her handbag in a cupboard and not allowed to take the cigarettes she had brought in for Declan, she was not in a good mood. As the younger sibling, after her mother had died she had run the house, had looked after their father when Declan was away in the Army and had the added pressure and ridicule from the neighbours when she fell pregnant by a local lad after a heavy drinking session one Saturday night. She wanted the child and had had Sian. Her father had passed away the following year and left Siobhan to bring the child up in an empty house. Her best friend looked after Sian each morning and took her to school while she went to clean in the local factory; not a lot of money but almost enough to get by on. All her money was spent of Sian. It was tough, but she never complained. Declan visited from time to time and gave her money; he adored his little niece. Life was hard for Siobhan, but she wasn't one to complain and did the best she could for her very small family. Declan spotted Siobhan in the middle of the room and made his way over. The moment he sat down she started on him.

'What the fuck do you think you've been doing you fucking bastard. I've had to come here to fucking see your sad fucking ass because you've fucked up with your stupid bastard mates. What am I supposed to do now? I can't afford to be looking after me fucking Sian and meself. I don't have any fucking money. 'Mother said, God rest her soul,' said Siobhan crossing herself, 'you would end up in fucking jail you fucking dickhead. What the fuck were you thinking? Where are your fucking mates now? Left you high and fucking dry I've no doubt. If you fucking think I'm fucking coming over here every other fucking month and bringing fucking Sian with me to visit you you've got another fucking thing coming Declan. I'm fucking pissed off with you. How long is this going on for and how long are you going to be fucking in here?' The tirade continued for another few minutes. Declan sat in silence and waited for her to stop.

After she caught her breath, she paused and in a much softer voice said, 'Are you alright, can I get you anything?'

'I'm fine,' said Declan. 'Thanks for coming.'

'I didn't have any fucking choice, did I?' said Siobhan, her voice rising again.

Declan raised his hand, 'That's enough, you've made your point,' he said sternly, looking round to make sure that no one was really listening to them now that she had calmed down. 'You will be looked after, so don't worry about money, and before you start again. . .' as Siobhan caught her breath to say something, 'you will take it and you will be looked out for, ok.'

'Now I need you to do something for me.' Declan talked her through who he wanted her to go and see. 'You know him, he will be in The Craic, he's always there. Ask him to get hold of Cole. Explain what's happened, although I expect he will already know, but Cole needs to "Pay my respects" to Tony Blackreach, right, Tony Blackreach.' Siobhan nodded.

Brother and sister continued to talk for another half an hour or so before the bell rang and Siobhan had to leave. Getting up and hugging his sister, Declan said, 'It'll be ok. I'll be away for a while but don't worry about anything.'

Watching Siobhan leave, he and the other inmates made their way back to their individual cells. Sitting on the bunk bed, Declan lit a cigarette, listened to the cell door bang shut, and pieced together in his mind a story of what Cole would do to Mr Tony Blackreach.

Siobhan stayed in London that night as Owen had booked her into a small hotel on the Cromwell Road. The following morning, she made her way back to Paddington and caught the train up to Liverpool. It was a long journey and she passed the time reading a few *Woman's Own* magazines, which she had picked up at one of the many newsstands. On arrival at Liverpool, she again stayed in a local hotel awaiting the ferry the next morning to take her back to Dublin, and then there was another long journey ahead, this time by bus, to her home town where she would meet her daughter Sian at the school gates and they would walk home together. It was a long trip and one that Siobhan wished that she wouldn't have to make too often but then, Declan was her brother and so she vowed to make the journey at least every other month. Occasionally, she thought, she might take Sian, maybe during the summer holidays. Declan wasn't sure if he would be transferred to one of the prisons in Northern Ireland, but he doubted it. She wouldn't make a special trip for the trial unless it came around at the time when she would normally go and see him.

As she had left the prison that night Owen had come by the hotel and given her a thousand pounds. Money, he assured her, that she would get every couple of months or so. It may be easier to give her the money when and if she came over, but if she ever ran short then to call him and he would arrange for some local money to be handed over.

The following weekend Siobhan caught the local bus to Talligary. On arrival, she stepped off and walked the short distance to The Craic. Pushing open the door, the room fell silent. Smoky and stinking of beer, the drinkers eyed her up with suspicion, but the moment Paddy saw her he waved, stood up and came across the bar to greet her and the pub regained its noisy ambiance.

'Darling, it's been a long time. How are you?' said Paddy, showing her to a seat. 'Let me get you a drink. What would you like? Gin?'

Siobhan nodded, 'Thank you.'

Paddy gestured to the bar and sat down next to Siobhan; the two men he was with moved away. Paddy leaned in, 'I've heard about Declan. I expect that's why you are here,' he said.

Paddy was a thick set man, pushing seventy, he had a reputation of settling people's problems. Working outside of the IRA, he wasn't bothered by them as they came to him from time to time to administer local punishment if appropriate. They preferred this because it lessoned tensions between them and the locals and was a way of farming out small fry problems. Paddy made his money from a variety of activities. He had never been in jail but had come close several times on liquor smuggling and once when he was close to being caught landing some arms from a small fishing vessel about 50 miles from Talligary.

Chapter 21

Easing himself back into the chair, glancing casually around him he took a sip of the hot Cappuccino. Nothing but trains and normal people. Wednesday midday, Paddington station was a hive of activity, briefcases in hand, commuters running for trains, backpackers staring at the departure boards, mothers with pushchairs, crying children, some bored some startled by the noise and the seemingly endless gaggle of people.

He liked the Reef Bar, as he looked around, good strong coffee, decent paninis, decent price, made a change from some of the overpriced outlets that purported to sell good fare. *That's a laugh,* he thought, *more like 'How little can I put in this sandwich and charge you the earth for it?'.*

Sitting on the mezzanine floor of the Reef Bar, he could observe the scene below whilst appearing to be one of the many transient people of the day. Drawing the occasional glance from people looking for a table, having thrown his coat over the opposite chair, all who looked assumed the table was taken and made no move to sit in the vacant chair by him. The Reef had about 16 tables seated for four on the mezzanine and he had chosen the one nearest the back, nearest the stairs.

It was highly unlikely that he would be recognised, having shaved off the beard he'd worn for five years. The last time he was in London was about six years ago and then only for a couple of months. *Mind you*, he thought, *that was a bit hectic to say the least.* Gathering his thoughts on the present, he pulled the small envelope towards him and looked at the two photographs. If anyone had walked passed and glanced at the photos all they would have seen was the picture of a young man. The picture appeared to be like the ones you would use in a passport or driving licence application, nothing unusual to see. If they had studied hard enough, which most people don't, they would have seen that the man in the picture was not the same as the man looking at it. And anyway, after a few minutes, like most people momentarily watching someone else, completely forgetting all about what they had seen, they moved on, lost in their own world.

Finishing off the coffee, grabbing his coat he turned and headed down the right hand side of the stairs, at the bottom, walking under the mezzanine, keeping close to the wall and exiting onto the main concourse. A quick glance upwards, taking in the camera locations, noting the obvious positions, he walked towards The Isabard pub. Like many stations across Europe, and for that matter cities and government office they had all increased their use of cameras, but like most others, Paddington had a finite budget for equipment and people so could only do so much, which left large parts of the station uncovered from the spying eye.

Walking on under the gantries to the end of platform eight, he moved into a walk with purpose, not rushing, just another commuter going home. Coming out from underneath the gantry, he made light work of the stairs and began crossing the bridge and down onto platform four, where a First Great Western train was waiting patiently for its passengers. He turned towards the front of the train, away from the main station, walked up to the last carriage and got onto the 4:30pm to Exeter St David's. Settling into a seat facing backwards, he could watch who came into the carriage whilst still enjoying the view of the Berkshire countryside and also knowing that he had boarded the train unseen by any cameras.

The train pulled into Reading at 12.03. Cole stepped off and made his way to the toilet; the least time spent on the platform the better. Having relieved himself and spending a few minutes dragging out the time washing and drying his hands, he made his way back up to platform two. The Birmingham train was due shortly. Picking a crowded section of the platform, he settled behind the commuters and waited. Boarding the train he took a seat in the first carriage and settled down for the 50-minute journey.

Breaking into his thought pattern, there was the announcement that the train would be shortly arriving at Kingham. Pulling himself out of his seat he made his way towards the door and, stepping off the train, walked through the gate to the bus stop. Kingham was an out of the way station purely for commuters who lived during the week in London and who dashed off to their Cotswold retreat at the weekend. The car park was littered with all manner of 4x4s. Over the years the locals of these beautiful villages had accepted the influx of townies. Sadly, many of the local children, once grown up, had been forced out, unable to gain a foothold on the housing ladder as the developers had seen an easy market of converting barns and outhouses into luxury accommodation, attracting the wealthy commuter.

Getting onto the bus, empty at this time of day, he settled in for the 45-minute ride to Cheltenham. As the bus trundled down the winding road to Stow and then onto the main trunk road to Cheltenham, his mind thought back to his contract in Bulgaria.

Tariq inhaled deeply, until his lungs were full, exhaling gradually, he watched the smoke drift up towards the ceiling aimlessly. Caressing the stark light bulb, it hit the ceiling and bounced across it like clouds slowly moving in the sky. Taking another deep intake he turned his head slightly and caught sight of the girl making coffee. Talking non-stop, he couldn't hear what she was saying, or was it he couldn't be bothered to listen, knowing full well that he was not expected to answer. She was dressed in his shirt. How old was she? Seventeen, 18, did it matter? Not really, they only came for his money and in this God forsaken country money talked. He knew he shouldn't smoke weed anymore but he liked the way the warmth ran through him, across his chest, into his arms and legs and slowly into his head, making him feel like he was living in slow motion, fully aware of his surroundings but unable to respond, a deep embalming, enveloping feeling, as intense and longer lasting than climaxing, warmer than lying on a beach, satisfying.

The smoke curled out of his mouth. He let his eyes close. *A few more minutes*, he thought.

She crossed the room and put the coffee beside the bed, leant forward and, with her right hand, touched his hair, intending to stroke him and make him feel as if she wanted to belong to him. The pain she felt in her wrist caught her by surprise, she'd not seen his left-hand fly from his side and hold her. With an overwhelming power she had not experienced before she was being pushed up and over onto the floor.

Tariq had acted out of reflex. As he looked down at her, gathering his thoughts as she screamed at him, he stopped short of pushing his right hand under her chin in what would have been her last act on this earth.

Realising she wasn't a threat he let go and she wriggled away across the wooden floor, holding her wrist and muttering obscenities at him. 'What's wrong with you, you prick?,' She scrabbled to her feet, the shirt riding up over her waist, pushing it down in a vain attempt to cover her modesty, she made for the bathroom, grabbing her clothes on the way. A parting shot of, 'I want my fucking money!' echoed through the slamming of the bathroom door.

Tariq looked around the sparse flat. Picking his trousers off the floor, he pulled his wallet out of his pocket and flicked through a sizable wad of notes. Picking a 100 Lev note, he threw it onto the bed. After the fall of communism, Bulgaria had experienced several episodes of drastic inflation and currency devaluation. When the average monthly wage was 200 American dollars, 100 Lev was about 50 dollars, so a good day's work for any girl, he thought.

Pulling his trousers on, picking up the coffee and the small cigarette butt he'd dropped, he took one last pull and crushed the remains into an ashtray on the table. Taking a mouthful of coffee, he looked out through the grubby apartment window taking in the huge residential complex of Poduyane. Living in the Suha Reka neighborhood, he could come and go without anyone casting a second look or passing comment. Some years earlier, at the time of their inclusion within the European Union, this area was quite smart with a lot of government money pouring in to rejuvenate the city. All that had changed of course, with the Mafia having a stranglehold on just about every part of national and local government, the construction industry, banking and finance, the money soon disappeared into consultancy pockets leaving expensive half-built projects. He'd been given the flat as payment for some job or other, he couldn't remember which one now, there had been so many. As he watched people scurrying around hunched over deep in their own thoughts, he heard the bathroom door unlatch and the girl walk to the bed, grab the money and slam out of the apartment. Glancing at his watch, he shrugged on his shirt, grabbed his coat and made his way down the stairs and became one of the many city walkers.

With a population of 1.2 million, Sofia, as one of the oldest capital cities in Europe, had witnessed many changes throughout its 1200-year history. Several name changes, several ruling dynasties and countless political upheavals had left its mark on what really is a beautiful city. Nestling at the foot of the impressive Vitosha mountain, it boasts imposing cultural and architectural sites, including the 10th century Boyana Church, Alexander Nevski Cathedral, which is one of the largest Orthodox churches, and the Church of St George, which is located within the courtyard of the large, central Sofia Hotel, which was where Tariq had made his way to. Pushing through the impressive foyer, he made his way to the fourth floor, knocked and waited.

He preferred to keep it tight. If they came to his hometown then they were serious, and more importantly, willing to pay: they wanted him not the other way around. In his hometown he could control the situation more easily; less chance of being exposed and taken out by old adversaries. Not that he was any less cautious, having posted his men at various locations feeding him info over that last four days.

Lists of businessmen entering and leaving the hotel, where they came from, how long they had been in the country, nationality and who they spoke to. It paid to be cautious and, whilst it cost him money, it always gave him the edge: never walking into a situation that didn't give him an exit.

Sitting in the square red sofa chair he faced the overweight, slightly balding Peter. Observing his demeanor, he saw no trace of fear or sweat of urgency, telling him that Peter was well versed with this meeting. Not overly confident but not characteristically nervous of who he was meeting, known only by reputation of course.

With just the two of them in the room, Tariq knew that his companion was in the next room, armed with the small but powerful SIG Saur. Clearly not intimidated by his surroundings, it was more a comfort knowing that showing no overt aggression would allow the meeting to take place cordially

Tariq looked at the sheaf of paper for the second time, absorbing the information. '$400,000 American dollars,' Peter penetrated his concentration, 'deposited now with a further one million on completion.'

'Yes.' Pausing and then looking at Peter, 'When?'

"July, possibly mid-August. We will confirm the dates by the end of March.'

'Ok,' Tariq rose to leave. Peter leaned over the arm of the chair and, grasping the coffee pot on the occasional table, poured himself another cup of coffee and watched Tariq leave the room.

On hearing the door shut, Peter pulled his mobile out of his pocket, hit the speed dial and waited for the connection to setup. 'It's on. I'm coming back, be with you Thursday.' Snapping the phone shut, he settled down to finish the coffee. *Not bad, bit strong*, he thought, peering into the cup. His eyes focussed on a red streak that was running down the edge of the cup to the coffee. Trying to concentrate, *why was that there?* he thought. He felt something fall off his nose and watched as a knob of red liquid dripped from his nose into the coffee. *This is not right*, his brain was still active for a millisecond before Peter fell forward, dead, hitting the floor and spilling the coffee over the sparse carpet that barely covered the hotel room floor.

The entry to the building was simple enough, he had watched the foyer for several hours over the last few weeks from the coffee shop across the road and knew when the concierge went for his breaks, when the shift changed and largely a fair proportion of the people who came and went from the apartment block.

Making his way quickly through the foyer to the lift, he stepped inside and went up to the sixth floor. Turning left out of the lift, the corridor was bare and lack lustre. It had seen better days, clean but still grubby through years of neglect. This was one of the buildings the city had chosen to forget.

Opening the door, he made his way in the dark to the expanse of windows facing the hotel. On any other day it was a fabulous view but today the view was obscured by his focus on time. The window had seen better days and opening it let in a blast of cool air. Cole took out the barrel, scope, magazine and stock, assembling the rifle quickly.

Clipping the magazine into place, he could hear, from the apartment next door, the beginnings of a song that he thought he knew. Lifting the rifle to his shoulder, securing the strap tightly around his left wrist and left arm, he raised the gun and slowly lowered the barrel through the small glass circular opening in the window

Adjusting the scope slightly, he picked out the hotel room and saw the two men sat in the comfy chairs. The range was close, an easy distance and with little or no wind. With another slight adjustment made, he brought the crosshairs to bear.

Flicking the cigarette butt out of the window and letting the smoke float one last time across his face, he looked through the scope. Cole fixed the cross hairs on the centre of the forehead, breathing slowly, and on the in breath he gently squeezed the trigger.

A single shot from 600 yards away at the top of a block of flats had easily flashed through the air, piercing the bedroom window and entering Peter's head at some 3000 miles an hour. It was not a particularly hard shot, not much wind, clear day and all the shooter had to do was compensate for the shattering window. A simple exercise for a moderate marksman, as Cole was. Upsetting the Mafia was a ticket to an early grave. Cole didn't care too much about his target, Peter, it was enough to know that for the likes of Peter, if you went up against the Mafia then you had to be pretty certain that they didn't know what you were planning. He was contracted for Peter, the other man in the room, Tariq, he was to let go.

Arriving at the bus station in Cheltenham, Cole walked the short way up towards the Queens Hotel, a grand imposing building overlooking Montpellier Gardens. He had stayed here once before some years ago when he was tasked to follow some people who worked in GCHQ. As he walked, he glanced around him. No threats were visible, not that he anticipated any, it would have been very bizarre if he had seen anything or if any threats had actually been made.

Arriving at the Queens' reception, 'Good afternoon, Sir. How can I help?' The receptionist smiled at him. 'I have a reservation in the name of Cardigan,' he replied. 'Do you have any messages for me?' The receptionist scanned the computer and printed out the register details. 'Can you fill these in for me please Mr Cardigan and yes I have a note, one moment please?' She said moving towards the end of the counter and opening a drawer.

Presenting Cole with the note and informing him that his room was on the second floor and the lifts were just through the glass doors on the left, Cole headed off towards his room, glancing at the note on his way. '6pm (Church) S.'

After checking into his room and having a quick coffee, Cole slipped out of the hotel and headed down towards the centre of town, walking quickly past the council buildings across the road, through the alley and into the church gardens. He made his way through past the church to a small road adjacent to the gardens. The second door on the right was nothing remarkable. Tapping lightly, he was let into the hall of what was once a grand entrance to a town house and ushered down into the basement. Stophies was stripping down a 45mm, oiling it and examining the firing mechanism. Oiled beautifully and restored, Stophies assembled the gun smoothly.

'Been a while. I have what you want,' he said. Reaching under the counter the gun rested on, Stophies pushed a switch and behind him a catch clicked, and a door revealed itself in the wall. Stophies opened it, went in and came back out with a duffel bag Carefully emptying the contents onto the counter, a SIG Sauer presented itself along with a short-nosed Glock.

'I've got you 60 rounds for each, standard issue, nothing out of the ordinary and all freely available.'

Cole quickly looked over the weapons, noticing the numbers filed away nicely and that the action moved sublimely on both. 'Thanks.' Stripping off his jacket, Cole fastened the holster across his back, loaded the Glock and slipped it into the pouch under his left arm. Not ideal but needs must. Pushing the SIG back into the bag, 'I'll just take the Glock,' said Cole.

Cole headed back to his hotel. Booked in for two days, he opened the bedroom door. The room had been made up as he had expected, so he pulled up a chair that overlooked the window and settled down with another coffee and waited.

Chapter 22

She didn't really know her grandmother or much about her other than she was a war baby. Her grandad had died during the Great War and she knew that her grandmother had suffered enormous hardship raising a daughter in the 1920s and '30s. It couldn't have been easy, never marrying again and living on the virtual poverty line. Her mother sent her out to work as soon as she could to bring in money to help them live; the age of the Charleston and ballroom dancing passed her by. As she sat there, contemplating the request, she thought too of her own mother, again another war baby: her dad and mum had married just before the outbreak of the Second World War. They had managed to get a small flat in Bethnal Green, and from what her mother had told her, small it might have been but they were happy for the two years they were together before he got called up.

He was one of the first to die in the desert when they battled the Italians in June 1940. Her mother never remarried, and they remained in Bethnal Green until she was old enough and moved to a flat of her own, in the late '60s, in Pimlico. She had been a bright child at school, one of the few who had passed her eleven-plus exam and went to grammar school. She benefitted from a headmistress, Ellen Sharp, who had been a member of the women's liberalisation movement during the late '40s and '50s. The group had made great strides in lobbying parliament to increase the rights of women: better education, fair working practices etc.

The war had seen thousands of women step into the places of men who had gone off to battle. In recognition of their dedication and commitment, the UK government, under pressure, had seen to changes that reflected women better in society as a whole. Ellen still participated as and when she could if there were rallies and marches. She saw herself mainly though as a woman who helped get the younger generation into better jobs and be taken more seriously in important roles, both in business and government. She had taken many young girls under her wing and helped them determine their paths, which led her latest young girl to secure a position within the Foreign Office during the 1960s.

Settling down in her position at the Foreign Office, she had never really thought she had time to marry. She had progressed in her career and soon came to the attention of Isaac Bedham, who also knew Ellen, and who noted her adeptness and analytical skills. Similar to the women he had recruited to Bletchley Park in the '30s and '40s, whilst the war was now over he felt that she could offer a great deal to the government and had her transferred over to the intelligence section, where she quickly became team leader and subsequently transferred to a new division being set up to monitor the IRA's activity in the UK.

Her father had grown up in Northern Ireland and had moved to London in the early 1930s to work for the British Army. He had met her mother one evening when they were both walking through Regent's Park, idly wandering and taking in the fresh air and the tranquillity the park offered. He had stopped to feed the ducks and her mum loved telling her the story of how she had laughed at him: it was the first time she had ever seen a man doing such a thing. The story always brought tears to her eyes. After his death and the war had ended, they began living a life in the rumble of London, and they watched the building restart and the capital come to life once more.

They had been to Ireland many times in the years following the war, mostly during the school holidays. They had stayed with her father's brother and she had become great friends with all his children, especially Peter who was more her age. Peter, along with his two brothers and two sisters, used to spend days out in the fields on the outskirts of a small town called Ballystally, which she always thought was a funny name. They used to make up simple, silly poems rhyming with Ballystally: fond memories of a childhood. The family had looked after her mother financially over the years ensuring that both she and her mother never went without, enabling them to live a reasonable life.

Peter had joined the RUC following in his father's footsteps and it was now, as she sat in her room, she contemplated what he had asked her.

The previous day, on the way home, she saw Peter approaching her. Startled and surprised, they hugged each other. 'Why didn't you ring?' she said. 'I wanted to surprise you,' he replied. 'Let's go for a drink. Do you know somewhere nice?'

'Of course I do,' she said. Holding his hand, they walked towards The Red Lion. She was delighted to see him and eager to find out about the family and why he had come to see her.

The Red Lion, typical of many London pubs during the '80s, had changed from having a simple bar and snug and had opened up its drinking area by knocking down some old walls, extending the bar, and it now offered a range of new lagers, beers and new world wines to cater for the demands of its lunchtime city trade. They went down into what was the cellar, now transformed into a semi-dark drinking den with high chairs and wooden tables adorned with candles and menus. The menus offered a list of the latest wines and beers with a few bar snacks to satisfy the myriad of drinkers. They ordered two beers and made their way to a small table at the back of the cellar, which was somewhat quieter.

'So, how are Lynn and Claire?' she asked.

'Doing well, they'd have loved to see you. It's been years since you've been over.'

'Tell me more about the baby.'

Peter got out a photograph. 'She's lovely.'

'Lar, I need your help,' said Peter. 'Lar' was the nickname they had given her when she first came over, as Peter's younger sister couldn't say her name properly. It came out 'Lar', so it had stuck ever since.

'Billy has gotten into trouble.'

'What's happened? I take it he's still doing dodgy deals?' said Lar.

Billy was slightly younger than Peter, hadn't done very well in school and was constantly in trouble with the teachers; he hadn't fared much better when he left. Peter's dad wanted him to join the RUC as Peter had done but he'd rebelled and decided that the police were fascists and he wanted nothing to do with them. He'd fallen in with a few older petty crooks whose main claim to fame was stealing a few cars and a bit of house burglary. They always got caught, fined, and on the odd occasion, went down for a spell. Billy had managed to avoid jail, but his father was convinced that he had been up to no good, but he couldn't prove it. A blessing in disguise really as it would have been extremely embarrassing for him if his son were arrested; although many of his colleagues were in the same situation, it never played well with the superiors.

'Billy has been caught smuggling fags and beer across the border,' said Peter.

'Well you knew one day he would get caught doing something stupid,' she replied.

'Yes, but this time it's not dad who caught him it's the other crowd.'

Startled, Lar looked at Peter. 'What do you mean? You don't mean. . .' she said, tailing off.

'Yes, I do.'

'For goodness sake, what has your dad said?'

'He doesn't know, they came to me.'

'You need to tell him and quick. Why are you here? You need to get back there, find him and sort it out. Why did they come to you?'

'I can't go back,' Peter paused. 'Listen, you're not going to like this, but they've threatened to kill him, me, dad, mum and the girls if I don't help them.'

'You're joking! They won't do that over a few fags. Can't you bargain with them, money or something, or just go to your dad, he will know what to do.'

'You don't understand,' Peter said harshly.

'They are going to kill him if I don't help them.'

'Help them, help them how? Do you have to look the other way one day? So just fucking do it. You can't let Billy get hurt over nothing, Peter. Just look the other way or something.'

'It's not that, they want information,' Pausing, Peter looked her in the eyes and said, 'From you.'

Taken aback, she stared hard at him. 'Me. . . me. I don't know anything, Peter.'

'They know where you work and say that if you don't help them then we are finished. You've got to help me,' said Peter, grasping her hand in desperation. 'Please, please, I'm so sorry I can't believe this is happening.'

'But I don't know anything. Yes, I work, as you know, in so called 'intelligence', but I'm a typist, I type stuff up, its meaningless to me, I pass it on. I don't have access to any secrets, Peter. I'm not that high up, honestly I'm not.'

Tears were starting to form on the edges of her eyes. Her lips began to tremble.

'Peter, I can't help,' squeezing his hand tightly.

'They want a picture of a man, that's all.'

'What do you mean a picture? I type, I don't see pictures or take pictures, where I work is all reports. They must have made a mistake, Peter, tell them. They've made a mistake. I, we just do typing, that's all,' she said, pleading with him. 'And how do they know where I work?'

'Billy told them, I think, to get himself out of trouble,' Peter said resignedly.

'Oh God Peter, you have to tell them I don't see pictures of people, it's only words and always has been.'

'They say you have access to files. It's a bloke called Tony Blackreach they want a picture of, that's all.'

'Jesus, this is getting worse, people's work files are all locked away, and anyway I don't have access to them. If you don't tell your dad, I'm going to have to tell my boss, Peter. There's no way I can get someone's file to you, let alone get it out of the building.'

'They just want a copy of his picture.'

'But they are all locked away, you must go back and tell your dad.' Desperation now coming through in her voice, pleading with him.

'I can't go back. I have two days, or they will kill him, and I know you know,' he said quietly, 'that they don't make idle threats.'

Sitting back and looking into space, she thought hard: *that's the end of my career, if I get caught, I'll go to jail. If*

I don't, well that doesn't bear thinking about, the thoughts flooded through her mind, tears rolled down her face. Peter hugged her, 'I'm sorry Lar, I'm so sorry.'

Chapter 23

Tony opened his eyes just as the alarm went off next to his bed. Reaching over, he flicked the off switch and swung his legs out of bed. Grabbing a towel, he walked out of the bedroom and into the bathroom. Turning the shower on, Tony looked into the mirror. *Nothing new there then*, he thought. Showering under the hot water, Tony picked up the razor and performed the daily functions of shower and shave. Dressing in a blue suit he had laid out the previous evening in the spare bedroom, so as not to wake his wife, Tony headed down the stairs and boiled the kettle for a quick cup of tea. The routine was always the same. Making two cups, he took one up for his wife and kissed her on the cheek. 'See you later,' he said. Murmuring, she turned over and pulled the quilt up around her neck; another few hours yet before she had to rise.

Still dark as he left the house, he got into his car and drove the three miles to the railway station. A season ticket enabled him to park and walk straight into the station and onto the platform: no need to queue for a ticket. As always, the train was standing ready to go. It started here in Cheltenham, the 6am to London. Looking around, Tony took in the ten or so other people scattered up and down the platform getting ready to embark and sit in their usual seats. Tony headed into the shop, picked up *The Times* newspaper and went towards the front of the train. Standing patiently, he waited for the doors to be unlocked. At five to six the guard whistled, and the doors were opened. Glancing along the length of the train, he headed towards the second carriage at the front.

The fourth table on the left, window seat. Taking off his suit jacket, folding it neatly, he put it on top of his briefcase, which he had already put onto the overhead rack, next to a supporting bracket. He knew that as the train progressed along its route more bags would be uploaded but his would not get moved or his jacket scrunched up as it fitted nicely against this midway holding bracket on the rack. Putting his paper on the table, he steadied himself as he felt the train pull out. Looking at his watch, 6am, on time. He sat down with his back towards the front of the train. After the short journey to Gloucester railway station the train came out the way it came in, meaning that Tony was facing forwards and was at the rear of the train.

His seat was calculated, halfway in the last coach. If the train became overcrowded, which it did on a regular basis now, he could exit the train at either end of the coach. In addition, he had looked at most of the train crashes that had occurred in the last decade or so and saw that statistically you were less likely to be injured if you were at the back of the train. A while ago, he used to walk the length of the train as it approached Paddington and got off at the front of the train, which then allowed him to access the tube network quicker. However, overcrowding meant that walking the length of the train after its last stop before Paddington, at Reading, was now almost impossible. Having studied the layout of Paddington at this junction, he concluded that by getting out of the train at the back, he was able to climb the stairs at the rear of Paddington Station, walk along the overhead gantry and get down to the tube that way. Time was everything in rush hour. Knowing where trains stopped, which doors were adjacent to which entrance and exit routes, what stairs to take, all allowed the savvy commuter to extract themselves from the transport mechanism, most of the time, in an efficient manner. Thereby getting to work on time.

Two minutes into his journey out of Cheltenham, he stood up and started to make his way through the four other carriages to the dining car. Waiting this short period of time enabled all the other passengers to get seated so his walk to the dining car was uninterrupted. It also allowed the staff in the car to open the shutters and make the counter ready for service. His coach, G, was empty, and as he made his way through F there was only one other person sat there, again facing the rear of the train. The doors sliding open onto coach E, no one, D, a couple, and then as he approached the half carriage of C, several more. C was split between the passengers and the takeaway counter. A few years ago you could get breakfast, served in First Class, on this train, but GWR had decided that they could make more money by cutting staff, the service and getting more seats on the train and halving the size of the kitchen area.

'Morning, Derek,' said Tony as he approached the counter.

'Morning, Tony, usual?'

'Yes please.'

He knew Derek as his brother was dating Tony's sister and they had bumped into each other a few months ago in the pub, which was when he found out that he worked on the railway. He'd not been with them long, had undergone several training courses and was destined to walk up the management path. GWR operated a very good system for employees to progress and Derek was going to, if he could take advantage of it. A keen railway enthusiast, he had a tendency to be a bit tiresome from time to time, as having a lecture on this or that train, which was coming through this or that station, and waiting on bridges to take photos etc. was not Tony's cup of tea, so although he liked the bloke, if he ever saw him in the pub he'd do a quick swerve.

Tea and a bacon roll were the order of the day. Paying and moving to the end of the counter, Tony put milk and sugar into his tea and stirred. Opening up the bacon roll, he squeezed the brown sauce onto the hot bacon. Wrapping the roll and picking up the tea, nodding to Derek, he started to make his way back down the carriages. C was now filling up and he had to wait as some of the newly embarked passengers at Gloucester sorted themselves out and settled in for the journey.

Cole woke before the alarm went off; looking at his watch, it was 4.45am. Getting out of bed, he entered the bathroom and switched on the shower. Walking back into the bedroom, he flicked the kettle on and picked up a sachet of coffee. Emptying the contents into the cup, he headed back into the shower. No razor, not that he was really bothered. He showered and towelled himself dry. Putting on the same clothes he had worn the previous day, he pulled the Glock from its holster and checked the weapon, sliding out the magazine and tapping the end, pushing it back and making sure the safety was on. He had ordered a cab for 5:15am. The receptionist had said that he could order a later one if he wanted, as the journey would only take a few minutes. Thanking her, Cole had said he wanted to be early as he had not been there before and wanted to make sure he wasn't late.

Walking down the ornate stairs of the Queens Hotel, it was very quiet. No guests were up and about yet and the only person he saw was the night porter, who was unlocking the front doors.

'Morning, Sir,' he said. 'Nippy out there today. Is that your taxi?'

'Morning,' said Cole. 'Yes, it is.'

'Have a good day, Sir. Thank you for staying and look forward to seeing you again.'

Cole opened the taxi door, got in and the driver nodded, 'Station is it?'

'Yes.'

During the few minutes it took to drive to the station, Cole quickly ran through in his mind the plans he had made the night before.

The options open to him would be dependent on several

things. He would kill him somewhere between Kemble and Swindon. He had studied the route and knew that the train got into Swindon at 6:45am. The train to Bristol arrived at 6:55am, which gave him ten minutes to exit his train and cross over to the other platform and catch the Bristol train. There were no stops between Swindon and Bristol. If Tony's body was discovered in the coach it would be some time before the police arrived, and even if he was seen on the CCTV system, by the time they had figured that out he would be in Bristol and long gone.

This was dependent on how many other people were in the carriage he and Tony were in. He suspected that the train would be more or less empty until it got to Swindon. If there were people and he couldn't shoot him then he would wait until they got to London and either follow him in the crowd and at a choke point do it there and make his escape. The other option was to wait until he got to the tube network. The chaos it would cause on a busy commuter platform would enable him to walk away easily. He had done something similar when he was in New York a few years ago and that went well.

He wasn't bothered about the noise of a gunshot. Whilst most people would look up if they heard a noise, recognising what it was would be difficult as most people have never heard one, apart from on the TV and in movies; in real life it was completely different.

The taxi entered the station car park. Paying the driver, Cole went into the station and looked for a ticket machine: he needed two tickets. Not figuring out how it worked, he went into the main ticket office and asked for the two tickets: one to Swindon and one to Bristol.

'You can go to Bristol from here directly or from Gloucester,' the ticket officer said. 'You don't have to go to Swindon to change.'

'I'm doing business in Swindon first,' said Cole.

Paying for the tickets, Cole made his way to the walkway overlooking the railway platforms. Picking up one of the free newspapers, he leant on the edge and waited, glancing occasionally to see if Tony had arrived yet and where he was.

He didn't have to wait long. He saw Tony enter the station and step down the stairs to the platform and walk along the side of the waiting train. He watched him go into the shop, come out with a paper under his arm and walk towards the end of the platform where the first carriage awaited.

Cole folded his paper and slowly walked down the stairs onto the platform towards Tony. Stopping at the carriage before, not looking at Tony, he waited patiently. The whistle blew, the doors opened, and he paused momentarily. Out of the corner of his eye he saw Tony enter the train two carriages down. Stepping onto the train, he turned left, the sliding doors welcoming him into the warm coach. As he slowly walked down the carriage, he saw Tony in the next one taking off his jacket and putting his paper on the seat. Tony slid into his seat. Cole put the paper he was carrying on the table and took a seat by the aisle.

No one had entered Tony's coach nor his and as he looked, the next coach was also empty, much as he had thought. Early morning, not many commuters to London from here at this time. Local people would be getting later trains to take them to their daily grind.

A few minutes later, Cole stiffened as he heard the swish of the sliding doors behind him. With his right hand he moved his hand under his jacket and wrapped his fingers around the Glock's handle. He waited, knowing full well that the only person approaching him would be Tony. Getting ready to draw the weapon and pounce, he inhaled slightly. Without looking around, he felt Tony pass his shoulder, and a fraction later he watched Tony continue his journey up the coach and into the next one. Relaxing his grip, he angled his head into the aisle slightly and watched as Tony kept going through the other doors. Cole guessed what he was doing.

With his tea in one hand and the bacon roll in the other, Tony felt it more than he saw it. As he walked through the sliding doors into the vestibule area, stepping across the join of the carriages onto the next carriage, he flung his left arm up and made contact with Cole's outstretched arm. With the tea flying out of the cup and onto Cole, his left arm carried on upwards and pushed Cole's right arm and gun hand towards the ceiling.

'Fuck!' cursed Cole as the hot tea caught the side of his face and went into his left eye. Not waiting, he rushed forward and tried to bring his right arm down. Tony snatched it and with as much force as he could muster slammed himself into Cole. Left hand struggling to keep a grip on Cole's right hand, they bounced into the train door. He grabbed at Cole's throat but his hand was brushed aside as Cole, quick to react to a frontal attack, punched Tony in the side of his face as he felt the weight of Tony on him as they both crashed into the door. Tony, with his grip around Cole's gun hand, banging his arm as hard as he could, the gun flew out of Cole's grip and across the floor. Ignoring the pain in his head and the stars that began to float in front of his eyes, he brought his knee up quickly and with a sharp stab aimed at Cole's groin.

Cole was quick and countered with his left leg up and blocked the knee kick, swung his head forward and went to headbutt Tony. Tony's head was slightly bowed and Cole's forehead smashed into the top of Tony's head, bursting Cole's nose; blood began to stream out, across his face. Hanging onto Cole's right arm, Tony brought his right hand around and slashed across his face, going for the eyes, with no time to think of who this was or why this was happening. Tony took a punch to the kidneys, which made him gasp for air. Slightly taller than Cole and weighing a few extra pounds, this little weight advantage kept Cole against the door. Cole jammed his foot on top of Tony's and twisted his left arm, releasing it from the grip, and with his right hand now free he punched Tony in the side and brought up an upper cut to his chin. The punch to the side swayed Tony slightly and the upper jab from Cole glanced his jaw. Tony renewed his effort in kneeing Cole in the groin; this time contact was made but Cole was made of fighting material, and whilst the pain made him wince, he threw another couple of sharp punches in Tony's direction.

Reeling now, the onslaught made Tony step back, which enabled Cole to get off the door and face Tony in a steadier stance. Not wanting to go down, Tony swung a kick at Cole's left leg blocking the kick easily, Cole swiftly chopped at Tony's neck. Tony blocked this with his left hand and repeated the kick to Cole's leg. Not expecting another kick, Cole took the blow, which would have broken his leg if done properly. Cole now knew that Tony was no walk over; his blows and kicks told him that he had been taught a few basic moves. Snorting at this assessment, Cole launched himself forward, going for a stranglehold, and almost succeeding. Seeing Cole dive forward, Tony blocked the assault with his right arm, and with his left hand, he made serious contact with Cole's face. Both men clashed in the centre of the vestibule, Tony striving to survive and summoning up the remnants of any self-defence moves he knew and Cole determined to end this as fast as he could. Cole hit Tony full pelt and knocked him into the opposite train door, following up with a kick to the stomach and a thunderous blow to the side of Tony's head. Tony reeled and slid slightly off balance. Cole moved forward and with a vicious punch went for the centre of Tony's face. As he saw the blow coming, he angled another kick at Cole. His foot connected, which put Cole a step back. Rising as fast as he could, Tony threw himself forward, catching Cole under the chin with a punch. The weight of Tony and the attack snapped Cole's head back; he hit his head on the doorframe, momentarily stunning him. Tony continued his forward movement, grabbing Cole's lapels and flinging him sideways and tripping him as he came past him, forcing him onto the toilet door, which flew open. This then tripped up Cole and, with the weight of Tony on top of him, Cole slipped and the pair smashed into the tiny toilet. As Cole fell backwards his neck landed on the side of basin. Even with his own weight, the speed of his fall, and Tony on top of him, the basin ledge held firm, but Cole's neck couldn't cope with the pressure and Tony heard a resounding snap. They both crashed to the floor, Cole lifeless and Tony breathing heavily, exhausted.

Fucking hell! struggled Tony as he lay on top of Cole, sucking in air as fast as could. *What the fuck was that all about?* as he looked down at Cole. Swallowing hard, still on top of Cole, he got to his feet and looked down at the lifeless body.

Stepping back and out of the toilet, breathing heavily, Tony looked around for help. As he looked, both carriages were still empty.

Tony caught sight of the gun: it was resting against the vestibule wall. Bending down, he went to pick it up but stopped himself at the last moment. Standing back up he looked again at the gun and at Cole.

What the fuck was that all about? What am I going do? Who is this? Why me? I need to tell the police. He tried to kill me. What have I done? The thoughts raced across his mind, each one requiring an answer, each one generating five others. Panic was beginning to set in and the shaking of his hands brought Tony back out of his closed mind, and as he looked, this time he saw what was in front of him. *How long have I been standing here?* he thought. *I've got to do something!*

'Shit! Shit!' he said out loud. Looking again at the gun and Cole, a way forward began to present itself.

I can't tell the police, he thought. *They will say I killed him, and I'll go to jail. It'll take ages to sort out. What's his face said I was on my own and he wouldn't help me out.* Tony struggled with remembering Geoffrey's name but closed the thought and moved on. *Maybe it was a mistake and he*, looking at the lifeless body, *has got the wrong man.*

Stepping forwards and into the toilet, Tony leaned forward and went through Cole's pockets: nothing. Reaching into the pocket of Cole's jacket, Tony pulled out a wallet. Two tickets, one to Swindon and one to Bristol, and a piece of paper, which Tony unfolded, and he saw a photocopy of his face staring back at him. Tony looked hard at the picture not believing what he was seeing. As he looked closer, he remembered when it was taken. Startled, his eyes widening slightly as he recognised it, it had been one that Geoffrey's staff had taken when he went to the London office that time.

Fuck me, he's trying to have me killed. Fucking bastard! thought Tony. Putting the wallet in his pocket, Tony pulled out his handkerchief, picked up the gun and put it in the toilet. Straddling Cole, he put his arms under him and dead weighted him further into the toilet, allowing the door to be shut.

Walking quickly back to his seat, he picked up his jacket and briefcase and he walked through the four carriages towards the buffet car where he waited with the other passengers to disembark at Swindon.

As calmly as he could, leaving the train and with a steady walk, he made his way along the platform and into the toilets. Bursting into the first cubicle, Tony threw up into the waiting basin, retching several times; after a minute or two he stopped himself. Nothing was coming up anyway. Tony opened the door and went over to the wash basin, looking at the man who had starred at him as he came out of the toilet.

'Too much last night,' Tony said.

Nodding knowingly, the man left the bathroom. Tony splashed water on his face and he quickly left. Deciding to use the ticket he had found on Cole, he walked over to the opposite platform and boarded the train to Bristol.

Having to stand all the way to Bristol, Tony had little time to put together a cohesive argument in his mind as to why the events of the last hour had come together. Leaving the train at Temple Meads, he walked through to one of the two main cafés open at that time of the morning, paid for a tea and took a seat near the window overlooking the main concourse.

Why would Geoffrey want him dead? was his first avenue of thought. Unless Geoffrey was corrupt then he couldn't think of a good enough reason. He hadn't done anything in the last year that warranted that sort of outcome, nor had he seen or reported anything that was that drastic. Also, he didn't believe that Geoffrey would do that or even if the UK government did that sort of thing, and to him, a nobody. *How, though. . .* thought Tony, *had he got the picture of him that was taken at the induction he had gone to? Maybe Geoffrey was corrupt, but why would he want him dead?* The thoughts swirled around Tony's mind as he sat and looked at his tea. Picking up the cup, Tony took a sip: cold. Had he been there that long?

He couldn't believe that Geoffrey wanted him dead. Apart from the mystery of the photographs, he concluded that it was highly unlikely that it was from Geoffrey, so if not Geoffrey then who?

Tony sat and pondered, thinking about the events of that morning. *Who was that guy?*

Finally deciding that although he believed in his heart it wasn't down to Geoffrey, he wouldn't tell him and if it ever came up, he would just deny it. Why would they think it was him anyway?

Catching the reflection of his face in the window, Tony saw the bruise beginning to develop near his eye and then began to feel the pain on the top of his head and in his sides. Looking at his left hand, he could feel the pain from his elbow to his wrist, just as he had been told it would on the day he went to Aldershot.

Tony drove up to the base gates, parked his car and walked up to the guard house. Signing in, he was told to wait. He'd been told that it was a couple of days, so he had booked the next few days off as holiday, having told his wife that he was on another training course. Not knowing what to expect, if he was going to be battered about, best to have a few days off as well on top just to recover. He looked around the tired, basic entrance room and at the soldier behind the desk. *Not for me*, Tony thought, *couldn't do this every day of my life.* He'd noted at the entrance booth that the soldiers had guns, but he doubted that they had ever been used. A few minutes later a corporal came through the door, introduced himself as Benny, looked at his pass, told him to leave the car where it was, he could move it later, and to follow him. Chatting amiably on the way through the barracks, Tony learnt that Benny had been in the Para's for about three years. After his basic training, which was shit, he was now enjoying it and told Tony that he thought he should join up.

'Jumping out of a plane is fucking brilliant!' Benny informed Tony.

'I love it, do it every day if I could. Off to Germany next month. You ever been there?' asked Benny.

'No, and you wouldn't catch me jumping out of a perfectly good aeroplane either,' said Tony.

Benny laughed, 'Not for everyone,' he said.

The walk took them through the barracks, past the parade ground where several men were practising marching and being bellowed at by a sergeant who, with a flurry and considerable dexterity, marched, swinging an upside down V-shaped stick smartly next to each of his steps as he showed the men how they should march correctly.

'What's with the stick?' said Tony.

'It's a measure, shows the length of each stride the squaddie makes, that way everyone marches the same. Takes a bit of getting used to especially if you are a bit smaller than the others, but once you get the hang of it, it works like clockwork. Takes time though, I seemed to be marching for six fucking months before we got it right,' replied Benny.

Leaving the side of the parade ground, they walked along the side of various buildings; the last one, Tony could smell bacon. As he passed by, he saw the entrance to the canteen and wondered if he would get breakfast first. *Unlikely*, he thought, *but you never know.* Leaving the buildings behind, they headed up a track and onto what appeared to be a vast field with several outbuildings in it. As they stepped towards one of the buildings, Tony recognised, from his time at Greenham Common, that they were walking onto an airfield towards one of the many workshops/hangers.

'Here we are,' opening a door and showing Tony through.

The door led into an empty hanger, one that had seen better days, Built just before the war, it had housed bombers. After the war it had become a machine shop until the REME had moved out and gone to Tewkesbury; it then had been seen as an ideal place for physical sport. There were two boxing rings, an assortment of wooden paraphernalia, which people jump climbed or fell over, a climbing frame and several large indoor mats.

Several people were in the hangar, some were just training on the bags strung up, a few were running around the indoor track, which had been painted on the floor. On the other side, six people were lined up next to one of the mats. Benny took Tony over to the group and called his name out to the main instructor, who Tony thought looked like a cross between a gorilla and a yeti.

'This is Tony, boss,' said Benny. 'See you later mate,' and with that Benny walked off and out of the hanger.

Tony looked around, the other six were more or less the same age as him. They all looked as if they were in some part of the military, it was the haircut that gave them away.

'Get in line!' said the boss.

'I'm Sergeant Brooker and I'm your instructor for the

next couple of days. Appreciate you are not in our lot,' he said, looking down the line with disgust. 'Don't expect any favours, you look fit enough to me so we should have some fun. We will try not to break any bones, but no promises. Do as you are told, listen, learn and put effort in. Not interested in your names. 'You. . .' the sergeant said, pointing at Tony, 'are No. 1,' moving to the next man in line, '2' '3' and so on, along the line to No. 7.

Tony and the others just nodded.

'Sorry,' barked the sergeant in a loud voice. 'I didn't hear you, it's yes Sergeant,' he bellowed. 'Let's try that again.'

'Yes, Sergeant!' the seven men shouted at the tops of their voices.

'Right you lot, four times around the track to loosen you up. Off you go,' commanded Sergeant Brooker.

Chapter 24

Tony called in sick. Placing the phone back on its receiver, he made his way across Lewins Mead into the main shopping centre and went into the Waitrose café. Buying a cup of tea and a doughnut, he sat at one of the booths overlooking the street. Calmer now and not dwelling on the man that he had killed, he began again to go over the main question, which was 'Why?'

After a while he concluded that 'Why?' was probably never going to be answered. He knew nothing about the man other than that he had his picture, so then he tried to make sense of how he got his picture. Logically, the only way was some member of Geoffrey's staff had given it to him. Assuming and wanting to believe that Geoffrey was not behind it, it then was going to be someone in his office. *Who though?* thought Tony.

Catching the train to London, Tony made his way to Gresham Street where Geoffrey was now based. On the corner of Coleman Street, one of the streets off Gresham Street, there was a small café overlooking the entrance to the building where Geoffrey and his team were based. Tony entered and ordered tea and a sandwich. It was close to the end of the day and the streets were beginning to get busy. Finishing up his tea, he saw the café closed at 5:30pm so Tony walked outside and waited, smoking a cigarette, trying to look casual.

After about 15 minutes, he spotted Sheila leaving the main entrance; discarding his cigarette he followed. They walked up past St Pauls Cathedral and along Fleet Street. The streets now were very busy as the office workers were all keen to pack up and get home. A typical busy Friday night, some were rushing and jumping onto the buses, others were swarming towards the entrance to the tube stations, all hell bent on beating the next person next to them to get home quicker. Sheila continued her walk down The Strand, over the road and into Covent Garden where she stepped down the flight of stairs into the pub, which was in the basement of the central arcade at Covent Garden market. Tony watched her make her way past the bar and saw a man stand up from one of the tables and greet her with a kiss, one of those kisses that meant they had known each other for a long time. Settling in beside her man, Sheila picked up the wine he had got for her and they began chatting away to each other.

Loitering near the bar, he ordered a Coke. Watching her, Tony sighed and shrugged his shoulders. *This is pointless*, he thought. *What am I going to find out? She's hardly going to be giving pieces of paper to the bloke next to her*, and even if she did, Tony had no idea as to what they would be anyway. He couldn't accuse her of anything and, at best, it would make him look like an idiot. Leaving the bar, Tony got back onto the street and made his way back to Gresham Street. *I have to tell him,* he thought. *I can't just act as if nothing has happened. He would hear about it sooner or later anyway, and he would just ask me.* The thoughts still swirling around in his head, Tony found himself once again on the corner next to the café. Unsure if he had missed Geoffrey, he decided to wait a couple of hours to see if he left. If not, then he would get back here early in the morning and wait for him to arrive.

Lighting up another cigarette, Tony waited. Darkness began to fall and as Tony looked up at the office block there were still several lights burning. Looking at his watch, it was just after 8pm. 'One more fag and then I'll go.' he muttered to himself.

Geoffrey, sat upright in his chair, glanced at the old clock on the wall and gathered up the papers he had been reading through. Placing them neatly into the three plain folders he stood up and walked over to his filing cabinet. Dialling in the code on the front of the cabinet, the lock popped open and he carefully placed them into the respected drawers and inserts. Sliding the drawers shut, he spun the dial and checked they were secure. Looking around the room to check he had not left anything open, he confirmed that each one of his desk drawers was tightly shut and locked, and he then picked his coat up off the back of the chair and put it on. Closing his door, the mortice lock sealed his office. Sheila had gone home a couple of hours ago as had the other members of the admin staff. Checking the main office door was also locked, he ignored the lift and made his way down the staircase to the lobby.

Priding himself on his fitness, Geoffrey rarely used the lift, preferring to keep a modicum of routine exercise by using the stairs, both up and down, every chance he got.

Signing out, nodding to the security guard, he pushed his way through the swing doors and onto Gresham Street. Pausing at the top of the steps of the office block, he buttoned up his coat and headed off towards St Pauls. He would stay at the club tonight as he did four nights a week. Journeying out to Godalming every day was quite time consuming and prone to delays. There were rumours that the government were planning on privatisation. *Got to be an improvement*, Geoffrey had thought.

'What do you want, Tony?' said Geoffrey, not looking at him as Tony closed onto Geoffrey's left side as they walked up the road.

Catching Tony by surprise, 'How did you know it was me?'

'I saw you when I left the office. What do you want?

'I've got a problem, well actually we've both got a problem. I need to talk to you urgently.'

'Go on.'

'Not here, can we go somewhere private?'

Geoffrey came to an abrupt stop, turned and looked at Tony, 'What do you want?'

Tony breathed in deeply.

'I've just killed someone.'

Geoffrey gasped, 'You fucking what?' losing his composure for a moment.

'There was a fight and the guy died.'

'Don't say anymore, come with me,' Geoffrey grabbed Tony's elbow and man-handled him across the road. Neither of them spoke as Geoffrey walked into Warwick Square and entered one of the majestic houses bordering the lovely garden square. The imposing houses, built in the late 1800s, were classic, sumptuous London residences. Situated over five floors, plus a substantial basement, they now enjoyed listed building status. The one Geoffrey walked into had been adjoined by the one next door and offered the London businessman private and discreet accommodation on an invitation only basis.

Providing a number of rooms for overnight stays, a private dining room and bar plus two beautifully adorned rooms with polished mahogany tables and an eclectic mix of leather chairs, a Victorian spoon-back, Oxblood bobbin and two beautiful English Bergere armchairs, amongst others.

'Evening, Sir,' said the doorman.

Geoffrey signed them both in and made his way through the large floor to ceiling doors into an oak panelled room which, as Tony looked around, seated about 20 people, men of roughly the same age as Geoffrey; some, read the daily newspapers, others just sat drinking brandy or whiskey, whilst a few were seated close together in armchairs in quiet conversation.

Geoffrey went over to the corner over the room and made himself comfortable in an early 1930s Art Deco Kilim chair, indicating to Tony to do the same. Tony looked around the room noticing only that they were several feet away from the nearest man, who was engaged in pipe smoking and a reading a very large newspaper. As they sat down, a man approached and enquired if they would like a drink. Geoffrey ordered two whiskeys.

'What happened?' said Geoffrey to Tony once the drinks had arrived.

Tony began his explanation, knowing full well not to leave out any details. He hoped that his belief in Geoffrey was right and the attack wasn't down to him, it was a difficult story to tell as much of the fight was a blur and it was only when they had crashed through the door of the toilet that Tony was able to recount a better description of the man.

'And there's this,' he said, pulling out of his pocket the piece of paper he had taken from the man's wallet.

Geoffrey opened it and looked, 'It's my picture,' said Tony, 'a copy of the one you took when I came to your offices at the beginning.'

'You are absolutely sure you don't know him or recognise him from any of your surveillance activities.'

'No, never seen him before in my life.'

Geoffrey stared at the picture.

'I wasn't going to tell you,' said Tony, looking down. 'I thought that you were behind it and were trying to get me killed. I know, I know,' he said, 'that sounds stupid, but I didn't know what to think.'

'You can rest assured it wasn't me,' said Geoffrey. 'We don't do that sort of thing and if we did. . .' looking up at Tony, 'you'd be dead.'

'Fucking charming. I came here straight away. I didn't want to ring because. . .' his voice trailed off.

Geoffrey picked up his drink and had a sip. He pushed himself back into the chair and just looked at Tony, thinking.

'Now tell me again exactly what happened.'

'I've just told you.'

'Tell me again,' said Geoffrey, curtly.

Tony relayed the story, recalling as best he could every detail of that morning. After he had finished, Geoffrey said.

'Do you take that train every time you come to work?'

'Yes, I do.'

'Have you ever noticed anyone unusual before?'

'No, not really. It's usually very quiet and there is occasionally the odd one who is new, but normally it's the same blokes, about a dozen of us every day.'

'I take it you, as with the others, have your favourite seat and coaches and do the same thing every day.'

'Pretty much, I like to sit at the front on the way out of Chelt and then when it turns around at Gloucester, I'm at the back, I prefer that.'

'Where were you going today?'

'Straight to work, got a couple of meetings, but that's all. I was then staying in London tonight going over to Ealing to visit a few of the pubs as normal to check in to see what's happening, same as, really,' said Tony. 'How did he get my photo and find me? It has to be either you or someone in your office, but I guess you've figured that out already.'

'Are you sure no one saw you at Swindon?' ignoring the question that Tony had asked.

'I don't think so, it was early, and people are just getting in and out of trains and like me not really looking. So who do you think gave him my photo? And what am I going to do?'

'You need to go to your hotel, call in sick in the morning and I'll meet you in the park tomorrow at midday,' said Geoffrey.

'Go now.' Looking up, 'David,' said Geoffrey, putting his hand in the air and beckoning the man who had brought them drinks. 'Yes, Sir.'

'Can you get a cab for my friend, he's just leaving.'

'This way, Sir,' said David, standing next to Tony. Tony looked at Geoffrey, sighed resignedly and got up.

'Tomorrow,' said Tony, looking at Geoffrey, and he followed David through the drawing room, across the hall and into the lobby where David hailed a cab for him.

'Goodnight, Sir,' said David, closing the taxi door.

The taxi drive to the hotel would take about 30 minutes. As they weaved their way through the streets of London, Tony recounted the conversation he'd had with Geoffrey. Fortunately, he had regained a lot of his composure during the day: his breathing was now Ok and his heart had stopped pumping heavily. He had looked at Geoffrey intently as he told him he'd killed someone. The look on his face was one of surprise and incredulity, both were fleeting but told Tony enough, in that micro second, that Geoffrey had not known about it.

Having studied hard on the many training courses he had been on, plus the dozen or so books that he had read, and was continually reading, and with the understanding of the behaviour of people and body language techniques and awareness gained through his job, he was able to size up an individual within seconds of meeting them; it had served him well over the last few years when it came to closing business deals. People were unable to hide that initial subconscious reaction that showed in their faces or the way they continued to act during a conversation. This understanding had spilled over into both his private life and surveillance that he had done for Geoffrey; this was not always to his liking, but it was not something you could just unlearn. Whilst not perfect, it was something of an ongoing skill that Tony was considerably adept at.

Geoffrey watched Tony leave, took another sip of whiskey and decided that eating tonight was not something he was going to participate in. Recalling the details that Tony had provided raised several questions that needed answers. Security and secrecy of the agency was of utmost importance in his life and to consider that it had been compromised was extremely worrying. There were two main issues that needed solutions: the death of a man by a known operative of the agency and secondly, the breach of security within the office.

Handing Tony over to the officials at this stage was a non-starter. Whilst no one is above the law, at this moment it would raise more questions than needed and potentially put Tony's life and family at a greater risk than they already

were, and more information was needed, Geoffrey concluded. This left the question: who gave Tony's photograph
to the assailant? Two of the 100+ other questions which
went through Geoffrey's thought process.

Chapter 25

The following morning Geoffrey arrived at the office as always by 7:00am. Walking along the corridor of the second floor, he passed a dozen or more other offices, each one housed a senior officer who reported through to him. Over the last few years the department had grown and the agents who worked directly for the agency were now being looked after by one of these men. Each man had between eight and ten agents to look after, and it was growing daily. The system worked well, information came in from the field, collected by a section head who passed it onto his senior's deputy who in turned had it typed up by their own secretary. This information was then acted upon as necessary; the report would then be passed to his office where the information was collated, an abridged version created, attached to the folder and stored.

Each week the senior officers met with Geoffrey, cross referenced, ongoing operations were discussed and fine-tuned as necessary; he then had his once a month meeting with the board.

Tony was one of a handful of the first civilian informants he had recruited and Geoffrey was still their usual contact;

however, a few weeks ago Geoffrey had made the decision to hand these last remaining few over to Carl Peterson, one of his senior officers, to handle, moving forward.

Carl deputised for Geoffrey when appropriate and at some point, when Geoffrey retired or moved on, Carl would assume overall responsibility for the unit.

Unlocking the main door to the office, he stepped inside and looked around. There were seven desks, all of which, by 8:30am, would be occupied by trusted staff, or so he thought, whose daily job was to support the administration staff of the officers. Each one reported directly to Sheila, who in turn provided him with the reports from the field and a raft of other information that came into the office. Who could he trust?

Each desk, as he went around the room, was locked, each filing cabinet behind each desk was also locked. *Well that's a good start*, said Geoffrey to himself, *at least that simple procedure is being adhered to*. There were no papers lying around and to all intents and purposes the office was bare. As he surveyed the office, he knew that probably one of the seven had betrayed their position, or it was one of the staff located in the various offices he had just passed, either way he had a mole. At this stage, his priority was not why, he needed to find who and how.

Crossing the office, he unlocked and went into his own office. Spinning the dial, he collected some of the papers from his filing cabinet, that he had been working on the previous day, and laid them out on his desk. Putting his coat on the back of his chair, he looked up: a plan already beginning to formulate. Walking back into the main office, he approached the security cabinets attached to the wall. A 15-foot-long, 3-inch wide metal bar was slid through brackets across the front of the filing cabinets, coupling all three together, and secured by a master lock at the end. Once opened, the bar was taken out and put on top of the cabinets and then resealed at the end of every day. This was a simple and effective method of securing the cabinets. He selected the middle cabinet and pulled open the fourth drawer. Picking out Tony's folder, he took it to his desk, sat down and opened the file.

Each one of the remaining 20 files in the cabinet were of the men and women he had selected to work with him on the same basis as Tony. Each file contained their initial interview, a number of papers relating to people who had first brought them to his attention, a picture, and various pieces of personal information. The back of each folder contained a typed precis of all the reports each one had filed since their engagement.

The main reports were archived, every six months, and they, along with other sensitive documents, were transported off the site to the massive underground installation just outside of Swindon. Each file was then microfiched, returned, and the fiche then went downstairs to the vault. The system was as secure as they could make it. They had considered, in the early days, using a private company to microfiche the documents but that meant outside eyes may be compromised, so it was safer and more secure to have their own system in place. They were also just starting to computerise these reports and were beginning to cross reference data from each. Using optical character recognition (OCR) was time consuming but necessary; it would be easily another year or so before every detail was on the system along with any new reports brought in from the field.

Great care had been taken at this stage not to name the informants on the computer as Geoffrey was still not convinced that computerisation was secure. Along with the men he ran who belonged directly with the agency, their files too were archived and had slowly been put onto the system, but again, no names, just numbers and pseudonyms. He had to keep the picture of each one just in case the unthinkable happened and they had to identify them. As he opened Tony's file, he saw his picture paper-clipped to the top of the first page. He got the photocopy that Tony had given him and compared the picture to the one on file. He knew it would be the same, but he had to make sure.

Geoffrey read through the notes at the back of the file; each one, less than a page in length, gave an outline of the report and contained only the salient facts. Some were shorter than others. Leafing through nearly 40 pages, speed reading, there were only two that stood out: one of the very first ones that directly involved Tony and one of the recent ones about the two men in Ealing. There were very few reasons why you would want someone dead. They either knew something, saw something or were responsible for something. As Tony wasn't in direct contact with any of the targets that he'd been set to follow or reported on, it was unlikely that it was what he knew. He was no threat to anyone as his role was minor, he wasn't actively involved with any long-term surveillance nor would his death have an impact on any operation that he was deemed to know about. So that left either something he had seen or was responsible for. Both were a contender. If he had seen something but had omitted to report it because he hadn't understood its significance, then it was a potential for someone to silence him before the information was reported or acted upon. The other scenario was something he was responsible for.

Looking over the sheet, which described his surveillance of the two men in Ealing, it could be possible that he had seen something. It was early stages so the responsibility line wouldn't apply. Picking up Tony's file, he returned it to the appropriate cabinet and pulled out his report file. This was a far bulkier file as it was closing in on the time it would be sent away for archiving. The latest reports were at the front of the file, which contained the reports on Ealing. Carefully reading the notes covering his surveillance, he concluded that it could be that Tony had been spotted. *But what had he seen?* thought Geoffrey

Visualising the report, Geoffrey focussed on being in Tony's place. The reports were detailed: the following of the two men from the pub, the shops, but the most significant report was the trip, on foot, across town to Covent Garden. *What had he seen?* The thought penetrated his conscious. There was no mention of contact with anyone else, no vehicle, no stops, no bumping into anyone accidently, no one collecting anything.

Closing the file, he got up and returned the file to the

cabinet, locked it securely and went back to his desk. Removing the files or taking out the pictures from each file would alert whoever it was who had comprised his office. Changing any routine or procedures would also be a potential flag. Picking up his phone, he dialled, 'Yes, hello, can you get me Sergeant Baxter, please,' he said to the operator. Cradling the telephone, he waited; less than a minute later, his phone rang.

'Morning Sergeant, Geoffrey here.'

'Yes, Sir, what can I do for you?'

'I need a file urgently, please,' Geoffrey relayed the information to the sergeant who confirmed that it would be with him tomorrow morning.

'Thank you,' said Geoffrey, replacing the phone.

At 8:15am he heard the office door open. He looked up and saw Sheila entering. 'Morning, Geoffrey,' she called, glimpsing him through his open door. 'Tea?' she enquired. 'Morning, Sheila, yes please,' he responded, the morning ritual accomplished.

'Here are the wires from yesterday,' said Sheila as she put down his tea on the desk.

'Thank you,' said Geoffrey as he began reading them. Noting a few skirmishes across the border, today, or rather yesterday was a light day and the information he was reading didn't have any impact as yet on his patch. Various other reports suggested increased funding activity by the IRA in New York, unsubstantiated at the moment but then if correct they could see some new activity in about a month or two when the money came through and they were able to re stock their armament.

'I need to see Carl when he comes in please, Sheila.'

'Of course,' Sheila replied.

Just after 8:30am Carl knocked on the half open door.

'Morning, Geoffrey, you wanted me.'

'Yes, come in,' waved Geoffrey. 'Need to run something past you, close the door.'

At the end of his conversation with Carl, Geffrey picked up the documents from his desk and put them all into the top drawer of his filing cabinet, closed the drawers securely and spun the lock.

Picking up his coat, he made his way out of the office.

By 9:30am he had scaled the four flights of stairs to the sixth floor and entered a conference room. The room itself was constantly swept and was soundproof. Reflective glass made it impossible for anyone on the outside to see in; however, given that it was on the top floor of the building and not overlooked, it was highly unlikely that they would ever be spied upon.

The daily briefing covered the known threats of the day. Chaired by the director, he made his way around the table with each member updating him on their latest activity. Geoffrey gave a short appraisal of his current position, as not much had changed recently. The meeting, after an hour, drew to a close, and as they were leaving, Geoffrey caught the arm of Gordon Armstrong, a section head who deputised for the Northern Ireland office. 'Can I have a quick word?' said Geoffrey.

'Of course.' As the others left the room, Geoffrey closed the door.

'Later today you will get a report of an individual who has died on a train which was heading into London. Information is a bit sketchy currently and I'm not sure if it is related to anything that I or anyone else is working on; however, it appears unusual. It may or may not be Irish related, but can you put out some feelers to see if they have anyone missing or if there has been some sort of in-fighting for me?' said Geoffrey.

'Yes, of course, do you know who it is?'

'Not at this stage, but I'm told it's a man in his late 30s early 40s maybe, and there was no ID on him, which is why I think it's unusual,' said Geoffrey.

'Ok, if anything crops up I'll let you know immediately, or if the info is slow, as it is sometimes, it will be next week.'

'That would be good, thank you.'

Geoffrey and Carl left the building and headed towards the park. His arrangement to meet Tony was at midday. They would be early, but he purposefully wanted to get there earlier just to see if he could spot anyone following Tony.

Sitting on a bench, slightly off one of the many paths that crisscrossed the area, newspaper in hand, they surveyed the park, across the lake, and from his vantage point he could see both paths that led to the meeting point. A couple of men reading a newspaper on a park bench was not uncommon, and knowing they wouldn't attract any attention, Geoffrey watched all activity intently. Sitting for over half an hour, he saw Tony coming down the path towards the small gravelled area next to the lake where, on sunny days during the summer, young boys would launch their boats.

'There's Tony,' said Geoffrey to Carl.

Keeping an eye on Tony, he continued to watch the people and new walkers in the park. From this distance, slightly hidden by the trees and across the lake, he doubted Tony would spot him. After ten minutes, Geoffrey was comfortable that Tony hadn't been followed and they made their way around the lake to him.

Tony saw him coming, somewhat startled that he was being accompanied by another man.

'This is Carl,' said Geoffrey. 'Carl works directly for me and is well aware of the current situation. He will be actively involved with you from now on. Carl is now your main contact and you will work with him moving forward. After this meeting we will not meet again, understood,' said Geoffrey curtly.

'Ok, what about that bloke?'

'You will not be arrested; however, that may change. You are not off the hook, no one is above the law and until I get a proper police report you will do as you are told and continue as if nothing has happened,' said Geoffrey.

'I need you to write down everything you told me from the time you caught the train until we met last night. Do you understand?'

'Who was he?'

'Do you understand?'

Tony looked at Geoffrey. 'I want it tomorrow. You stay in London, write it up and do not and I repeat do not leave anything out, is that clear? Carl will meet you here at the same time tomorrow.'

'Yeah Ok.'

With that, Geoffrey turned around and left the park.

'Hi,' said Carl, holding out his hand.

Taking his hand Tony said, 'Why are you taking over and what's going to happen now?'

'As you know, you are not the only one Geoffrey has taken on. It was always the plan that Geoffrey would start taking a back view and that I would become your day to day contact at some point, just a bit sooner than we thought. I know what's happened and I want to make sure that you are safe and, of course, so is your family. Have you any idea as to why you?'

'No, it's been going round and round in my mind, but I can't think of anything.'

'Ok, well, as Geoffrey said, write it up as much as you can, and we'll meet again tomorrow. Don't worry,' said Carl, putting his hand on Tony's forearm. 'It'll be fine. See you tomorrow.'

The two files on his desk were closed; it had been a week since his initial conversation with Tony. As he sat back in his chair, Geoffrey contemplated the contents and the telephone call he had just received from his counterpart in six. The first contained the report from the Met Police of the man they had found on the train in London. They had been alerted by the cleaners when they went about their business once the passengers had disembarked. The area had been cordoned off, photographs taken, and body removed. The autopsy had revealed that the man had several bruises on his body, which could have been the result of a fight, but his death was certainly caused by his contact with the cubicle's wash basin and resulting broken neck.

His personal effects had revealed a wallet containing £90 and a passport in the name of Wallace Calbrow. His name did not appear on any registers that the Met Police had; however, during a wider search it was found that he entered the country the previous week from Germany. No one had come forward for a missing person nor could the police trace any family within the UK with the name Calbrow. His body is in the morgue and will be for the next six months unless it is claimed. If it is not claimed, then he will be buried in a simple grave out at Bexley Heath. Further forensic evidence would be taken and stored in case new evidence came about and moved it from an unsolved cold case to an active murder investigation.

The name had gone to the various agencies, with Geoffrey flagging the file if anyone had any further details. The call he had received was from Jordan Smith-Hodgson, his counterpart. Jordan had also read the file, and whilst the name had meant nothing to him, his staff had searched their foreign files of known individuals who were suspected of terrorist activity in the last two years. Filtering it down to white males, English speaking, ex-army, for hire, it was the 'for hire' that proved fruitful. Jordan had confirmed that they thought it was a man called Cole.

Gordon had also rung him, there had been nothing from his contacts nor any reports that had come in from the field about anyone missing, or any rumours about the death at all. In fact, it appeared it was business as usual; the man was not known, as far as he was concerned, to anyone on their radar.

'Come in,' said Geoffrey, responding to a knock on the door.

Carl came into the room and sat down opposite Geoffrey.

'Conclusion?' Geoffrey asked.

'I think it has to do with Tony's first encounter in Reading. I don't think it has anything to do with the guys in Ealing. It's too close for comfort for them to do something like that, plus what if anything had he seen and either forgot to report or didn't report? It's highly unlikely, in my opinion, that it's Martin. So that leaves Reading and when Sean Keating was killed and Declan escaped. Of the four of them, again I don't think it was anything to do with the O'Dowd brothers. In my opinion, it's a revenge kill on Tony ordered by Declan. I think Declan and Cole got to know each other when they met in one of the training camps in Libya. Somehow, Declan has got to Cole and asked him to get Tony for him, given that he is now banged up for a while and will be for the next few years or so. I also don't think that their command knows anything about it. Otherwise they would have sent one of their own to do it and it would have been done a lot sooner.'

'I think you're right,' said Geoffrey. 'Had a call from Gordon over in Belfast and there has been no word or rumours etc. after the papers ran the story.'

'Plus, Tony made him look a fool. He had him in his grasp a few weeks earlier, before the raid, and I suspect he's put two and two together,' said Carl.

'Still leaves us with a few problems. What do we do with Tony? Who gave them the picture and what do we do with Cole?' said Geoffrey.

I'll get Sheila to reorganise the office. It's time we moved people about anyway, sectioned some off, allocated different roles, and we need some more people. While she's doing that, we can get all the personnel files out of here, down into the archives. Only you or I can release them on receipt of a signature. It's the easiest way of moving information around without tipping our hand to whoever it is,' said Carl.

'Good idea,' said Geoffrey. 'I tell you now, Carl, it's one big screw up, not only the fiasco with Tony but to have some bastard in the office who's against us.'

Nodding, Carl agreed.

'Ok, keep Tony in play. I think the risks are small given the likelihood that it's a Declan vendetta. Do the office move and we will set some bait for our little mole. I'll take this upstairs.'

The following week, a Wallace Calbrow bordered a flight to Beirut. Leaving the airport, he made his way to the Achrahieh district and entered a small hotel on Rue Monnot. Three days later, Michael Steward, a war correspondent for *The Times* settled back into his seat on the BA flight from Beirut to London Heathrow.

Chapter 26

It had been almost three and half years since the incident on the train. Tony rarely thought about it these days, but every now and again it cropped up in his thoughts, so he sat, drinking his coffee, reflecting for a moment on the events that had occurred. Carl had offered no solutions as to the identity of the man nor had he given any opinions as to why it had happened. As to who gave the guy the picture, Carl said that that the investigation was ongoing. He'd brought it up a couple of time this past year or so but had got no further, so either Carl was stalling or genuinely didn't know. Either way, he had more or less put in behind him and Tony had been concentrating on expanding his visits around the London pubs and clubs. He had benefitted from a number of training courses and there had been no pressure from anyone in BT about his activity or performance.

He had been putting in routine reports, photographs and observations to Carl Nothing had cropped up, and whilst the bombings were continuing within the UK, all he could do was carry on doing what he was doing. This weekend he had told his wife he was on another training course, which gave him a full four days to do the rounds and spend some proper time in some of the pubs he visited. A quick couple of pints in each was useful to keep his face in front of some of the regulars, but every couple of months or so he had decided that to get deeper into the local gossip, he needed to spend more time in each one.

This strategy had proved very useful, or it would have been if he had been a private detective or police officer investigating who was selling dodgy cars, stolen property or who was having an affair with who. As to anything that fell into his brief, it was in short supply. Not unexpected, but it had been a tad boring. This weekend, the plan was to visit three local pubs and a couple of nightclubs: The Feather & Firkin, The Cross Hands and The Lion. Two or three pints in each, Friday and Saturday night, then Sunday lunchtime possibly in The Cross Hands as it had now become part of the Beefeater chain. *Might be able to get a bit of lunch in there as well*, he thought.

Finishing up his coffee, he went back to the office. Some of the guys were going for an early evening drink down on The Strand, which was a usual occurrence on a Friday night before everyone headed off home. Tony joined the crowd in one of the noisy bars. About 7pm, people were beginning to drift off to catch trains, so Tony jumped into his car and drove out to Ealing. Booking into his bed and breakfast, he showered and changed his clothes then he walked to The Feather and Firkin.

The pub was busy as expected. It was a Friday night, people had been paid and it was time for a few drinks. Tony exchanged greetings with the landlord, picked up his lager and walked over to the fruit machine. He lit a cigarette and began playing. Over the course of the next half an hour he got through about £10. Not winning, he picked up another pint and had a chat with a couple of the locals who were nailed to the bar stools. The bar was full, a mixture of people, all local. Some young men and women had started to come in. Their next stop would be a trip up town to a nightclub. One or two of them were with girlfriends, but mostly they were single. A dozen or more locals drinking and chatting about the week's events; mainly the topics of conversation were football. The pool table was busy, and after another pint or so, Tony had a couple of games. Looking at his watch, he downed his pint, shouted goodbye to the landlord and a couple of people he been drinking with. 'You off then Tone?' said Mike, one of the guys he had been playing pool with.

'Yes, thought I'd go over to The Cross Hands for a quick one before they shut.'

'You going up town later?'

'No, not tonight. Been a busy week so I'll be up there tomorrow.'

'Ok, mate, see you tomorrow,' Tony waved and left.

The Cross Hands was not as busy as The Feather, mainly now because the bar was more geared up for food and not so much for regulars. Tony ordered a pint and wandered over to the fruit machine; sliding in a few coins, he started to play. Lighting a cigarette, he looked around: it was so much quieter and an older group of people, no youngsters or manual workers. If they had been in they'd gone, but he doubted now that this place was going to be anything more than an eating house with local drinkers pushed out. Getting in another pint before last orders were called, Tony finished off the evening chatting amiably to a couple of blokes stood at the bar, agreeing with him that the place had changed and not all for the better. Tony finished his pint and headed back to the B&B for the evening, grabbing a kebab on the way.

Pushing his empty plate away from him, savouring the last morsel of bacon, his breakfast had consisted of bacon, egg, sausage, fried bread, mushrooms and beans all delivered with a cup of tea and toast. He sat back, the smell of the greasy spoon café kitchen wafting across his nostrils. The place was ideally situated for Tony: just down from his B&B. Tony looked around as he lit up a cigarette. Another one of the local places he visited, watching the people come and go, regulars, people like him needing some blotting paper from the night before, a few construction workers grabbing bacon rolls and tea. The customers, many of whom he recognised, were just going about their daily Saturday morning routine. Finishing up, Tony spent the next few hours in town, picked up a few new shirts, had a couple of pints in The Admiral, which made him feel better, and then ambled through some of the busy streets. Seeing and registering, causally looking for the unusual, he spotted a couple of pickpockets. They were working together, a young woman with a baby asking a tourist for directions whilst her accomplice picked the tourist's bag. *Wrong, but relatively harmless*, he thought.

That evening, Tony's plan was to go into The Lion, have a couple until about ten and then go uptown to one or two of the nightclubs. His favourite, after The Empire, was the club above Ronny Scott's. It was loud, dark and stayed open until the very early hours. You couldn't get in until 11pm, and then it was down to the bouncer on the door. Fortunately, Tony had, like Winston in Reading, got to know the guy, so rarely had trouble getting in. It wasn't a place Tony expected to see or hear anything useful, it was just clear escapism on his part. The music was so loud that, on occasions, it almost turned your insides upside down and damaged your eardrums. Just the way he liked it.

Changing for the evening, he collected his keys, money and cigarettes and headed off to The Lion. It was an easy walk, slightly cold now, the air, but no rain was forecast for the weekend.

Rounding the corner of the street about 100 yards from where The Lion was located, he looked across the road and was startled by who he saw: Martin Dempsey. He had come from the opposite corner and was walking steadily along the pavement heading in the same direction now as Tony. Martin had no real distinguishing features as such, about six foot two, short brown hair, walked with confidence, nothing to really draw your attention to him, but Tony recognised him instantly.

Martin had not taken any notice of Tony, as he was just another man walking along on a busy road. Tony carried on his side of the road and then watched Martin enter The Lion. Tony followed. Spotting Martin in the middle of the bar as he came in, he made his way to the other end of the bar and waited for Robin to serve him.

'Hi, Tony,' said Robin.

'Hiya, lager please. How's it going?' he said, catching out the corner of his eye Martin picking up his pint and going around to the lounge area.

'Been good, always like this at the end of the month. People have plenty to spend. How've you been?' asked Robin.

A few minutes of idle chat and then Robin turned his attention to his story of the week, which he'd obviously related a dozen times to the unsuspecting locals about how he had had a fight with a bloke and his dog. He droned on and Tony half listened, nodded in the right places and gave the occasional grunt. At the end of the story, Tony praised his bravery and moved quickly away from the bar to the fruit machine. Robin moved onto the next new customer, an old man and his wife who had just come in. Tony smiled, *that'll be fun*, he thought, *old Billy is deaf.*

As the fruit machine spun, Tony idly glanced around the room. He couldn't believe he had just seen Martin again. The last time he stayed outside of the house where he last saw Martin there was no sign of him, in fact, he had made a point of almost two weeks of watching even after Geoffrey had told him to leave it. He had come to the conclusion that either Martin had done what he had had to do, or he had just gone home, maybe back to Ireland.

Either way, Tony thought, *there is no such thing as coincidences. This guy was not on holiday, he's here for reason. I don't care what Geoffrey thinks,* Tony reasoned.

Martin was sat next to a man who Tony didn't recognise.

The man was smoking, talking amiably, or so it seemed to Tony. Drinking every now again from his Guinness. After about 20 minutes they were joined by another, again someone new to Tony. Racking his brains, he had been going over the photos he had seen but he could not place either man. This one was short and wiry, nervous, skinny, hair a mess, and when he sat down, he immediately began grabbing at his scruffy coat jacket. He produced a roll up tin and proceeded to make himself a smoke. The other man got up and went to the bar, brought back another pint of Guinness, of which the man took a hefty swig.

Tony went to the bar, got another drink and a handful of change. Slowly he put the money in the machine. He could either stay until they left and follow them or go and get his car and park it outside of the house that Martin was staying in the last time. Both options presented difficulties. If he went and got his car and they weren't staying at the same place then Tony potentially may never find them again. On the other hand, if they left the pub and he followed, they might spot him. Watching the men cautiously, it was obvious that Martin was in charge. 'Wiryman', puffing vigorously on his rollup, interjected occasionally and was glared at by Martin's other companion. Martin retaliated quickly and harshly, which quietened the man down. It was almost impossible for Tony to overhear what was being said apart from the brief exchange when Martin told him to do as he was told.

How long they would stay was also in the mix. They were drinking at different rates; Martin, after about forty minutes, had finished his pint. Tony noted that the other two still had some left. Guessing that they would have another, Tony watched Martin get up and order three more drinks. *I can't afford to lose them,* thought Tony. The decision made, Tony slipped a few more coins into the fruit machine. Drinking as he played, he watched as they began to finish their drinks; this time they were in unison. Tony judged that they were either now going to leave or one of the others would buy another round.

Opting for the former, Tony finished his drink, waved goodbye to Robin and went outside. He knew where Martin's old house was and began to walk in that direction. As he came to the corner, he waited, lit a cigarette and watched the entrance of the pub. A few minutes later all three men emerged. Wiryman immediately turned away and walked in the opposite direction to the other two, coming towards him. Tony turned and carried on his journey to the next intersection and again watched. Tony sighed with relief that moments later Martin and his companion turned the corner and again headed towards him. *Good,* thought Tony, *he's going back to his old house.* With that, Tony quickened his pace, and a few minutes later he passed Martin's house. Taking up a stance three quarters of the way down the road, slightly hidden by a lamp post, he watched as they both entered Martin's house.

The following morning Tony rose early, grabbed his camera and went back to Martin's house. Parking up, he had a good view of the front door, angled as he was it would be difficult for anyone to see him through the car window on leaving the house. Tony settled in. Around 9 o'clock he watched as Martin and his mate left. Taking as many pictures as he could of the other man, he saw them get into an old BMW 5 series. Tony scrunched down as they came past, started the car and did a quick U turn and shot up the road after them. They turned left onto an artery road which lead up to the A40. The roads were relatively quiet, and Tony gained on them quickly. Turning onto the A40, both cars headed into London. At an easy pace, Tony followed the BMW as it turned off and headed down towards the river. Across Waterloo Bridge, they cut left driving almost parallel with the Thames as Tony saw signs for Rotherhithe.

Tony backed off, there was virtually no traffic at all, and he was an easy spot. The road swung round in an arc and he just saw them turn left on a small road heading down towards the riverbank itself. The whole area, for many years, had been engaged in ship building; however, after the boom years many of the yards were timber yards having easy access to the deep part of the Thames that washed alongside the docks in that area.

Tony pulled up about 300 yards past the entrance of the road he saw them go down. Pulling in between a couple of lorries, he grabbed his camera and made his way back to the road. Looking cautiously, there were several small lanes and alleyways adjoining the road. He quickly got to the end of one and poked his head around the brick wall. Scanning the area, he couldn't see them. Moving forward, he walked further down and onto a path overlooking the river. Looking and slowly making his way, he edged along around a small bend and suddenly he saw the car. It was parked outside of one of the yards, the gates to which were closed.

Climbing over the small hedge next to the river, he settled down with his camera. Breaking a few branches, he was able to position his camera on the gate to the yard. He sat and waited. Not daring to smoke, patience was his natural friend. Looking behind him along the hedgerow he saw there was no access to the river, so he was in a blind spot to anyone who came down either the alleyways or road to the yards. About an hour later he saw movement at the gate as it swung open. Tony pressed the camera button and got off a dozen shots of the two men as they came out of the yard. Martin locked the gate behind him. The two men got into the car, and with Tony taking more pictures, they drove away.

Tony lit a cigarette and waited. *Half an hour*, he thought, *I've got all day so no need to rush.* He guessed that Martin may well go back to his house and wouldn't be back. As it was a Sunday, the place was deserted. Getting up, climbing over the fence, Tony approached the gate. A new lock. Tony held it in his hand. The lock was attached to a double chain through a small hole in the wooden gate. Trying to peer through the small hole, he couldn't make out anything apart from that the place looked abandoned and had been for some time. Walking along the fence, past the locked gates, took him to the river's edge. Peering round the side, he could see that the fence seemed to go a long way along the river's edge. The path up the other side went on for about 40 feet and attached itself to an old building. Not knowing if this building was part of the yard, Tony walked back up the road Martin had driven down, to the end, and looked at the front of the old building.

'Grayson Small and Son' said the sign on the front. Tony followed the building to its end, and this gave way to a car park. Signs in the car park stated that parking was for the Grayson Small & Son company only, suggesting to Tony that the yard was separate to this building. Tony walked up the road, past the car park, in the direction he had first come. There were no further lanes, roads or alleyways down to the river. The only way, it seemed to Tony, to get into the yard was either via the gate or by boat. Drawing a blank for the moment, Tony headed back to his car. He planned to spend the rest of the day watching Martin's house.

Chapter 27

Two days later, Tony was positioned behind several cars out of a direct line of sight from Martin's house. He watched as the two men walked down the steps and got into their BMW. Driving off, Tony surmised that, as both were going, then it was no shopping trip and he guessed, hopefully, that they were going back to the yard in east London. Watching them drive past and disappear around the corner, Tony waited for five minutes before getting out of this car. Making his way up the steps of Martin's house, he saw that the lock on the door was a standard Yale. Pulling out a couple of small, flat metal picks, he inserted the first into the lock creating a slight tension, and the second slim, curved pick he pushed into the recess above the other one; within a few moments he was able to turn the lock and the door sprang open. Looking up and down the street, he stepped into the hallway of Martin's house. Closing the door quietly behind him, he stopped and listened. No sound came to him so he went straight upstairs: the top rooms were bare, maybe once occupied but now no furniture just bare walls and old carpets. Going down the stairs to the next landing, there were two more bedrooms, one on the left, the other on the right. Both doors were open, and he went into the first. Looking around the bedroom was nothing special, a double bed with the covers thrown off, a few clothes scattered on the floor, a wardrobe door slightly open and a dressing table on which stood a bedside light.

Pulling the wardrobe door open, it contained several coats, a couple of pairs of trousers and a small suitcase on the top shelf. Tony pulled this down, but as he did so he felt the weight and guessed that it was empty. He was not surprised when he slid the latches and opened it up: empty. Putting the case back carefully, he ran his hands through the pockets of the coats that were on hangers: nothing. Turning his attention to the bed, he ducked down and looked under: nothing. The bedside table drawers contained nothing of interest: a few underpants, socks. Sliding his hand under the clothes revealed nothing hidden at the back. Taking the drawers out, he looked underneath and on the back, again nothing. Making sure they went back properly, he peered over the back of the dresser, again nothing.

The carpet, such as it was, slightly threadbare, was firmly attached across the whole floor and had not obviously been lifted. The windowsill, as Tony carefully pushed the net curtain to one side, again contained a few odd and ends. Noting the empty street, he took one last look around the room and walked across into the second bedroom.

Another double bed, wardrobe, bedside cabinet; it was pretty much the same as the other one. The only thing that was different in this room was that it was slightly larger and had flower patterned paper on the walls. Seen better days, this was the main bedroom. The carpet, again wall to wall, was fitted and was slightly better but still getting threadbare. It had also seen better days and was probably 30 years old, if not more. Making a note of everything in the room, he opened the wardrobe: this one contained a few more coats, a couple of shirts and some trousers. Searching through the pockets, again nothing. The larger case on the shelf was also empty, nothing under the bed and the cabinet again provided nothing. Satisfied that he had searched the room but disappointed that he had found nothing, he went downstairs. Looking at his watch, he had been in the house about ten minutes.

At the bottom of the stairs he turned right into the front room. Approximately the same size as the bedroom above, it contained an old upright piano, a settee and two chairs, a small bookcase with several ornaments, a couple of pictures on the wall and an empty fireplace. *Bit like his grandma's,* Tony thought, *a room that was hardly ever used.* Mainly births, deaths and marriages and there in case someone important called, this was the typical room that was polished, hoovered, but never used. Looking at the pictures on the wall, they were mainly sea-based. A picture of the sea with an old fishing boat; the other two pictures were photographs. As Tony looked closer, one was of a naval boat with some sailors stood to attention; the other was of a small barge type boat with two men standing at the front waving to whoever was taking the photograph. *Memories,* Tony thought, *of whoever lived here before Martin.*

Closing the door to the same position as when he opened

it, Tony went into the room opposite. The door creaked as he opened it. This opened up into a larger room the length of the house. As he walked in he saw the curtains were drawn and the room was quite dark. Tony paused; it had that old smell, well used, and it was obviously the room that everyone used. A quick sweep of the room, Tony saw a dining table by the window with a couple of chairs, a sideboard by the wall, an empty fireplace, a settee with bed sheets and a pillow on, which at first glance appeared odd to Tony, but not worth taking a great deal of notice of, and two armchairs facing a TV, which was off. Adjusting his eyes, he walked into the centre of the room. The room carried on round to the back of the first downstairs room he had gone into, and as he got closer, he could see that this was the kitchen. As he walked slowly towards it, Tony stopped abruptly: he could see half a head poking out of the top of one of the chairs positioned in front of the TV. Next to the chair was a small table full of pill bottles and on the other side an oxygen tank that was hidden by the chair, which accounted for why he hadn't spotted it when he walked in. From the tank was a tube going to whoever was sat in the chair. *Shit!* thought Tony, *who the fuck is that?* as the man moved and groaned in his chair.

Moving closer, Tony lent forward around the chair; he saw an old man, face mask on, asleep. Doing a quick scan of the room, he backed up and knocked against the sideboard. Freezing. 'Is that you, Martin?' called out the man.

As low and as guttural as he could manage, Tony said, 'Go back to sleep.'

The man didn't move, and Tony edged himself back towards the door. Closing it quickly, he opened the front door and pulled it shut. Striding down the steps, Tony hurried back to his car, jumped in, lit a cigarette and breathed an enormous sigh of relief. Hands slightly shaking, he took a few quick drags of his fag and settled down. *Fuck me!* he thought, that *was close.*

After a few minutes, Tony wound his window down and lit another cigarette. Replaying what he had just seen, the room with the old man in it was sparse. The dining table by the window contained a newspaper and a couple of opened envelopes. There were a few more pictures on the walls, a few ornaments and, apart from several ashtrays, there didn't appear to be anything that was out of place: just a standard living room. Not being able to go into the kitchen, Tony thought it unlikely that anything of interest would be stashed there anyway. Kitchens weren't really a good place to hide things, and an old house like that would have a smallish kitchen with a cooker, a few wall cabinets, a sink and a possible pantry, but that's about all. The house appeared to be just a place for the two men to sleep and eat whilst they looked after, or helped, the old man who seemed to sleep on the settee.

Looking at his watch, he had been in the house for 15 minutes. A calculated risk, he thought, and one worth taking even though he had found nothing. It at least ruled out that Martin, unless in a shed outside or under the floorboards, was not keeping anything at this place, which, Tony thought hard, meant that the yard was the main location of any information about what Martin was up to. If he was going to find anything at all, the yard was the place to look. Reflecting on the old man, Tony wondered if he was the man in the picture by the ship and the barge boat. Maybe it was Martin's dad or old relative who had served in the war and then worked on the boats on the Thames during the '50s and '60s. *That would explain the yard, if they were related,* thought Tony. He needed to get into the yard. Tony wound the window up, started the car and drove off. Making his way towards the yard, he contemplated informing Carl of what he had done but quickly dismissed that course of action. As of yet, he didn't have any proof that Martin was doing anything wrong, and as for breaking into a house, he guessed Carl would have a fit and probably ban him from doing anything else. Also, could he trust Carl? No one had actually said yet whether or not they were closer to finding out who had given his photo to the bloke he had encountered on the train. 'I'll wait,' he said out loud.

As he approached the road that went down towards the yard, Tony slowed and looked as he passed by. Not seeing anything, he carried on and parked up as he had done before, along the roadside in front of a couple of lorries. Leaving his camera under the seat, Tony got out of the car and went down the alleyway he had used before. At the bottom he headed down towards the yard. Looking cautiously around the bend, he saw the BMW parked up outside. The gates were closed, and Tony could see no sign of activity. Climbing over the hedge next to the Thames, he positioned himself in the same location as before and waited. Having a clear view of the gate and the road, over the next hour or so there were a few vehicles that came down the road and either turned around or went along the road he had walked along. The area wasn't busy, and fortunately there were no people wandering around either. It wasn't the sort of area that attracted attention, just another old part of London that was rotting, and in the main, vacant, apart from a few die hard businesses hanging onto the factories or warehouses that they had owned for years and years.

Not wanting to smoke, Tony waited patiently and was rewarded after about an hour as he saw Martin and his companion open the gate and come out of the yard. Locking it behind them, they got into the BMW and drove away. Tony looked at his watch: *Five minutes*, he thought. The minutes passed slowly, but when they had gone Tony climbed over the hedge and, looking around, made his way to the yard gate. The padlock was a new one and easily picked. Pushing the gate open and stepping through, he closed the gate behind him and relocked the padlock. Scanning the area in front of him, the yard opened out. Walking across the yard, there were four of five buildings attached to what was Grayson's back wall. At first glance, the ones closer to him were single height and appeared to be offices, next to these were a couple of storage warehouse type buildings, small in size both with double wooden doors that opened out. At the end, again, there was another small single height building. No windows in the storage units and the windows on the offices were closed with a few broken and cracked windowpanes. The building at the end had a couple of doors and looked like someone had converted them into toilets.

On his right, as he looked at the Thames, the fence, which he had seen at the side of the yard, stopping him from walking along the river to get into the yard that way, finished and gave way to a wooden jetty. Walking over to it he saw that it was about 20 feet in length, and, on closer inspection, he saw that some new boards had been fitted so the deck was good enough to walk on. *So, they've been repairing the jetty*, thought Tony, *I wonder why?*

Turning around, he went to the first building that looked like an office. The door was closed but not locked; it gave way to an empty room. Quickly walking through, it was attached to the next, which again was empty. At the bottom of the room was a small door, which Tony guessed led into one of the storage type buildings. Trying the door handle, the door swung open and he went through. Skylights in the roof provided plenty of light, which flooded down across the room. On the side of one wall closest to him there were several fading posters – a few that looked like old information leaflets – and a calendar: it was new. The 14th and 17th were circled and the current month, although no note was written, was just circled in black. Next to the calendar were several cabinets. Opening these, Tony saw that they used to be lockers for clothes; a few discarded boots lounged at the bottom of one of the lockers but that was all. As he looked around, apart from the work area, there was nothing here.

Walking over to get a better look at several of the benches, he saw that they randomly contained a variety of tools, some looked like woodworking tools and drills, others were spanners, wrenches, and there were also a couple of vices clenched to the work benches. There was an oxyacety-lene canister with a welder's mask on the bench. The room smelled of a mixture of oil and wood, and Tony felt an acrid taste form in his mouth of someone who had been welding.

Tony noticed that on the floor near one of the benches there was sawdust. Obviously this was where they had recently renewed the boards in the jetty. A few bits of discarded metal plates were on the floor, and in the corner, Tony noticed some sheets of metal about four-foot square. *What have they been doing?* wondered Tony. *Obviously, the jetty, but what have they been welding?*

Walking back over to one of the further benches, he saw there was a large piece of paper which had the outline of a drawing on it, not particularly well-drawn but sketched out. It was a box; the measurements were 5ft x 4ft x 3ft. Wooden, with metal corners, racked inside and with a wooden top with a latch that could be padlocked. It looked sturdy, from what Tony could see, but looking around the workshop he couldn't see any of the boxes. *This solved the question about the welding*, thought Tony.

Nothing was obvious in the room, so whatever they had done they had moved on to somewhere else. However, Tony thought, he had only seen them in the car and no van, which meant . . . as his eyes locked onto a small door near the front of the building next to the double doors. This door was in the wall and led, Tony knew, into the next storage area. Moving swiftly, Tony tried the handle of the door, it was unlocked, and he pushed it open.

Chapter 28

Entering into the second workshop warehouse virtually the same size as the last one, Tony saw, as he quickly surveyed the room, about 20 boxes brightly illuminated by the sun shining through the skylights. Most of the crates were the same size but there were four or five which were more cubed than oblonged. As he looked, he took in two more benches with cans and rags on. Ignoring these, he went up to the first box in front of him. Each one had 'MACE Agr' sprayed on the side, and each one was closed, there were no padlocks; in fact not one, as he looked, had padlocks on. Opening one up, it was empty apart from racks. Pulling one of the racks out, he saw that that there were a total of three racks on top of each other with slots for four items in each rack. Having no idea as to what they were for, Tony put the top rack back and closed the lid. Stumped for a moment as to what he had found, he wandered over to the bench. Picking up one of the cans, the label read 'Oil'. *Half a dozen cans of oil, what on earth are they doing?* he thought. The spray tins were obvious.

Putting the can down and turning around, he surveyed the room: the double doors were locked. He could see the padlock from where he stood, same as the room before. *What are they doing?* He checked a couple of the other boxes, but they were the same: empty but with racks. That was it. 'Well, nothing illegal here,' Tony muttered to himself. Making boxes isn't against the law. The thoughts swirled around in his head. There must be something, there just has to be. Martin is IRA, he's here with someone else, he met someone else, he's built boxes, why here? All unanswered. Tony's gut feeling was that something was going to happen and then the calendar came into his mind: the 14th and the 17th. Whatever it was it was going to happen then. The 14th was a Sunday.

Taking one last look, Tony made his way out and into the first workshop area. Taking a last look in case he had missed something, he went through the door into the office, closing the door behind him. That's when he heard the shout.

'Wait, someone's here!' the shout was loud and came from somewhere in the yard. Tony froze. 'Fuck!'

Spinning around, he dived back into the workshop and shut the door. Looking around, there was no back exit, the front double doors were locked from the inside, and then, worryingly, he heard someone run to the doors and start shaking them to see if they were open. Fortunately, locked from the inside, this gave Tony breathing room. Rushing now into the second area which contained the boxes, he closed this door behind him. Again, looking around, almost panicking now, he saw nothing, nowhere to hide, no back door, and he couldn't get out through the front.

'Shit! Shit!' hissing through clenched teeth.

Spying the last door in the opposite wall, knowing that it led to the toilets, he ran across the concrete workshop floor and tore the door open. Toilets! He ducked down as he scurried down the short corridor, hearing the outside door handle being wriggled vigorously and the door banged.

'Every where's locked!' he heard the shout. 'Must be still inside.' Hearing the man run away towards the other end of the yard, Tony burst into the first cubicle. The window was barred. 'Shit!'

The second one was the same; the third, as he dived in, held no hope either. With nowhere to run, he crashed into the fourth cubicle and looked at the window.

Martin unlocked the gate, and with Niall at his shoulder, they came into the yard. 'Why didn't you pick it up when you were here?' said Martin.

'I forgot. I was going to put it in the car but by the time I'd locked number two I forgot all about it.'

'Ah you're a fucking twat, you know that. Go and get it, I'll wait,' said Martin. Lighting a cigarette, he watched as Niall walked towards to the office door.

'Wait, someone's here,' shouted Martin.

'The fucking door's open,' drawing his gun from his belt, he ran towards Niall. Niall turned, looked at Martin and drew his own weapon. 'You sure you shut it?' said Niall.

'Fucking right I am.'

'There's someone here. Go and check the doors.'

Martin burst through into the office, gun pointed: nothing. Making his way quickly, he opened the next door and the second office: nothing. Striding purposefully to the end of the office he opened the door into the first workshop. Crouching and pointing his gun, he looked under the benches. He heard Niall shout that the doors were locked, and he could hear him running on the gravel outside in the yard past the double door. Any second now, he would be with him.

Niall burst into the workshop, saw Martin and stopped. Martin put his finger to his lips and motioned for Niall to go over to the door that led onto the next work area. Pulling the door open quickly, Niall ran in with Martin at his elbow. Both men ducked and scoured the room: nothing.

'Check the boxes,' said Martin.

Niall cautiously went to the first box and pulled open the lid, pointing his gun in as he did so. Nothing, second box nothing, third box the same. The other boxes were piled three high and would be difficult to get to. Martin considered firing into each of the top ones but decided against it. Looking quickly around, the last place would be the toilets. If anyone was in the top boxes then he would hear the noise of them coming out, and they wouldn't get very far. Pointing to the last door, Niall swung it open and crouched down; the stench of twenty odd years of waste hit him. The two men quickly slammed open cubicle one, cubicle two, then the third: nothing. Martin poised himself. Last one, Niall kicked the door open and both men jumped forward, guns pointing.

Tony closed the window as quietly as he could. *Options, options*, he thought. Looking around, running back to the main gate was possibly not the best idea; he could be heard, he could also be caught. The river, Tony ran towards to river. If I jump in, I can't swim to the other side as it's far too wide, and I would probably drown, and they would see me. Looking at the jetty and then turning and looking at the yard gate, he could hear the two men in the toilet. *For fuck's sake*, he thought. They will be out any second now.

Kneeling on the end of the jetty, he lowered himself into the water, grabbing hold of the wooden leg supporting the end. The current was quite swift, and Tony was in danger of being pulled, not only out into the river itself but, if he wasn't careful, under water. Taking a deep breath, he sank under the edge and came up under the jetty. Head room was a few inches, enough to breathe. Looking at where he was, he decided to push off from the end wooden pillar and grab the second one along next to the bank. Clawing at the wooden pillar, he wrapped his right arm around it and kept his head as low as he could, He slowly raised his head above the water as he clung to the pillar. He could hear the two men now shouting in the yard. They were getting closer.

'On the Jetty!' shouted Martin. Both men ran onto the jetty and surveyed the water. Guns in hand, they stared at the Thames as it flowed by. Martin leaned over and looked up and down along the water's edge: nothing.

'Would he have jumped in?' said Niall.

'I fucking would have, if it had been me,' said Martin.

'We would have heard it and I can't see anything,' said Niall, taking a knee to get a lower eyes view of the water. 'Are you sure there was someone?'

'I'm fucking sure I shut that door before I left,' said Martin.

'Well', said Niall, 'if you did you did but whoever they are, they are long gone, or the door wasn't shut properly, because they ain't inside and they ain't here. The gate was locked and it's a bit of a stretch for anyone to climb the fence,' said Niall.

'Maybe I'm paranoid, maybe you're right,' said Martin.

'Let's have another look.'

The two men headed towards the buildings. Tony breathed a sigh of relief.

Martin and Niall spent the next ten or fifteen minutes going through the buildings.

'You could be right,' said Martin. 'It was only the front that was open; all the others were closed as I went through.'

'Let's go,' said Martin. Martin closed the door to the office and pushed against it, hard. It gave a bit, enough for Martin to doubt that he had shut it tightly when they had left.

Padlocking the gate, Martin and Niall got into their car and drove off.

Tony looked at his watch. He was cold now; the water was lying heavy through his clothes. He swapped arms. *I'll give it half an hour if I can*, he thought, *just to be on the safe side.* Waiting patiently, he listened intently for any footsteps on the yard gravel. He could see a little through the wooden slats of the jetty, but not a great deal. The sun was going down now, and it shone through some of the cracks. To stop his muscles from completely seizing up, he slowly pushed himself from one pillar to another, then back again, careful not to make any noise. He'd been in the Thames before fully clothed. He'd fell in a few years ago; that was a shock to the system. It's all very well being able to swim but it's a different story when you are fully clothed in a flowing river, and cold.

Tony was freezing now. Looking at his watch, it was well over 30 minutes since he had jumped in the river and his whole body was now aching. Fortunately, it wasn't winter and whilst the water wasn't warm, it wasn't freezing cold. Clawing his way around the bottom of the jetty, he stretched up and with one foot on the bank, he hauled himself up and rolled onto the wooden deck. Breathing heavily, he tried to stand. The lack of circulation in his legs and feet made it difficult, so he just sat. He took off his jumper and shirt. He threw the jumper in the river and squeezed out his shirt. Taking off his shoes, socks and trousers, he did the same, squeezing out as much water as possible. Rubbing his arms and legs, he struggled with putting the wet clothes back on. Standing now, he walked over to the yard gate and sank his hand into his jean's pocket; thankfully, the picks were still in there. Flexing his fingers and blowing on them, a bit of feeling beginning to come back, he managed to pick the lock, open the gate and relock the padlock. 'Thank fuck for that,' he said to himself as he made his way back to his car, again thankful that he had left the keys on the top of the back wheel.

Putting the heater up to full, he dropped the glove box and hunted around. Finding a pack of cigarettes, he lit one up and sucked in greedily. Letting the smoke slowly whisp out of his mouth, he slid the car into gear and drove off onto the main road. Instead of going back, he took a right onto the A100 and crossed over Tower Bridge. Turning right, he headed off into the Isle of Dogs. The road wound its way along, adjacent to the river, and he pulled down one of the tributary roads to see how far he was away from the yard. Not quite seeing it properly, he carried on until he judged that the next right would take him down to the riverbank, almost opposite the yard.

Pulling his car up, he climbed out of the car and surveyed the area: a quiet road adjacent to the river, very similar to the opposite bank, a few derelict buildings, some new work regenerating the area a couple of hundred yards away. Walking towards to bank, there was no fence or hedge between the road and the water's edge so, looking around, a short distance behind him he could park up and watch the other side easily. Deciding that this was the ideal spot, he drove back to his B&B. The next morning Tony went into town and bought two pairs of binoculars and a couple of extra rolls for his camera.

Chapter 29

The ship reduced its speed to 12 knots; at best it could achieve 18, but as it manoeuvred into the left of the English Channel, it slowed. On its last legs, the ship, during the second world war, had been an oil tanker. Converted into a container ship just after the war, its deck could, fully laden, hold 500 containers. As countries around the world had secured trade agreements and with the wealth of the west growing by the day, consumers were flexing their spending muscles, and due to demand, a vast range of goods were being shipped from the sweat shops of the far east to the massive markets of Europe and the United States. This demand had seen the creation of bigger and better container ships, some able to carry upwards of 6,000 containers. IO5467, however, was bound for the breaker's yard at Bremerhaven after its last stop in Amsterdam.

It had started it final journey out of Shanghai, stopped at Hong Kong, where it picked up 200containers, and then made its way through the Suez Canal into the Mediterranean. It docked briefly at Mersin for fuel, stopping at Tripoli and then into the Atlantic and up through to where it was now, ten miles off the coast of England, some 70 miles from the Thames estuary. Daylight was beginning to show, the channel was relatively calm, and although the wind was picking up and rain was expected across Portland, Wight and Thames – as forecasted by the BBC that morning – it would be another hour or so before the sea became overly choppy. Decreasing the speed, an old fishing vessel came alongside where the deck hands on the container ship and fishing boat lashed the two together.

A calm morning enabled the transfer to go smoothly. The wooden crates that were put onto the deck at Tripoli were broken open and the contents carefully lowered down to the deck of the fishing vessel. The operation took about an hour, and when finished, one of the deckhands let the rope go and the boat powered up its diesel engine and motored away from IO5467. The captain increased his speed marginally once more, and two of the deckhands on the container ship broke up the wooden crates and tipped them overboard to float as driftwood in the English Channel. As they hadn't really entered the choke point of the English Channel between Dover and Calais, the radar would have picked up both vessels, but as they had sailed apart before they got to close to Dover, they did not attract any attention. The fishing boat pulled away from the container ship and was several miles ahead of it as it turned into the Thames estuary.

Tony rose early on the 14th. Armed with several rolls of film, two pairs of binoculars and several packets of cigarettes, he grabbed the sandwiches he had bought the day before and left his bed and breakfast. He looked at the sky. Although it was a bit chilly and overcast, he hoped that the rain would hold off until much later in the day. Driving through town, he pulled up alongside the Thames, more or less directly opposite the yard. No one was around, although there were a couple of lorries that had parked up overnight waiting for some local factory to open so they could deliver whatever they had on board. This side of the river, not far from some houses, was a slum. Regeneration was muted, as with many parts of London, but he imagined that when Canary Wharf took off then this area, along with others along the Thames, would be rife for redevelopment for house and flats. However, now it was quiet and a borderline dump.

Settling in, he opened the window of the car and lit a cigarette. He adjusted the binoculars, changed to the other pair and found that they had a better zoom on them. Adjusting them, he could see the yard, jetty and the buildings very clearly. Looking at his watch, it was early and he no idea at all what to expect. Lighting up another cigarette and pouring himself a cup of tea from the flask, he sat and waited. The river was quite busy. Tony had no idea if the Thames was always like this, but he pondered the contents of some of the boats as they passed up and down over the next couple of hours. Most, it seemed, were some sort of barge weighed down and going out towards the sea. There were a few fishing boats and a couple of what Tony decided were just boats. He checked the yard every few minutes just in case his eyesight had missed anything. Although he could see the yard entrance and the road coming down, it was a semi comfort to see through the binoculars.

He spotted the car as soon as it entered the road, *Here*

they are, he thought. He put the binoculars up to his eyes and saw Martin's companion get out of the car and unlock the gates to the yard. Pulling them open, he saw Martin's car enter the yard and the gate locked behind him. He couldn't see the car as he guessed he had pulled alongside the fence on the right as you entered the yard. He did see Martin and his mate then emerge from behind the fence and walk towards the building that Tony had been into previously. The door unlocked; he watched as the two men went inside. A few moments later, the main door of the first warehouse/workshop was opened. Both men disappeared and Tony could make out one of them in the workshop doing something on one of the benches. A few minutes later, the second door was opened, allowing a view of the interior, and Tony saw the wooden boxes.

Picking up his camera, Tony started taking some photos. *Nothing incriminating here*, he thought, *but might as well get some shots off anyway*. There was very little activity for about half an hour or so as both men went back and forth between the workshops. Focussing his attention on the yard and Martin, it caught him by surprise as a boat came into his line of sight as it closed onto the jetty alongside the yard. Tony grabbed his camera again and started taking pictures. As it docked, Tony saw both Martin and his mate come to the boat. Some activity between the people on the boat and Martin, and then he watched as they started lifting what appeared to Tony to be large and long duffel bags, the sort he had seen in a few films, a type of soldier kit bag. They were obviously heavy as each man could only carry one. There were over 20, then Tony lost count, and then there were several smaller case type bags as well. Changing the roll in the camera quickly, he took some more photos. Within about 30 minutes everything was off loaded and the boat left the jetty and headed back the way it had come. The whole delivery operation was done without any fuss and had not attracted any attention from any of the half dozen boats that had sailed past in the meantime. As Tony watched, the doors of both the warehouses were pulled shut. *Now what?* Tony wondered. So today is delivery day. I wonder if they are going to have another delivery on the 17th. Whatever had just been delivered would not go in Martin's car, that's if whatever was in the bags was going to be taken somewhere else, and Tony wondered, *Where is Mr Wiryman?*

Tony sat and waited, drinking his tea, smoking the cigarettes, eating the sandwiches; the day passed without him seeing any further activity at the yard. Just after 6pm, Tony sat up, and he watched as the two men came out of the building, locked it up, and then he saw the car leave the compound, Martin's mate had locked the yard gate and the car drove off.

Deciding that he needed to see what was in the building, Tony waited. Just before midnight Tony checked the yard once more, as he had done many times during the last few hours, started the car and drove out of the Isle of Dogs. Driving across the river, he made his way to the spot he had used before, alongside the road near the entrance to the yard. Carefully checking his mirrors, he got out of his car, lit a cigarette and walked up past his car, casually checking any vehicle as he walked along. The road and the few cars that were there were deserted. Satisfied that the area was empty, he went down towards the yard gate.

Unpicking the lock, he slid the gate open, stepped through, closed the gate behind him and relocked the padlock. Taking a small pocket light from his jacket, he walked over to the door he had picked before, made short work of the lock and entered the building. Knowing the layout, he went through the door and into the first warehouse. Flashing the torch across the open workshop, he saw the bags that had been off loaded from the boat were stacked along one side of the wall. He flicked the torch around the workshop, taking in the benches: nothing much had changed. Before checking the bags, he went through to the next workshop and saw the crates pile up. There were three that had been separated from the rest and these were now by the main warehouse door. The air smelled of oil. The silver 'MACE Agr' lit up as he swung the touch around the open space and across onto the crates. Tony went to the ones near the door; putting the torch in his mouth, he lifted the lid of the first crate and looked inside.

'Fuck me!' he exclaimed. Taking the torch out of his mouth as he slid the lid off and onto the floor, he shone the torch slowly over the contents. The smell of oil wafted up; the torch illuminated four guns. Inspecting them closely and touching one, it had a very fine coating of oil on it. Tony guessed that they had just been cleaned. Not knowing guns, the closest Tony could guess was that they looked like AK-47s similar to the ones he had seen in the film

Commando. Shining the torch in the box, he could see that there were 12 of these guns, four to a rack and three racks. Looking closely at the guns, from what he could remember of the film, they didn't appear to have the magazine for the bullets in them. Pulling the box lid back, Tony surmised that the other two boxes were also filled with these guns, and looking around, it became a lot clearer to Tony as to what actually was now going on in here. The guns in the bags were delivered, they were then cleaned, the moving parts maybe tested, oiled and then put into the crates that had been specifically made by Martin. Walking back through to the first workshop, Tony went over to the long bags next to the wall. Kneeling down, the bags were piled on top of one another. Pulling one down, he unzipped the first and then several more: each one contained the guns. Making sure that he put them back as he had found them, his attention turned towards the smaller bags at the end of the wall. Unzipping one of these smaller bags, he shone the torch inside. He pulled out one of the magazines. *Not unexpected*, he thought. Turning the magazine around, he could see that it was loaded. Putting this back and picking up another couple, these too were fully loaded.

The last three bags were a different shape and had been put next to each other. unlike the others piled on top of each other. Tony carefully unzipped one of these bags and shone his torch inside. Gasping, he took a step back. The bag contained grenades. 'Fuck me!' he said again, out loud. Nervous now, he re-zipped the bag and decided it was time to leave as fast as he could. Shining the torch around the workshop one last time, he made sure the doors were closed as he backed out of the workshops, through the office, and closed and relocked the door. Walking quickly to the gate, he re-picked the padlock. Flashing his torch, he relocked the gate and again shone the torch to make sure everything looked Ok. Satisfied, he went back to his car. Shaking as he opened the car door, he lit a cigarette and drove away.

Chapter 30

'I need to see Carl urgently,' said Tony into the telephone.

'Put the phone down and wait there,' said Sheila.

Tony cradled the phone and lit a cigarette, going through his mind the events of the previous evening. Still unable to believe what he had actually seen, he knew that it was desperately important to see Carl and tell him in person as opposed to dropping the information through the system, as was routinely done.

The phone brought him out of his thoughts. 'Ten-thirty at the lake,' said Sheila.

Putting the phone down, Tony looked at his watch.

Walking into the office in Newgate Street, Tony put his jacket on his office chair and went down to the canteen. He nodded at a few people and passed a few minutes of idle chat with one of the admin staff about the weekend's football results. Taking his tea back to his desk, he looked around the office. Heads down, many were busy opening the mail or answering phone calls. He sat at his desk and logged onto the computer in front of him. Checking his own emails and some correspondence that had come in that morning, the hour passed quickly. Looking at his watch, he gathered his coat and made his way out of the office and along towards the park.

Carl, as punctual as ever, caught Tony up as he walked causally alongside the lake.

'What's up?' asked Carl.

'Have you read or do you remember one of my reports some time ago about an Irish guy called Martin Dempsey. I followed him for a while. He was in Ealing with another bloke, but Geoffrey told me to drop it as there was no real evidence of the guy doing anything wrong.'

'No, I don't remember. I've read some of your reports but not all of the earlier ones. So what's the relevance and why the urgency to see me? said Carl.

'Ok, well a couple of weeks ago . . .' Tony told Carl how he had spotted Martin, how he had met up with two other people and Tony had followed him to a warehouse in Rotherhithe. Omitting the part where he had gone into Martin's house, he also skipped over the part where he had nearly got caught by Martin at the yard, but he told Carl he had been into the workshops and saw the calendar.

'So yesterday I waited all day and. . .' Tony continued about the boat and then his account of him going back to the yard late last night.

'The crates are full of guns, bit like the AK47. There are magazines fully loaded and I also found a couple of bags with grenades in them. They are being put into the wooden crates. There are a couple of small wooden boxes and I'm guessing that they are for the grenades,' said Tony.

Carl looked at him and shook his head. 'Tony, for fuck's

sake how many times do you need to be told? I know for a fact that Geoffrey has told you and I've told you to watch, look and report, no engagement. Anyway, for now I'll let that go, we can cover that later and your ability to pick locks which, I might tell you, is breaking and entering. So, you say the next date is the 17th?'

'Yes. It could be another delivery; I really don't know. Also, I've not seen Wiryman either.'

Pulling the camera rolls out of his pocket. 'This is the film I took. Wiryman isn't on any of them, but the boat, Martin and the unloading is. I've also got this.'

Tony pulled out a piece of paper and gave it to Carl. It was a drawing of the buildings, the office and jetty, where the doors were and where he last saw the crates and benches. Carl took the paper, looked and nodded at Tony.

'Tell me again what you saw and what you've done,' said Carl.

Tony relayed his account again, careful to keep to the truth but dropping, once again, his entry into Martin's house and his near miss at the yard.

After Tony had spoken, they walked alongside the lake for a few minutes. Carl stopped, turned and looked at Tony.

'Ok, don't go back to Martin's house and don't go back to the yard. Stay away from now on and leave this with me. I don't want you anywhere near either location for the next few days. Is that clear?'

'Yes, of course. What are you going to do?' asked Tony.

'Is that clear, have I made myself understood?' repeated Carl.

'Yes, very clear,' said Tony, slightly annoyed.

'I'll be passing this on. Whatever action is decided we don't want them to get any idea that they have been rumbled, so the last thing I need now is for you to be spotted by Martin. Ok?'

'Ok.'

'Right, meet me here tomorrow, same time,' said Carl.

With that, Carl turned and walked away, across the park and headed back to his office.

Tony smiled to himself. Pleased about what he had achieved, he lit a cigarette and went back to work.

The following morning, Tony met Carl by the lake.

'The Met will be raiding the place on the 17th. They will wait until some activity takes place, more than likely when the boat turns up. Make sure you stay away Ok. I don't want you going into Rotherhithe.' Emphasising *Rotherhithe*. 'You understand?' said Carl looking at Tony. 'I'll let you know how it goes. Meet me here again on Friday. Write your report and give it to me when we meet. Apart from breaking the rules,' Carl paused, put his hand out and shook Tony's hand. 'Well done, Tony, it's been noted. See you Friday.'

The morning of the 17th Tony woke early. *Not allowed to go to Rotherhithe*, said Tony to himself, *didn't say anything about the Isle of Dogs, did he?*

Driving through the early morning traffic, Tony pulled up between two lorries on the opposite side of the Thames, in the Isle of Dogs, a few feet from where he had been parked before. It was very early. He slid across to the passenger seat in his car and reached for his binoculars on the back seat. If anyone on the opposite side of the river saw the car, they would not be able to see him sitting in the passenger seat. The driver's seat next to the pavement, which was several feet from the edge of the river, the river reflecting onto the driver's window, deflected any presence of him in the opposite seat.

He scanned the area: nothing. No activity in the yard and no vehicles anywhere to be seen in the road near or adjacent to the yard. Tony waited. Three hours passed. Boats, barges and a few fishing vessels sailed passed, as they had done previously. Tony began to wonder if anything was going to happen at the yard or was the date for something or somewhere else. He hoped not; he also hoped that the guns inside the workshops had not been moved. Moments later, he saw Martin's BMW come down the road and pull up outside the yard. Martin's mate got out, unlocked the gate, and he watched as Martin drove his car into the yard. This time he pulled it over next to the jetty. Thinking that was a bit strange, Tony watched and waited. The two men went into the building, and a few minutes later, the double doors of the second workshop were opened. Tony looked through his binoculars and saw that many of the crates were now at the front of the building. He scanned the area, still no activity and he couldn't see anyone who resembled anything like the law.

As he watched, he saw a lorry come down the road and go around the corner, past the yard. It stopped and then started to reverse back towards the yard gates. He saw Martin come out of the workshop and head towards the entrance. Guessing that Martin had opened the gates, the lorry backed into the yard and came to a halt as Martin's mate waved him to a stop outside the front of the double doors. The driver got out, and as he rounded the back of the lorry, Tony recognised him straight away: Wiryman.

The men got to work. Wiryman lowered the elevator on the rear of the lorry and the back doors swung open. Martin and his mate brought the first crate, then a second and third one. Wiryman pressed the lever and the back lifted the crates up. He then jumped onto the lift and started to slide them into the back of the lorry. Tony scanned the area. Where were the police? What are they waiting for? He started to panic a bit as this process of loading the lorry was not going to take very long and if the police didn't get a move on then these guys would be long gone.

The tail lift came down and they put more crates onto to it; the lift was raised and the process repeated. Tony lowered his binoculars. 'What the fuck, where are they?' he said out loud.

Glancing to his right and along the Thames, his eyes were drawn to the white spray coming out of the back of two power boats. Hurtling round the bend in the Thames, they were now speeding towards the yard. The spray out the back was high: the power these boats wielded was impressive. What was more impressive, thought Tony, as the boat came closer, was the crew: each boat had six men sat in the bows. The driver of the boat was raised in an open cockpit with a partner who looked like he was on a radio. Both boats bristled with flying antenna, a spinning radar dish and blue lights flashing across both sides of the boats. The men, as

Tony focussed on them with his binoculars, were masked and looked heavily armed.

Tony spun his binoculars at the yard; unsuspecting, Martin and his men were still loading the crates. It wasn't until Martin heard the roar of the boats as they came storming up to the jetty that he knew something was wrong. The landing of both boats on the jetty was incredibly co-ordinated, and as the men leapt from the boats to the staging, Tony saw, as he flashed his binoculars towards the yard gate, a massive Land Rover type vehicle with a cattle grid on the front had sped down the road and crashed straight through the gates of the yard, sending them in tatters to the floor. The vehicle was followed in by two other Transit type vans and what seemed to Tony like two dozen other police offices, armed to the teeth and running across the small yard. Tony could hear the shouts from the police. Martin had been ambushed on both sides. Wiryman was in the back of the lorry and couldn't go anywhere and it appeared to Tony that, with the speed of the raid and the overwhelming force of the police officers, Martin had no option but to drop the box he was carrying with his mate and they both put their hands in the air.

The adrenalin rush surged through Tony; he breathed out not realising that he had held his breath for the last minute. 'Bloody hell!' he exclaimed. 'So, that's how they do it.' Getting out of his car, he walked around to the water's edge and watched the final scenes unfold. All three men were in handcuffs and were being led away out of the yard, each into a separate police van. They were driven away with blue light flashing and sirens filling the air; an escort front and back joined in the cacophony of sound. The men from the boats had been into the workshop and, satisfied there was nothing else for them to do, they had climbed back into their boats and sped off. A separate police boat arrived and was secured to the jetty. The big Land Rover that had burst through the gates reversed and drove off. *No damage*, thought Tony, to its front. In its place, several unmarked police cars arrived along with what Tony thought was the bomb squad van and some other officers in white overalls. Both the roads, he could see, were being blocked off and quite a few of the original police raid team were making their way back to their own vans. Fifteen minutes and it was all over, you would never know, apart from what had just happened. *Clearly a job well done,* thought Tony. Not a single shot fired.

Tony lit a cigarette and sat on the bonnet of his car, reflecting on what he had done, what he had seen and what had just taken place. *Pity it's not on film*, he thought, *it would make a good movie.*

Chapter 31

Tony wrote up the report, once again drifting away from the actual events but reciting everything he had said to Carl when they met earlier in the week. Scrunching his cigarette out in the ashtray, he folded the written notes and put them in his jacket pocket. Gathering his coat, he made his way to the tube and through the underground system to the park. Walking up to the lake, he spotted a bench and sat down, idly watching the ducks as he recalled the events and smiling to himself as he saw Martin in handcuffs being put into the cop van. The speed of the boats and the way they had landed at the jetty had impressed him. He wondered if it was the Met Police, as Carl had said, or maybe some military unit. Either way, they achieved a fast result.

Looking around, he spotted Carl as he closed in on him. Walking by the lake, he had another man with him. Tony noticed nothing unusual about him, *pretty ordinary really*, he thought. He stood up as they approached.

'Morning, Tony,' said Carl,' 'this is Leonard.'

'Morning,' responded Tony, nodding at Leonard.

'Do you have your report?' asked Carl.

Pulling out the report, 'I've put it together for you as you asked,' said Tony.

'Thank you,' putting it into his pocket.

'Did you get everything?' asked Tony.

'Yes, we did: the guns and ammo, grenades etc.'

'Who was Wiryman?'

'We don't know yet,' said Carl. 'Investigations are ongoing. All I can tell you is we think the weapons were going to be trucked over to Ireland but as I said, investigations are ongoing.

'Did you go to Martin's house?' said Tony.

'Yes, we raided Martin's house and found his uncle in there, he owns the yard. Apparently, he was a timber merchant in the '50s and kept the yard after he retired. He's not well, but we don't think he's involved. That's all I know. It's in the hands of the Met Police now.'

I expect you know more, thought Tony, but he wasn't going to push it. Martin and his mates were banged up and they got the gear, so as far Tony was concerned, he had done what they had wanted him to do.

'Right, I'm off. Maybe speak to you later, Tony. Leonard wants a word,' said Carl as he turned away and left the two men together.

'Leonard Hewes-Smith,' said Leonard to Tony.

'Nice to meet you. What can I do for you?'

'Let's sit down,' said Leonard. Tony got out his cigarettes, offering one to Leonard, who declined.

'Do you work with Carl and Geoffrey?' said Tony.

'No, separate area. Although we do the same sort of work,

my role is focussed on terrorism. I know a lot about you, Tony. You've been of interest to me for some time and I think now is the right time for us to have a chat.'

'Ok,' said Tony, slightly puzzled.

'Let me explain.' Pursing his lips, he looked at Tony.

'The overriding priority in this country is to keep it safe. The different departments within the government, like Carl's and the police etc., along with others, are constantly striving to get information on any individual or group who pose a threat to not only the security of the country but also the general public. As you know, the IRA have been a major source of concern for many years and may well be for some time to come; however, there are people who think that they may not be as difficult in the next few years or so. Hard to tell, of course,' said Leonard, 'but we are hopeful.'

Tony just nodded.

'The world is changing, we've had the bombs, the hijacking of airplanes and kidnappings etc., but threats come in many shapes and forms. I'm not sure how much you keep up to date with world events, Tony, but the drug cartels from South America, although not classed as terrorists, sell vast amounts of their products in the UK, and they are sold and distributed by hard core gangs. These are a problem, and with the growth of the economy, will become more of problem as time goes on.'

'So I heard,' said Tony, beginning to wonder where this conversation was going.

'On top of that, we are seeing more and more groups that are religious-based and are driving their message to radicals whose sole aim is to destabilise their own governments and, in some cases, looking to overthrow and install their own leaders. All these threats are real, and we think, will lead to many more problems as they breach our shorelines in the coming years,' Leonard continued.

'Ok, so what's that got to do with me?' said Tony.

Leonard looked at him. 'To fight terrorists we need to think like them, we need to be in their field of view, we need to engage with them and we also need to make sure that we reduce their ability to recruit members and foil any terrorist activity that might take place.'

'That's wishful thinking,' said Tony. 'You need to be part of them to find all that out and that is unlikely unless you can get people from a young age or in the same country as them to gain their trust etc., which as far as I can see is a non-starter,' said Tony.

Tony looked at Leonard. This was not a polite, easy conversation. Leonard's tone was dark, hard and authoritative, and Tony was beginning to realise that this was not going to be an ordinary chat about his past endeavours, an overview of the future of terrorism, nor about his role of observing and informing, as he had been doing previously. The question was: where was this leading?

'That's true,' said Leonard, 'however, there is more than one way to skin a cat, so to say. If you are ahead of them and can provide them with the resources they require then you can second guess their moves and act on them before they seek any terror advantage. That, of course, requires considerable forethought, skill and patience.'

'Ok, that's sounds logical, but how can you do that? It also sounds as if you want to collude with them in some way,' said Tony, 'because providing them with resources could go either way, either you win or you lose track of what you gave them or what they wanted and they win. I'm not getting where you are going with this. Who do you work for?' said Tony.

'I work in a similar department to Carl, but we look at things slightly differently. The people we have are a small group who have the ability to act on their own initiative and have some considerable latitude in what they do,' replied Leonard. 'It's the sort of group I think you would work well in; however, it can be dangerous and exacting.'

'Did Carl provide you with *all* the information I've sent in over the last few years?' said Tony, emphasising 'all'.

'Yes, I've seen it all, and if you are referring to the man on the train, then, yes, I know about that as well. Everything that you have done and with, who, plus the evaluation reports and assessments, which is why we are having this conversation,' said Leonard.

Tony looked at him closely. *No expression on his face at all,* thought Tony, *a difficult man to read.*

'In which case, you know that my photo was given out by someone, and if you are the same as Carl and going after other people then it's likely that whoever gave out my info will do it again, which, as you can imagine, I'm not overly keen on,' said Tony.

'You don't need to worry about that, as I said, the group is small and we act differently. The information I'm about to tell you is confidential. If you repeat it or I get to hear that it's been talked about then it will be denied strenuously and you will be subjected to prosecution and you will go to jail,' pausing, 'understand?' said Leonard, looking hard at Tony.

'Ok, I understand.'

'We operate on a face to face basis. There are no reports filed from the unit, information such as photos, documents etc. once used and seen, are destroyed. There will be no record of anything you do deep in some archive naming you, dates place etc. I report directly to the minister, and he in turn reports, if required, to the PM. We are not outside of the law; however, from time to time our activities require hard choices and can have severe consequences on those who oppose us. We are not in the limelight nor do we have a section name, like Carl's for instance, so 99.9% of the time we go unnoticed and mostly undocumented. We are, however, required, on occasion, to act to preserve the integrity of the security of the country.'

Tony had listened intently to what Leonard had just said to him. He had never heard of anything like this before and was trying to read between the lines as to what really was the message here. Leonard let him sit for a moment to absorb what had just been spoken about.

'So, Tony, would you like to come and join the team? There will be no medals, no plaques on the walls, no pats on the back; in fact, no one will ever know what you do or will ever have done. There will be no recognition at all, ever. I also need to point out that if you say yes, then this is a lifetime commitment. You don't get to leave, you will work with new identities when you are in the field, which will put you under considerable pressure. This job is difficult, dangerous and could, in the worst case scenario, result in you being put in harm's way.'

Tony sat for a moment; the decision was easy as far as he was concerned. He wanted to do more and he knew he could. What he had seen so far had made him all the more determined in the role he had forged for himself with Carl. This opportunity seemed to Tony to be an ideal way of making more than a difference.

'Absolutely, yes I would,' said Tony.

'Good, nice to have you on board,' said Leonard, holding out his hand. Tony took the proffered hand. 'What now?' said Tony.

'I'll talk to Carl; he will put a note on your file saying you are no longer active. Also, you will need to put in your resignation on Monday.'

'What about my job or money? I have a mortgage, bills and so on.'

'You will still work for outside firms. Over the next few years most of the companies that you will work for you will only be there for a year or two and then move on. The salary will come from these companies so you will not be on the payroll of the government, but don't worry, you will always have work, Ok,' said Leonard.

'Fine.'

'Take this,' Leonard pulled out a piece of paper and gave it to Tony. 'Ring me on this, end of next week and I will give you an address to go to after your notice has been served.'

Tony took the paper, committed the number to memory and burnt the paper as he lit up another cigarette. Leonard stood up, nodded and walked away.

The following week, Tony had picked up his tea, took a sip and finished the bacon sandwich he was eating, the café in Fleet Street was run by an old Greek guy who Tony thought was on his last legs; the food was Ok though. Finishing up his roll, he took out the letter he had written over the weekend. His boss wouldn't be in until 12pm so Tony re-read and then folded it up and put it away: straight to the point. It was time to move on and further his career, four weeks' notice, standard stuff. Sat by the window, Tony watched the flocks of people walking up and down outside, some hastily trying to make up time to where they were going others walking from their office to appointments, Tony guessed. An assortment of people, not that he was really interested in them, but it gave him time to watch and see the variety of individuals who graced the streets of London.

Watching, his thoughts turned once again to his conversation with Leonard. *Dangerous*, he said, *well there's danger with everything*, thought Tony. The number he had given him was from the Woking area, which surprised Tony as he thought he would be going to an office in London. A face to face meeting seemed a secure way of doing things, probably better, that way it was less likely for anyone to read what they were up to. Looking at his watch, he finished his tea, left the café and made the short walk back to the office.

Logging in, he sorted through a few emails and waited for his boss to turn up. *It was going to be a quiet couple of weeks,* he thought, *before he started his new role. Looking forward to it,* Tony said to himself.

Chapter 32

It was a decent day, thought Tony, *not too cold, bit of sunshine and it had been a good week as well*. Coming out of his client's building, he walked along the high street and into the multi storey car park. The meeting had gone well and he had explained that Rupert, Tony's colleague, would be taking over from him. He would meet Rupert at the seminar next week and would ensure that his order would be installed as discussed. The last one, thought Tony, that's it now, hand back the car tomorrow, week off, start the new job at Brakes on the Monday then meet up with Leonard at the new place on the Thursday. He had spoken to Leonard the week before, apprehensive that he could get him a job so quickly; however, Leonard had come through and it had been arranged for him to take a position at Brakes, similar to what he was doing now. The manager there was a nice guy, he had met him over lunch, he had seen his CV and was happy for him to start. Neither of them mentioned Leonard, apparently, he had received his details through a recruitment agency. Tony didn't push it. He was just happy to get the job under his belt; at least for the foreseeable future he could pay the bills.

He had left his car on the top floor, caught the lift and at the top headed over towards his car. The car park was relatively empty at this time of day as most people had left work and were on their way home. There were about four or five cars left in the bays, a couple of vans and that was it. Not paying any particular attention, he took the keys from his pocket and opened the door. Chucking his briefcase in the back, he went to take off his jacket. The pain in his right leg was instant; his right leg buckled as he started to go down. He saw, out of the corner of his eye, the bat swing across and smack into his left leg, just below the knee. Again, the pain was brutal. Virtually on the ground now, the second hit made him sink to his knees. He took a massive blow to the back and then heard the bat hit the floor; a fraction of a second later the world went dark. A hood had been pulled over his head and the noose done up violently at his neck. Trying to claw the hood away from his throat, he was knocked sideways with a punch to the head and a kick in the back. He fell forwards and hit the side of the car. Dazed, he felt both of his arms being pulled behind him and then his wrists being bound together.

A strong arm went around his throat and he was dragged a few feet, manhandled and thrown into the back of a van. The man knelt on his back, quickly looping a rope around the underside of his arms, and Tony felt himself half dragged up onto his knees as the man attached the rope to a ring fastened to the underside of the roof. The position was painful, he couldn't stand nor could he kneel as the rope behind his back made it impossible for him to do either. He heard the van door slam and the driver getting in, starting the engine and powering off down the ramps of the multi storey car park. Every movement of the van swung Tony back and forth, crashing into the sides. Disorientated, and with pain in his legs and back, Tony was tossed around like a leaf in a force ten gale.

The journey was punctuated with spells of stability. Tony guessed they were on a straight road, but every now and again the van swerved, and Tony crashed, not standing nor kneeling, into the sides of the van. Each movement he was taken by surprise. With darkness around him, he cursed with pain every time. Tony had no idea how long he was in the van for, but by the time they stopped he was semi-conscious through all the abuse he had taken during the journey. He heard the driver get out, vaguely heard some noise, then the van start up again, jump forward and come to an abrupt halt. The driver got out, slamming the door. Silence, then the door opened, and Tony felt a blast of air come into the van. The rope around his arms was untied and he fell to the floor. Another blow to the head and then Tony was dragged out and he hit the concrete floor with a resounding bump. He had fallen and landed on one knee. A two foot drop from the van to the floor wasn't much, but when you are blindfolded and the drop unexpected, the pain sparkled through his knee, up his thigh and into his groin. He winced with pain and involuntary cried out. An arm around his throat, he felt himself being pulled up. With a quick movement, his arms were cut free, but before Tony could react, he took three powerful punches: two to the face and one to the stomach. Thrown into a chair and unable to offer much resistance, he felt first his right arm being taped to the chair and then swiftly his second arm secured the same way.

Another punch to the head and Tony saw stars and passed out. The water was ice cold. Tony thought he was dreaming about swimming with his arms tied when the water shook the last remnants of the dream away as his head snapped up and his vision cleared. The man was behind him; he heard the bucket being chucked across the floor. Tony quickly took in his surroundings: both arms were taped to the arms of the metal chair, his legs were free, but he couldn't stand up, the chair, he saw, was bolted to the concrete floor. His mouth had tape over it, and Tony tried to calm down so he could breathe normally through his nose. The pain in his legs and head was dull and aching. He looked around: it was some sort of warehouse. The van that had brought him here was parked just inside the roller doors. As he switched his gaze the man came in front of him and punched him across the face.

'Hello fucker, awake are ya?' said the man.

Tony focussed. *Fuck! Fuck!* he thought. He recognised the man: Declan Cassidy.

Declan, seeing the recognition in his eyes, bent his face forward so it was within inches of Tony's face.

'Yes, it's me you fucking cocksucker.'

Tony tried to head-butt him, but Declan was quicker and slapped his head away. A slap was better than a punch. He tried to talk, but with the tape across his mouth, just garbled noise came to Declan's ears.

Declan laughed and turned away and walked towards a bench. Selecting an item, he turned back and came towards Tony.

Plyers, Tony's eyes widened.

'Yes, this is going to be very painful for you,' said Declan in his deep Irish accent.

'Let me explain what's going to happen, because I really wouldn't want you to have any surprises during our short time together,' said Declan sarcastically.

'Seven years I've waited for this,' Tony frantically looked around the space.

'You can look as much as you like, you bastard, but you're not going anywhere. Seven years, seven long years, you killed my friend Sean, you made me a laughing stock and I've been stuck behind bars for seven fucking long years. I should have taken care of you the first time we met. By the way, just so as you know, I killed your mate Pete, bullet to the head. He begged and begged me to let him go, wet himself, crying like a baby he was, little prick. Had to put him out of his misery. Shit himself when he took the bullet.' Declan laughed as Tony furiously tried to swing his legs out and kick Sean, pulling with all his might at the tape restraining his arms.

'Too tight, don't bother,' said Declan.

'Anyway, where was I? Oh yes that's right.' Declan walked behind Tony and grabbed his right hand. Yanking his hand flat, he took hold of Tony's little finger, leant over and closed the plyers on his nail. Tony started to scream, struggle and thrash about, but the restraints held tight and Declan's grip on his finger was strong. Declan closed the plyers tight and yanked the nail straight out.

The pain was unbelievable; it forced tears down his face. The pain stabbing up his arm into his neck and brain, Tony began to shake. He had never felt pain like it before. Declan threw the plyers back onto the bench, picked up the pail, filled it with water and threw the contents over Tony.

'Shut the fuck up, you wimp. We've not even started yet.'

Tony felt the pain fractionally easing and he looked at his finger: the red raw skin under his nail was oozing blood. The pain, he thought, got worse every time he looked at it.

'As I was saying,' continued Declan. Tony spotted the batteries near the chair.

'We'll be using those later,' said Declan as he saw Tony look at them.

'I've had many long hours to decide what your death is going to look like,' said Declan. Tony stared at him, hate filling his eyes.

'I'm not going to torture you for information because I'm not interested in anything you have to say. To me you are just a fucking shithead who needs to die. What I'm going to do is make it as painful as possible.' Closing in on Tony, he quickly swung a left then a right. Tony tried to roll with the punches; the first was not so bad, but the second caught his nose and blood started to flow.

Declan picked up a hammer from the bench. 'This is what we used to use on any of the squaddies we used to catch, painful and very effective.' The blow landed on Tony's thigh, then on the other one. The pain jarred like lightning, another full swing and he felt as if his leg was going to fall off. He was helpless, he couldn't move and couldn't talk his way out. He tried to sink the pain into the back part of his brain and rise above it. Closing his eyes as Declan took pleasure in punching first in the stomach, working round his side to deliver blows on the right then the kidneys. Five or six blows to each side, the pain was overwhelming and Tony barely remained conscious.

The punches came thick and fast. Declan was talking all the time, but Tony couldn't make out what he was saying. Trying to drift away, the pain of each attack bringing him back to reality swiftly each time. Declan tore the tape from Tony's mouth. Tony heaved and spat onto the floor involuntarily. Blood spewed out and Tony caught a glimpse of what he thought was a tooth, his vision now fading as the pain and brutality was taking its toll.

'Doesn't look like you're going to last too long does it?' said Declan.

Tony couldn't talk, he just mumbled and spat more blood out of his mouth.

Declan behind him, grabbed his hair and yanked his head up and swung his face to look next to the bench. 'See those,' said Declan. A couple of jerry cans were set aside the bench.

'Full of petrol, just for you. You are going to beg me to finish you off, you motherfucker, or I'll burn you alive. In fact, I may just decide to burn you alive anyway. That's your fate, that's the way you are going to die, a gruesome ending to a shitfaced lowlife.'

Declan flung Tony's head out of his hand and walked over to the bench, looking for another tool to inflict pain with.

Tony heard a phone ring, he saw Declan look towards the ringing. Ignoring it, he picked up a screwdriver looking at its point, flicked it with his finger, put it down and picked up another one, slightly smaller and with a thinner handle. The noise continued; the phone kept ringing.

'For fuck's sake,' said Declan, chucking the screwdriver onto the bench.

Picking up the phone 'What?'

Listening, 'No, I've told you, I'm done. I have a bit of business to finish here then I'm gone, so fuck off and find someone else.' Slamming the phone down, he went back to the bench and the phone rang again. Declan walked over to Tony, stood by his side and began to push the screwdriver head into the muscle on Tony's left arm. With nowhere to go, Tony felt the pressure and the pain began. The ringing kept on. Declan swore again, 'Bastard!'

Striding over to the phone, 'I've just told you, no!' he shouted into the phone.

Tony saw Declan pause. The pain in Tony's left ear made it difficult to hear exactly what was being said but he could make out Declan protesting.

'Why can't he do it himself? I've shown him twice for fuck's sake,' said Declan.

He listened for a few more moments. 'Fine, you are fucking useless. I'll come over but that's it. Twenty minutes.' Slamming the phone down once again, Declan strode over to Tony and with two swift punches to his forehead, rendered Tony virtually unconscious. Tony felt his arms being freed but then being dragged unceremoniously across the floor. The door swung open and Declan threw Tony into the room and slammed the door shut.

Tony crawled across the floor; his hands were shaking. He rubbed his face and his little finger touched his nose. He screamed with pain as the agony in his hand flared up. Putting his little finger in his mouth, he dribbled onto the raw skin. In his mind it gave him some pain relief. His head pounded, his whole body ached, he thought he was going to be sick, and every move he made felt like a thin bladed knife scouring his stomach and sides. He touched his left thigh: the pain was like squeezing a lighted cigarette between your fingers by mistake. He dragged himself to the wall, turned, sat against the wall and took in his surroundings. The room was a cold storage unit. He could tell by the size and the lock on the door that the room fortunately was not operational and had been left in disrepair for some years. The old temperature clock was by the door. The door itself was large, large enough for a pallet to be pulled through; it had a small window in it. Other than that, the room was bare: no windows, no furniture and no way out.

Declan picked up the baseball bat and looked through the window of the cold storage room. He could see Tony was squatted against the back wall, head down, rocking slightly. Declan snorted; he'd been gone an hour. He knew Tony would have recovered a bit, but the beating he had given out would have taken its toll. Gripping the baseball bat tightly, he unlocked the door and swung it open. His plan was to run in and smash the bat into Tony. His own strength and speed would be too much for Tony to counter. Once done, he would get Tony back to the chair and finish him off for good. He was done with this country, had had enough of all their bollocks. He had a ticket for the ferry tomorrow. He would drive down to Spain and then maybe across to Africa. He knew people there; from Africa he would go onto the States. He was not going to jail again that's for sure.

Tony didn't move as Declan opened the door. Striding in, he raised the bat above his head and went to swing at Tony. Tony pushed himself off the wall as hard as he could. He dived headlong into Declan and grabbed him around the legs. The bat came down and hit him on the shoulders but the force of his move pushed Declan backwards and he crashed to the floor. Declan wasn't expecting a low attack, if anything he thought Tony would go for his face or the bat itself. The baseball bat spun out of his hand and he hit the floor hard. Tony, with his shoulder, used a battery ram into Declan's legs, a classic rugby tackle that took Declan off his feet. As he did so, Tony slammed his right fist into the side of Declan's thigh, making Declan wince. Rolling slightly to his left side, Tony freed up his right hand and plunged it into Declan's groin.

Declan felt the punch and some pain. *Smacking me in the bollocks isn't going to work you fucking dickhead*, thought Declan. As Tony had rolled slightly to his left, Declan grabbed his head, turned him completely over and pulled him up so they were both facing the ceiling with Tony on top of him. Declan had him round the neck and got Tony in an arm lock, pressuring his throat. Tony struggled and punched his fist into Declan's left leg. Declan felt pain; he also was now feeling more pain from his groin area. The two men struggled on the floor, Tony now thrashing his arms to try and rid himself of the powerful lock Declan had on his neck. Declan was holding Tony as hard as he could, knowing that it would only be a minute or so before Tony was unconscious as he was too strong to let Tony gain any grip at all. Tony elbowed Declan in the side. Declan felt strange, he had too much pain in his legs now and he could feel himself losing the strength in his arms and body; his eyesight was fading. Starting to panic, he tried to increase the pressure on Tony's neck but couldn't. Tony felt Declan weakening slightly and he back kicked him and elbowed him twice. He felt Declan ease his grip slightly. With all the strength that was left in him, Tony literally spun round on top of Declan and slammed his right fist into Declan's neck. Declan was fading, he could feel his strength disappear, but he didn't know why. His eyes began to close; he felt as if he was floating. Declan's life drifted away.

Tony drew back his fist from Declan's neck; the blood dripped from the knife securely wrapped around his fingers. The knife wound in Declan's neck, small and effective, was not, however, the killer blow. The four-inch blade had penetrated the femoral artery near Declan's groin. The blood had pumped out, draining his body, and the wrestling had increased the blood flow. Declan didn't stand a chance. The blood seeped through his trousers and across the floor.

Tony pushed himself off Declan and rolled away. Breathing heavily, the pain began to come back. He looked at his hand. The knife, glistening with blood, hidden in the buckle of his belt – he had worn it every day since the day Pete had bought it for him – had saved his life.

'Thanks Pete,' he said.

'Motherfucker!' said Tony out loud as he looked at the lifeless body of Declan. Unwrapping the belt from his hand, he struggled to his feet. Bending his knees a couple of times, he stepped over Declan and went into the warehouse. Rolling up the belt, he put it into his pocket and walked over the bench. Picking up a rag, he tied it around his little finger, wincing and trying to ignore the pain. The blood had stopped but banging it on something would be agony. Looking around, there was very little. He saw a table with some food on it, next to a camp bed. Declan had obviously been sleeping here. The van was still near the door, and Tony went over and looked outside: there was another car parked up. Going back to Declan, he searched his pockets and found some keys.

Going for good was he, thought Tony, *well he is now.* Picking up one of the jerry cans, he emptied the contents across the floor; the contents of the second one, he poured onto Declan, into the van and then just left it on its side to spill out. The unit was in an industrial estate and it was dark, no one was about and the whole place looked derelict. No wonder Declan had chosen such a place. Checking the car, he saw a packet of cigarettes were on the dashboard. Tony took one and lit up. Inhaling deeply, he regretted it immediately as the pain made him gasp. He tried again, gentler this time. *Not so bad*, he thought flicking it away.

Going back inside, he took another rag, soaked it in petrol and left it on the floor by the entrance to the unit. One last look around, he bent down set fire to it and watched the flames snake along the concrete floor, onto the van and across to the cold storage room to where Declan lay. Closing the door, he left, got into the car and started the engine. It started first time; the radio came on. Tony wound down the window, the music playing in the background. Soft, gentle, soothing music.

Tony lit another cigarette and put the car into gear. Adjusting the mirror, he watched as the smoke began to billow out of the top of the roller doors of the unit. He could smell burning; he could smell death. *Fuck me*, he thought to himself, *not so quiet after all*. Sliding it into gear and with one last look as the flames breached the top of unit he drove away.